PAYBACK IS A CART
FORMER MARINE AND H
FIGHT FOR THEIR LIVES
A HUMAN TRAFFICKING ORGANIZATION.

Five years ago, Drew, a former Marine sniper, his partners and an on-the-run sicario joined forces in the desert to rescue a group of children from human traffickers. The shootout in the desert left a trail of dead federal agents, cartel members and a high level cartel boss in prison. The cartel never forgets and are now out to avenge the deadly indiscretion. This time it's personal as they target family members and Drew decides the only way to guard against violence is to inflict it on a deadlier scale.

Picking up where *The Silence and The Dark* concluded, *The Silence and The Death* puts Drew and his friends with their backs against the wall and follows them on their lethal plan of justice.

Payback is a Cartel Virtue but that doesn't mean it comes easy.

Drew scrambled over the top of the rock and took up a position. He pulled the rifle out of the bag and locked a round in the chamber. He dropped to a shooter's position—on his stomach. With his left hand, he dropped the small bipod attached to the barrel end and sighted. It was not a night vision scope, but he was close enough to the targets and had enough moonlight to make out the outline of any body. His heart rate was still elevated, and he knew that he would have to lower it before shooting.

Drew went back to his training. He closed his eyes for two seconds. Clear your mind, he told himself. He let out a deep, cleansing breath and opened his eyes. He scanned the area where he had seen Katie running. He followed the path with the scope until he saw the two figures nearing the road. The one in front was a female. The male pursuer was gaining. No time to think. No time to consider technical aspects to the shot: wind, distance, elevation, humidity. No time to think about the fact that he had never fired this weapon. Even if he had a spotter, there was no time to consult about drop and angles. The only thing to consider was that Katie was running for her life. The only thing for him to believe was that he was a weapon.

I am the Weapon. I am the Dark. I am the Silence. I am Death.

The Silence and the Death

Marc X. Carlos

Moonshine Cove Publishing, LLC

Abbeville, South Carolina, U.S.A.
1st Moonshine Cove Edition December 2020

ISBN: 978-1-952439-00-1
Library of Congress PCN: 2020922980
Copyright 2020 by Marc X. Carlos

Cover image used with permission of the author, cover and interior design by Moonshine Cove staff.

Dedication

For Moms

About the Author

Marc Carlos is a career criminal defense trial attorney. A veteran of over two hundred complex jury trials, Marc has made a career of defending a wide array of individuals charged with crimes ranging from capital murder to white collar offenses. His novels draw upon his experience in defending and investigating drug and human trafficking cases in the border region.

Marc is a graduate of the University of California, Berkeley and Santa Clara University School of Law. He lives and works in San Diego, California.

www.marccarloslaw.com

Acknowledgment

Writing and maintaining a full time legal practice is difficult without the support of family. Special thanks for their encouragement and, of course, to my wife, Tonya, for putting up with the early morning typing and "just let me finish this one thing..." . Also, a special thanks to John Cannon at JCannon Books for his editing and sense of place and authenticity. Finally, a special thank you to my dad, a non-fiction devotee, for acting as first reader and not telling me to stay in court where I belong.

THE SILENCE
AND THE
DEATH

ONE

He ran. He didn't think. He didn't look back. He just ran. He increased his foot turnover to ramp up his speed. He had trained for this. The trick was not to go into an all-out sprint but to control your gait and breathing while increasing your speed. He never knew where or on what type of surface he would have to run, but he knew that one day he would have to run. For his life. He always wore soft, rubber-soled tactical boots in case he had to do just this. Run. The adrenaline kicked in, and he felt as if he was moving faster than he ever had. In a way, it was cathartic. He heard nothing except the sound of his breathing. His feet bounced off the pavement, each step propelling him farther.

He came home from work. The normal slow climb up the exterior stairwell to his apartment. But before he reached the top step, he saw the front door to his apartment was slightly ajar. He knew he shut the door and locked it, just like he did every time he left. The small, white, folded piece of paper that he wedged into the jamb was now lying on the mat in front of the door. No, he was not mistaken. Someone was inside. Waiting.

He stopped dead. For a second, he couldn't move. He couldn't breathe. He began to back slowly down the steps as quietly as he could. Retracing his path as if backing out of a minefield. He kept his eyes trained on the door.

When he reached ground level, he stopped. Still no movement above him in the apartment. He looked out to the street. Normal, residential. Nothing out of the ordinary. The apartment complex across the street had a few people milling about, but no one looking over at

9

him. Maybe he overreacted. Maybe he left and forgot to shut the door completely.

Then he saw it.

The vinyl blinds were drawn as usual, but for a brief second, he saw one of the slats move. Someone was looking out.

He turned and ran.

Witness protection, he thought, *puta madre*!

He knew they could never truly protect him, so he was always ready to run. What were the chances that Cicatriz, the Sinaloa Cartel, or any of the other assorted low-life criminals that he had wronged would not come looking for him? He remembered one of the last things that Caritas had taunted him with.

"We know who you are, *Detective*!"

Gerardo had no reason to doubt him.

How far had he run now, half mile? Mile? He didn't know. What mattered was that he didn't hear the ping of bullets or the roar of car engines. Still, here he was running like a crazy man down an orange-tree-lined road in Riverside. Maybe not such a good idea for a Latino to be sprinting fully clothed on a Southern California street with a bunch of trigger-happy police on patrol.

The hot August night, with the daytime heat and humidity still hanging low against the pavement, stuck to his body. Every breath seemed to be a swallow of hot steam. He spotted an orange grove to his right about a hundred meters away. He had passed the set of groves connected to UC Riverside on countless occasions on his way to work. The grove extended off the road for a few dark blocks. That had to be his play. He increased his speed and did not look back. He knew every foot of distance he put between himself and whoever was chasing him could save his life. His heart was screaming out of his chest, but he pushed past the pain. He came up alongside the grove and saw an opening in the wire fencing. He cut hard and veered into the grove. The moment his feet hit the grove soil his pace slowed. The dirt was loose and thick. The smell of a recent watering permeated the air. Gerardo zigzagged to a dark place in the grove's center. He dropped to the ground. He leaned his back against a large orange tree, his heart pounding, his lungs gasping for oxygen. He tried to moderate the citrus- and earth-tinged air. What was it that the Marine told him? Deep breath, focus on controlling your heart rate.

He remembered back to that night in the desert. He knew then his involvement in rescuing the children would haunt him, but he had plenty of other things that kept him up at night. He dropped to his stomach to get a better view of the street. The moist soil had a healthy, fertile smell. As his hands dug into the dirt, he remembered his neighbor telling him the groves had been here over a hundred years. One hundred years of Mexicans like him tending this rich, black soil. Still, here he was running for his life, lying face down in the dirt. It was still dirt. He could never escape it.

He stayed still, his dark clothing melting into the night. He could see the roadway about one hundred yards away. Cars passed by sporadically, the drivers oblivious to the execution awaiting the man in the grove. Then he saw a vehicle slow to a stop. It was a Suburban or some other equally oversized vehicle. The doors opened, and three men got out. Gerardo was far enough away that he could not make out any facial features. He had no doubt they were here to kill him. One of the men turned on a flashlight. The powerful beam traversed the grove. Gerardo lowered his head into the earth and pressed hard. The dirt entered the side of his mouth as he kept his head turned to get a partial view. The beam passed right over him. His heart started pounding faster. Breathe. Deep cleansing breath. Like the Marine had told him. He debated whether to get up and run. He had a good hundred yards head start. They, on the other hand, had guns and an SUV. This was an urban place not open farmland, despite the old stand of citrus he found. Once he left the grove, he would be exposed. He decided to wait. What was the worst that could happen? Two bullets in the back of the head out here in the dirt where he deserved to die?

Just then, with his head still pressed against the dirt, he heard the doors of the vehicle shut and the engine start. He didn't lift his head or move for a solid three minutes. A single ant casually crawled across his face, but he could not move to knock it away. When he lifted his head, he saw the SUV was gone. Still, he remained face down in the dirt and darkness another thirty minutes before he lifted himself to lean against the tree. During that time, Gerardo had time to think about his past, his decision to get involved with those men in the desert, and whether this would truly ever end.

Gerardo took one more long look around the grove for signs of the men or the vehicle. When he was certain he was alone, he reached into his front pocket and pulled out his phone. He looked one more time toward the road to make sure his eyes had not deceived him. He pulled the phone up close to his chest and turned it on. The glow from the phone lit up his face. If there were anyone out there, they would certainly be able to see the light beacon he created. With the phone powered up, he opened his contacts. He found the numbers he was looking for and began to text.

He typed one word. ALAMO. Gerardo looked out at the dark expanse of orange trees and hit SEND.

TWO

Hector Ramirez sat at his desk reviewing reports of investigation, ROIs, that his agents had prepared. They were the usual alien-smuggling arrests and investigations, apprehension of deported aliens found in the United States, and narcotics seizures. Things hadn't changed much since he was in the field. Now, as agent in charge, Ramirez was responsible for seventy agents assigned to the San Diego border region. His desk was piled high with thick manila files and white three-ring binders filled with ROIs, crime scene photos, and rap sheets. Each file represented active investigations over which he was ultimately responsible.

Ramirez removed his reading glasses and rubbed his closed eyes with his thumb and index finger. He leaned back in his chair and took stock of his office. The walls were covered with memorabilia from old cases he had worked. Photos of elaborate smuggling tunnels his agents discovered, including one that showed an underground passage with wooden supports and a rail system complete with a flatbed cart powered by a motorcycle. Framed certificates of recognition for his valuable service to the Border Patrol and task force investigations. To his right, a large, mahogany-bordered blow up of a newspaper feature story. The photo showed Ramirez, five years younger, receiving an award and shaking the hand of the attorney general of the United States. The headline read: Hero Border Patrol Agent Receives Recognition for Valor. The piece was a gift from his wife, which is probably the only reason it hung on the wall. He had read the article hundreds of times by now. It reported the award of special citation for valor and exemplary service for his actions in rescuing twelve immigrant children being trafficked for sexual exploitation. According to the account, Ramirez had been captured and held by dangerous cartel traffickers when he stumbled upon the operation. He managed to escape from captivity when another group of criminals stormed the ranch where he was being held to rob the traffickers of an unknown sum of money. During the shootout that ensued, Agent Ramirez managed to escape with the children. After the vehicle stalled on a desert road, Agent Ramirez singlehandedly confronted and killed five smugglers who followed him to retrieve the children. Two other Border Patrol agents were killed during the incident. Agent Ramirez was credited for the rescue of the children and the capture of a cartel leader, Vicente Corriente-Torres, aka "Caritas."

The agents in the office took to calling him Wyatt Earp for his courage in the western-style standoff. Not to mention a shared physical attribute with Marshal Earp.

Ramirez leaned back and his chair and brushed his thick mustache. Half true, he allowed.

He thought back to that night five years ago. Waiting to be executed. There was no other outcome. While patrolling alone in the backcountry outside of Jacumba, he came upon an isolated ranch in a box canyon. He noticed another Border Patrol vehicle in front of the main house. He drove up to the house to investigate and was immediately confronted by armed men. With automatic weapons pointed directly at him, he had no choice but to surrender. Ramirez was taken inside the house. He was gagged and wrapped like a mummy with duct tape. He couldn't move. He couldn't believe it when he saw two of his fellow agents walk into the room. Two of his friends, in uniform. They had been to his house for barbecues, for Christ's sake.

He tried to talk but could not get any words out. One of his fellow agents walked over to him and gave him a look a disgust.

"Fuck!" he said back to the group of ten or so men in the room. "This is not part of the plan!"

"You have no choice," said a young, confident man. One of the other men had called him Caritas. Clearly, he was the leader. "He has seen you and everyone in here. More importantly . . ."

He walked over to Ramirez.

"He has seen me." At that moment, he delivered a backhand blow with the barrel end of his handgun to the side of Ramirez's face. He felt his cheekbone cave, and the blow sent a sharp burst of pain that immediately engulfed his head. Ramirez could not see anything.

"Once they bring money and pick up the children," the man said, "take him out and make sure he doesn't get found!"

Even though he was in excruciating pain, Ramirez could do the math. He had seen the operation and the two Border Patrol agents who were working with the smugglers. He was dead, and he knew it. They had him wrapped so tightly in duct tape he could not feel his arms. He couldn't move. This was it. He would never see his family again.

Almost two hours went by. Ramirez drifted in and out of consciousness. He had seen two other men come into the house. One carried a canvas duffle bag and dropped it onto the ground. Money. There was no mistaking the soft landing of the bag. Ramirez found it odd that the leader complained they should have used a nicer bag to carry *un medio millón.*

Children, dirty federal agents, an exchange for half a million dollars. He was in agony but did not have to connect too many dots to understand that this was a human-trafficking ring. Trafficking children. There would be no good end to this.

He couldn't recall how long he was out when he heard loud voices and screaming inside the room. His right eye was badly swollen, and his vision was hazy, but he could make out that they had captured someone else. He was some chubby guy in blood-drenched Lakers basketball gear. They him tied to a chair. The leader was cracking him across the face with a handgun. He drove a knife through a bullet wound in the guy's shoulder. The sound of the knife twisting in the flesh was sickening. The screams from the poor sap were unnerving.

Ramirez knew he was next. They would need information out of him, and that was the only way to get it.

And then it happened. Like a bolt of lightning. In this case, more like the bolt of a nine-millimeter Glock automatic.

He saw the flash then heard the boom. He watched the splinters fly as bullets exploded from underneath through the wood floor. Men went down, and others were firing in every direction. Then two men came in from separate doors firing away at the traffickers inside the house. In seconds, they were all dead. All except one. Caritas, the leader, was still alive. He was badly injured on the floor, screaming and holding what was left of his foot.

The room, filled with smoke and the distinctive sulfur smell of expended ammunition, was littered with dead bodies. The two men who had burst in did not notice him at first. Ramirez's heart was pounding so hard he could feel it bounce on the duct tape across his chest. Another group of narcos, he thought. He was a witness to this shootout and now would probably die at their hands. Then he noticed the heavyset, ex-military-looking man with the gun walk in his direction.

"Listen to me very carefully," he said. "You are going to be all right. The less you know about us, the better. Just know that we are on your side, and that you are going to come out of this alive. Do you understand me?"

He watched the men free the guy who had been tortured, gather the weapons and load the children into a trailer. A fourth man with the look of a Marine arrived, and he seemed to be the leader. The conversation he heard revolved around needing to get the children away from the house.

The men loaded him into a pickup along with the injured narco. He watched the Marine lead children out of the barn. There were twelve of them. Six boys and six girls. They looked to be between six and eight years old. They looked tired and scared. The children were loaded into an off-road racing trailer. There was a sense of urgency because they all knew others were on their way.

He was in the truck driven by the man who told him he would be safe. As they sped down a backcountry dirt road, the trailer carrying the children fishtailed and caused the truck and trailer to stall.

The rescuers seemed desperate. They knew more narcos would come after them. They could have left the children and ran but that discussion never happened. They decided to confront an unknown number of armed smugglers. Ramirez could not believe it. These men were not professional law enforcement. They were low on ammunition, and one of them had been tortured. During their conversations, he heard their names. Drew, the leader. Short, brown, military-style hair. In his mid-thirties. He was self-assured, fearless, and made it clear they were not leaving the children behind. Chino appeared to be Latino, but his face had Asian characteristics. He was powerfully built and quick to support Drew without question. Gerardo, a Mexican in his forties, had the look of someone who knew how to use a gun. His three-day stubble offset coal dark eyes. He appeared to have extensive knowledge of cartel activity and smuggling organizations. Finally, there was the man named Chance, whom they also called "Gordo." He was the one who had taken the savage beating and torturing from the smugglers.

When it was clear the men would make a stand against the smugglers, one of them looked over to Ramirez and handed him a gun.

* * *

When the gunmen arrived, Ramirez concealed himself in the brush behind Drew and Chino. Ramirez moved off along a low ridge and noticed a footpath that would take him behind the traffickers. He had no sooner reached the bottom when the gunfire began.

Even after four years with the Army and four years with the Border Patrol, Ramirez had never discharged his firearm in a real-world situation.

"Flanking!" he yelled out to let them know he was coming from behind.

Ramirez could not remember how many shots he heard or how long it took him to come up behind one of the gunmen. What he did remember was how time slowed at the instant he leveled his weapon at the back of the trafficker who was about to shoot the Marine. He remembered his eyes moving from his hands holding the grip of the gun, then down the barrel and to the target. Ramirez remembered his mind registered he was four to five feet away from the man who had his back to him. He remembered his finger hooking the trigger and pulling twice. He was not expecting the kick he got from the weapon since he had only ever fired his own service revolver at mandatory range sessions. The chemical signature of the weapon was different than his own. What he would never forget was the image of the man he shot. Both arms flew out up and forward. One of the rounds must have hit an artery because he remembered the fountain of blood as the body fell forward to the dirt.

Then it was over.

Standing on a desert road near three dead bodies and with twelve children, not to mention several dead traffickers and two federal agents in a nearby burning ranch house, all the men were silent. Ramirez knew that if they waited for law enforcement, the men would be swept into an investigation that might not end favorably for them. He also knew if their names were released to the public, it would be certain that the head of the smuggling ring would send *sicarios* to kill them and their families.

It was Ramirez who proposed or, rather, imposed the solution. He told them Gerardo would stay behind with him and notify law enforcement. Ramirez told them they both would be heroes for saving the children and that Gerardo would no doubt be awarded legal status and witness protection. The surviving narco with the mangled foot was on a federal "most wanted" list. He advised the others to take the money and disappear.

That was when things got strange. It turned out that his new-found partners in crime knew nothing about the half million dollars in cash in the canvas duffle bag on the floor of one of the SUVs. He was almost speechless. These guys had really risked their lives to save the children!

Drew told him the story. He met Chance through Chino. Drew had lost all his savings in a financial fraud and was out of work. His home was about to be foreclosed on. Chance proposed that they meet with Caritas. They were only supposed to drive a load from point A to point B. Somewhere along the way, Drew decided they had to know what or who they were carrying. They opened a compartment on the load vehicle and found twelve young children, all drugged. As they were trying to figure out what to do with the children, Caritas's men arrived and held them at gunpoint. They were about to be executed when Gerardo came out of the brush and saved them. Three of Caritas's men were killed and more were on the way, so they had to leave the children behind. One of the trucks had a GPS locator for a unit they found on the trailer. They decided to use the locator to follow the children and get them back.

Ramirez had difficulty believing that these four men, with limited ammunition and handguns, could hope to be successful against an unknown number of cartel gunmen with automatic weapons.

"I'm assuming you all are former Marines," Ramirez had said to them.

"Chino and I, yes. Sniper unit. Chance," Drew hesitated, "just a badass out of Walmart."

He remembered Chance letting out a laugh that sounded like it hurt.

Drew explained they had the element of surprise. It worked.

* * *

Ramirez watched Drew, Chino, and Chance part ways with Gerardo as if he was a lifelong friend. Near death experiences have a way of doing that. Ramirez and Gerardo wiped down the weapons left at the scene and the vehicles Drew and his companions had driven. Then came the hard part. The story. Ramirez needed to come up with something that would sound plausible and account for a live witness. Gerardo would be interviewed, so his story had to be exactly in sync with Ramirez.

"So," Ramirez had said to Gerardo, "tell me how the hell you got involved in all of this."

Gerardo told him how as a Mexican federal officer detailed to the Culiacan Municipal Police he found himself drawn into the cartel run by the notorious kingpin, El Cicatriz. It began with the mindless passing of information at a cantina regarding federal police activities, but when he was tasked with delivering his childhood friend to the *sicarios* and witnessing his execution, Gerardo had enough. He knew that Cicatriz, who happened to be Caritas's uncle, would be enraged. No one peacefully left his organization. They left when they were dead.

"Why are you part of this?" Ramirez had asked with a sweeping gesture toward the bodies in the road near Jacumba.

Gerardo recounted how he paid smugglers to take him across the desert outside of Tecate into the United States. His group had about twenty or so other crossers. Along the way, he noticed twelve children, six girls and six boys, bound in pairs, being led through the desert with them. The adults were loaded into a refrigerated food truck. Something went wrong and the traffickers left them stranded inside the truck in a false compartment. Hours passed and people began to panic. Gerardo was able to shimmy up the interior wall of the compartment and break through a weak spot. As the migrants escaped from the truck, he decided to run up a hill and hide. It was a few hours later when he saw a trailer come to a stop below the hill. Two armed men in a pickup arrived. The first group, whom he later knew to be Drew and his companions, were forced to kneel in the dirt.

Gerardo told Ramirez that men kneeling in the dirt soon meant bodies lying in the dirt. He could not articulate his reasons to Ramirez, but he described how he came down the hill firing and hit one of the armed men. Drew's group overpowered a guy in mirrored sunglasses who had pistol-whipped the man they called Chance. Later, it was Chance who calmly walked over and executed the man in the sunglasses with two shots to the head.

Ramirez took it all in and was silent for a minute. He was even more convinced now he had done the right thing. There were too many moving parts. Too many things that might ensnare the group in a criminal prosecution.

"Here's the way this is going to play out," Ramirez said to Gerardo.

The story was mostly true. Gerardo would say he escaped the refrigerated truck after the smugglers abandoned them to die inside. This would be easy to corroborate since the truck had not been moved and the Border Patrol no doubt picked up several of the crossers who would confirm the story. Before leaving the truck, Gerardo would tell whoever asked, he searched the cab for anything of value and found a handgun. He separated himself from the group to have a better chance of slipping away. He would tell investigators he made his way up to the top of a ridge and saw the trailer that the children were loaded into earlier in the evening.

"How would I have done that?" Gerardo asked incredulously. "Am I supposed to say I chased the trailer and these kids on foot?"

"That's the thing," Ramirez answered. "I have been working this area for five years now. All of the ridges and dunes look essentially the same to anyone here for the first time. Crossers sometimes wander for days, lost, with no sense of direction and end up only a few hundred yards from where they started. It is very believable that you wandered a few miles and ended up on the ridge above the ranch house."

Gerardo immediately figured out the next problem.

"What, I am some sort of Super Cop who took down all these men by myself?"

"No. The way I see it is that there is no way that you burst in with one gun and took out all of these *pistoleros*."

Ramirez paused and thought for a moment.

"I can say that another group of bandits arrived and shooting started, so I slid back behind one of the couches. When the firing was over, I heard the survivors rustle around looking for the money that the smugglers were discussing while I was tied up and slated for execution."

Gerardo followed the line of reasoning.

"That would have left just a couple of men standing when I came shooting," he said.

"Right," Ramirez said. "After you shot them, you helped me, and we went into the barn and found the children and decided to get them out of there."

"And on our way out of there, the truck and trailer stalled."

"Exactly! Then you and I had the showdown at the O.K. Corral."

"But," Gerardo hesitated a bit, "how will I be able to stay here in the US?"

"That's where I come in," Ramirez said, smiling at his ingenuity. "You are a witness to the smugglers and their organization. I will tell everyone who will listen that the gunmen told you that they knew who you are and where you lived."

Ramirez paused and gave a short laugh.

"How many times did we hear that from pretty boy sociopath?"

Gerardo nodded in agreement.

"The feds need you to make the case against our bleeding crime boss back there. I know my supervisors will get you into witness protection, and then we can get some Justice guys to work on getting you some sort of legal status."

"You think it will work?"

"What choice do we have?"

"I could take my chances on the run," Gerardo said.

Ramirez let out a breath shaking his head.

"You would be running your entire life," Ramirez said as he placed a hand on Gerardo's shoulder. "Look, I owe you and your friends my life. I was dead. I was a rotting body in a desert ravine until you guys came along. I can never repay you enough but rest assured I will do everything in my power to make sure you come out okay."

Ramirez paused to look out over the crime scene.

"This is your chance to get legal status. I say you take it."

"What about Caritas?" Gerardo asked.

"The bleeding narco is not going to be a problem because no one is going to believe anything he says. Just in case, though, I have an alternate plan."

"What's that?"

"I will prepare an ROI outlining my discussions with our little crime boss while we were waiting for the cavalry."

"What's that?" Gerardo asked.

"Report of Investigation. It will outline how he proposed a sincere desire to cooperate against his uncle and related cartel associates. I will visit the asshole in lockup and show him the report. I will impress upon him the need to keep you all out his story otherwise I will be forced to file the report. Once a report like that gets out, Gerardo will get the immediate snitch jacket, and word will travel back to Sinaloa so fast he won't know what to do."

Gerardo began to grin.

"No amount of whining or explaining to his uncle or his cohorts would make them believe he is not a snitch. He would live out the rest of his days in the Bureau of Prisons in a snitch yard with a bunch of child molesters and confidential informants waiting for someone to stick a shank in his kidney."

They stuck to the story. Gerardo was interviewed by Homeland Security, DEA, ICE and, for some reason, the Postmaster Inspector General. He told the same story over and over. His ties to Cicatriz were of extraordinary interest to the DEA because they had been looking for reliable intel on his organization for years. Over the next six months, Gerardo lived in the family housing section of Camp Pendleton while he was shuffled between agencies. In the end, in exchange for his cooperation against Caritas, Gerardo was placed in the Witness Protection Program. He was given a new identity, temporary legal status, and relocated to Riverside, about one hundred miles from San Diego. With his new indistinguishable name, Ricardo Garcia, legal status, ability to speak English and help from the feds, Gerardo secured employment as a city maintenance worker. He liked doing it. He was outside and, more importantly, in public. He could keep an eye out for anything he thought suspicious and, at the same time, never be in the same place.

Five years had passed since that night in the desert, and there had been no resolution of the case against Caritas. Every month, Ramirez monitored PACER, the United States District Court e-file system, to chart the progress of the case. The entries showed numerous "status hearings" with no substantive motions filed. Ramirez had been around long enough in the federal criminal justice system to know something was unusual about the case. A pretrial delay of this length could only mean that the defendant was cooperating with the government in exchange for a lighter sentence. As a leader of a conspiracy to transport illegal aliens and children for sex-trafficking purposes, Caritas's federal sentencing guidelines were off the charts. He would also be held responsible for the "natural and probable consequences" of the conspiracy, which included the death of nine of his men and two federal agents. Caritas was looking at consecutive life sentences. There was no question in Ramirez's mind that he was cooperating.

It was also clear to Ramirez this was no normal cooperation agreement. Defendants who turned snitch to receive a sentence reduction usually had their cases resolved within a year, year and a half max. The US Attorney would provide a "substantial assistance" letter, filed under seal, outlining the defendant's cooperation. With minimum mandatory sentences and the United States Sentencing Guidelines, it was fairly easy to read between the lines and determine whether someone cooperated. In Caritas's case, there was no sentence, no trial, no dismissal. Five years and nothing.

The question then became what was he saying and about whom?

Ramirez knew his name would be forever associated with the case. Although his safety was a concern, Ramirez had an added level of security because he was federal law enforcement. More importantly, he had been associated with a specific case and an identified cartel. If Cicatriz moved against him, the law enforcement blowback against the cartel leader would be enormous on both sides of the border, and that was bad for business. While the fear of reprisal was still always on his mind, Ramirez was more worried about the possibility that the others—Drew, Chino, Gerardo, and the punching bag they called "Gordo"—would be drawn into the mix.

Whatever happens, he thought, I owe them my life.

THREE

It started as "Taco Tuesdays" at El Gordo's. It was Chino's idea. Tijuana-style street tacos with no bullshit. Chino brought in a semi-legendary taco maker from National City named Luis Barbera, known locally as "El Pepino," the cucumber, for reasons known only to him and his now deceased wife, to head up the taco experiment. The concept was simple. They set up a wood and charcoal-burning grill outside and let Luis go to work. He made only chicken, pork and beef tacos, or as El Pepino so elegantly shouted at the uninitiated customer, "*Solo pinche pollo asado, adobada y carne asada, pendejo!*" He was easily in his late seventies, but Luis could stand behind his grill for hours making tacos. His ten inch meat cleaver that he called "El Chingon" was always by his side so he could chop the grilled meats as they came off the grill.

The popularity of the Taco Tuesdays led to Taco Wednesdays, then Thursdays, then to every day but Monday. He needed at least one day off. The result was that El Gordo's soon became one of the most popular cantinas in Santee. They converted a stand-alone, drab stucco building a few blocks from Las Colinas Detention Facility, the women's jail. Drew, Chino, and Chance agreed on the location because they thought Santee would be a low-key place to start a business. With their new-found money, five hundred thousand dollars of liberated narco- and human-trafficking cash, there was an incentive to keep things low key.

On the outskirts of San Diego, the city of Santee had a rural feel to it even though it was a mere fifteen miles from downtown and the coast. In 2018, the housing there was relatively affordable for Southern California, and the population was mostly middle class. There was a famous rodeo in nearby Lakeside every year and there were more trucks with gun racks than cars with surf racks. This suited Drew just fine.

As partners in the now popular cantina, they all took turns managing the bar each night. Chance proved to be a natural, constantly coming up with promotions and specials to increase the clientele. Drew and his wife, Katie, came up with the décor. Although Katie was a little unsure of how the new business partner, Chance, fit it into the big scheme of things or why Drew and Chino called him Gordo, she threw herself into the project. She decided on a Mexican cantina motif. She researched historical photos and documents and was able to get sepia-toned photographs of Mexican settlers and citizens from the area where the restaurant was located. They tiled the floor with two-foot by two-foot saltillo tiles from Tecate, Mexico. Katie went down to custom furniture makers in Rosarito Beach to recreate a bar from a photo of the legendary Hotel Caesar in nearby Tijuana in the 1940s. She made sure that the tequila glasses were from Jalisco, the birthplace of tequila. Finally, she commissioned a mural that dominated the rear wall of the cantina. The mural depicted the glory days of the California ranchos—a sprawling adobe with elegantly dressed men and women watching the roping of cattle in a large holding pen.

The success of El Gordo's was almost immediate. The patrons appreciated the effort the new owners expended in creating something new and authentic for the community on the outer limits of the large city. Soon word got out and not only the locals patronized it but also urban dwellers and hipsters who wanted to experience an Old California setting. Still, with all the success and positive reviews, Drew and his partners shared an unspoken apprehension. They knew that Caritas's case had not been resolved, and they worried about what he may have told the feds about them. Worse, Drew wondered if Caritas got word back to his uncle about their identity.

The unspoken burden the three men shared was the knowledge that someone might come looking for them at any time. They could do nothing about it. Drew thought often about that evening and the events that led up to his decision to cease criminal activity and become a vigilante.

The fallout from that night in the desert took some time to resolve. The most pressing was getting Chance medical attention. Showing up at the emergency room with a gaping gunshot wound in the shoulder held together with duct tape would require a difficult explanation to law enforcement. It was Chino who remembered Billy Briggs, a former corpsman in their unit, was living in Alpine, only thirty miles away. He remembered the corpsman's parents lived in the same town and most likely still had a listed home phone. Chino contacted them and quickly got Billy's cell number. Billy didn't ask any questions and told him that he would be ready for them.

They arrived early in the morning. Briggs was living in small, two-bedroom prefab home on a half-acre of dirt off the Interstate 8. Drew and Chino were covered with dusty dirt and reeking of sweat. Chance looked like he had been in a car wreck. His face was caked with dried blood, both eyes were swollen nearly shut and his upper torso was wrapped with silver duct tape.

Briggs met them outside.

"Holy shit!" Briggs said. "Get him inside before some local fuck gets eyes on him."

The three of them had been in combat together and did not need time to reacquaint themselves. Briggs moved quickly, opening his aid kit and cutting through the duct tape to expose the wound. On the scale of combat injuries, he had seen worse.

"Okay," he said looking into the wound with a penlight, "what's your name, Chief?"

"Chance," he said in a low voice, "but you can call me Gordo."

Drew and Chino laughed.

"Well, Gordo, it looks like you are in luck." Briggs pulled back from the wound to look at Chance. "The entry is pretty clean, no major bones or arteries hit, and the round is still intact and fairly easy to reach."

Briggs looked back to Drew and Chino.

"I can clean and debride the wound. I will pull out the round and sew this poor bastard up, but I can't write you a script for antibiotics. I've got enough here in my kit for three days, but one of you is going to have to make it down to TJ to pick up a one-week supply."

"I'm on it," Drew responded, relieved at the prognosis.

The pain of the cleaning, extraction of the bullet and suturing of the wound paled in comparison to the extreme level of violence and pain that had been inflicted on Chance the previous evening. He didn't even make a sound. Drew was even more impressed with his new friend.

"Remember," Chance said looking up at Drew, "my number one skill is being able to take a beating."

Drew laughed.

"You would have made a good Marine," Chino said.

"And you are one badass motherfucker," Drew added.

Chance, still looking like the loser of a bare-knuckles boxing match, brushed off some of the blood caked over his forehead.

"Copy that," he said with a smile.

* * *

It was Saturday night at El Gordo's, and all three partners were present to celebrate four years in business. The evening was still warm from the hot August day. A beautiful San Diego evening, a light breeze out of the east and no humidity. They shared a table in the back. Katie managed the books and was excited to relay the news of the profits of the venture. Drew watched her beaming from across the table. She seemed to only get prettier over the years. The youthful roundness of her face had given way to elegant, chiseled features. Her eyes, still cobalt blue. She had her hair pulled back in a ponytail, a few strands crossing her forehead. Her light blue summer dress enhanced the unavoidable Southern California tan. She was simply beautiful. Chino was there with his girlfriend, Sonya. They had been together for four years and, as Chino put it, as serious as a Mexican in need of Tapatío hot sauce. Chino hadn't changed. His close-cut hair clung to the top of his scalp with just a few gray strands. His bulky frame had been unaffected by the years. Tonight, he was dressed in his usual—San Diego Padres T-shirt, faded jeans and flip-flops. Sonya—dark, long hair and dark, almond-shaped eyes—was a Mexican beauty. Chino always told anyone who would listen that she was slumming it by hanging out with him. Chance was seated at the far end of the table. He had abandoned his XXL Laker gear and wanna-be gangster mentality. Tonight, dressed in board shorts, flip-flops and a Tommy Bahama camp shirt with a cigar lounge logo on the pocket, he looked like a relaxed and completely normal inhabitant of Southern California. The only visible remnant of that night in the desert was a two-inch vertical scar that ran down the outside of his right eye. Under his shirt, a six-inch zigzagging scar. There was no question that the incident had jolted him emotionally. Being shot, tortured, and facing imminent death makes for an evening that is hard to forget. His demeanor was now more reserved. No hip hop bravado or street talk. Chance stayed quiet and, to others, appeared to keep things buried. Chance and Drew had seen this before. It was the way most warriors acted returning from war.

Drew took in the scene around him. His three friends enjoying feelings of normalcy and success. He couldn't help but smile. It was the best way to erase the memory of the death they were all responsible for as a result of their involvement with Caritas. They did right, he would always tell himself. They saved twelve children from certain physical and sexual abuse and saved the life of an honest Border Patrol agent. Any time that Drew felt ambivalent about his heroic actions, he remembered what Ramirez said to them:

"My kids will still have a father because of you men."

Despite the success of the cantina and the justification for his actions, Drew could not shake the uneasy feeling that things could fall apart at any minute. In a way, this was worse than thinking about the men he killed in the desert.

"Well," Katie said lifting a shot glass of Patron, "here's to you three idiots."

She slid a butcher block tray with sliced lemon and lime wedges across the table. Drew picked up a slice of lime.

"You would have never thought we could pull this off" Chino added.

29

Drew smiled, taking in the moment.

He reached for his shot glass. As he pulled it across the table, he felt the familiar vibration of a message alert from the phone in his front pocket. Twitter alert, news update, messenger notification. Who cares, he thought, it could wait.

Drew raised his glass to the others and reached across the table to tap the other glasses.

"To good fortune and good friends!" Drew said.

"Copy that!" Chino said.

Drew threw the shot back and felt the warm burn of the tequila slide down his throat. He bit into the lime, and the immediate shock of acid and tartness brought the burn back up to his mouth. Drew chased it all with a little salt from the shaker on the table.

His phone vibrated again.

Drew leaned back and pulled out the phone. The screen read "message received." He did not recognize the identifying phone number. He entered his access code, read the message and, for a moment, sat stunned. He looked down again to make sure he was reading the message correctly. At that moment, all the good feelings of success, camaraderie, and safety were crushed. He looked up at Chino. As his Marine Corps sniper spotter, Chino knew all of Drew's moods and could sense something was wrong.

Katie and Sonya got up from the table to use the restroom. They laughed and chatted on their way toward the back of the cantina. Drew maintained eye contact with Chino and slid his phone across the table. He said nothing. Chino picked up the phone and read the message. It was one word in all capitals.

ALAMO.

FOUR

Gerardo walked the three miles to the storage unit he had been renting for the past four years. It was on the east side of Riverside near the 91 freeway. The single-story structure spread out over a few acres next to a public park. Gerardo chose the location for the proximity to the freeway and his apartment. If he had to leave on foot, he could make it to storage without the need to hail a cab or use a smartphone. It was ten thirty in the evening, so no people were milling about the facility. The lights to the main office were on, but he could see no movement inside. He could hear faint music coming from one of the units, but he detected no sign of other people. He knew one day he might have to make a run for the unit and when he did, he might not have time to find his keys. For this reason, he buried a key container in the plant bed directly across from his unit. At the raised bed, he turned back to his unit and sighted a direct line to the lock. This was his way of marking the location of the key. He cleared the debris off the surface and began to dig with his hand. About five inches in, his fingers felt the metal of the key box.

Gerardo brushed off the key and inserted it into the lock. Pulling the sliding door up, he reached over and flipped up the light switch. Everything was the way he had left it. In the center of the room stood a black motorcycle. He purchased the 2007 Kawasaki Ninja four years ago in case he needed to run. The bike had 47,000 miles on it, but he didn't need it for long-term purposes. He needed it to run in a hurry, and he needed it to be fast. He paid four thousand dollars cash and had it fully serviced before storing it. The bike had a 1400 cc inline motor with a top speed of 135 miles per hour. A full gas tank could get him 330 miles. It was jet black with a smoke black wind guard. Its lines were refined and aerodynamic, but it had a just a bit of a praying mantis appearance. The Ninja looked fast standing still.

Off to the side of the motorcycle was a workbench that was clean except for a backpack. To the right of the bench hung a leather riding jacket. Below it, a brand-new pair of black tactical boots. A box next to the boots held a supply of clothes. Gerardo unzipped the backpack to check the contents. In the inner pocket was a bundle of cash wrapped with rubber bands, a leather wallet with a California identification card. His photo but under the name Gustavo Chavez. He pulled a blue LA Dodgers cap and a dark zip-up hoodie out of the main compartment. He unrolled the hoodie and found what he was looking for—a matte black Glock nine-millimeter. Reaching back further into the main compartment he found the extra clip and the box of ammunition.

It was time to go.

FIVE

Hector Ramirez was in his backyard watching the San Diego Padres play a meaningless game against the Rockies. Both teams were at the bottom of the division and now, in August, had no chance of making the playoffs. Not that the Padres ever had a chance. Ramirez had taken out a second on his home in Eastlake, a modern suburban neighborhood in Chula Vista, south of San Diego, after he was rescued from certain death five years earlier. When he made it home that night, Ramirez vowed to devote more time to family. A precocious ten-year-old daughter and always hungry twelve-year-old boy became his number one priority. To that end, he decided to create a backyard where he could enjoy family and social gatherings. He built a large rock grotto-style pool with a cascading waterfall and slide. Next to the pool was a large gas fire pit surrounded by outdoor sofas. The covered portico was his favorite part. It was his own little paradise. There was a built-in, eight-burner gas grill. Off to the side, a custom, Argentine-style wood grate grill was attached to the end of the cooking island. A refrigerator stocked with sodas and water. A Kegerator. God, he loved that beer. The best part was the sixty-five-inch screen against the back wall.

Ramirez spent hours in the backyard, particularly in the warm summer evenings, watching baseball with a cold beer and cigar. He was doing exactly that when he heard the buzz from his phone. The phone was in the kitchen, but Ramirez was so attuned to the vibrate alert from the phone that he could hear it from far away. He ignored it. He wasn't on call. It was after hours. The phone buzzed again. He knew it was a text and that it would stop alerting after the second vibration. Good, he thought, now I can finish my beer. He looked up at the screen. Just another slow-moving game in one of the most beautiful ballparks in America. Nothing really happening.

Shit, he thought, might as well check the phone.

He put his cigar to rest flat against the rail of his ashtray and walked into the kitchen. Ramirez picked up the phone and saw a message from a number he did not recognize. He slid the notification banner back and looked down at the message.

For a moment he couldn't move. He couldn't breathe. He stared down at the message. The feelings from five years ago, the pain, desperation, resignation to certain death, came rushing back to him.

He put the phone down on the granite counter. He leaned in and placed both his hands on the edge and glared at the phone. Maybe the message was an error, or he did not read it correctly. He picked it up again, just to make sure. It was the same. One word, all caps.

ALAMO.

SIX

Drew sat stunned. Katie and Sonya had come back from the bathroom and continued to carry on about the success of the cantina and the bright future. Chino did his best to smile and respond appropriately to Sonya, but all he could think about was the very real possibility that *sicarios* from Sinaloa were headed their way. He tried to rationalize. What did the *narcos* know about them? He remembered that Caritas took photos of their driver's licenses. His memory was quick to defend. We crushed the phone and SIM card. We got the licenses back. What else did they have? What did we miss?

"Chino?" Sonya snapped her fingers at him. "Are you paying attention?"

"Huh?" he said. "Sorry, I was just zoning on something."

"Well, it would be nice if you were part of the conversation."

Once again, he seemed to not take in what Sonya was saying to him. He looked down at the table and took another long sip from the Tecate.

"Sorry, girls," he said. "I need to speak to Drew and Chance for a minute."

Sonya and Katie looked at each other.

"Not a big thing," Chino said, "just some stupid guy shit."

Drew did not wait for a response from Katie. He walked toward the empty area near the back of the bar. Chino and Chance followed.

"I don't know what to . . ." Drew started to say.

"Fuck, Drew," Chance said, "he wouldn't have contacted us unless they got to him."

"I know, I know," Drew said.

"What's our play, Boss?" Chino asked.

"We wait," he said. "Wait for Gerardo to get to us.

"Do you know where he is?" Chance asked.

Drew remembered the postcard that came to the cantina two years ago. It was a photo of the historic Mission Inn in Riverside. One word was scrawled on the back. *Saludos.* Drew figured that Ramirez told Gerardo about the restaurant. The postcard was Gerardo's way of letting them know where he was.

"My guess is Riverside," Drew said.

"That's about ninety minutes away," Chino added.

"Look," Chance said, "you guys get your ladies home. I'll stay and wait for him to show up."

Drew was about to say something when the bartender came over to the group.

Trey had been working at the Cantina for two years and was very popular with the clientele. He was young with the intentionally disheveled good looks of an actor.

"Hey, Drew," he said, "telephone for you."

Trey handed over the phone.

"Hello, this is Drew."

"Drew," the voice on the phone sounded serious, "this is agent Vincent Ramirez, I'm calling . . ."

"Hey Ramirez, why are you calling me on the landline?" he asked.

"I don't know, not used to this cloak and dagger crap. Just thought it would be safer."

"You got the text?"

"Yeah," he said, "I specifically gave him that phone in case something happened."

"Did you speak to him?"

"No. We always figured that if something happened, he would have to move quick. We agreed that we should meet at a specific place. The text to me means that he is on his way."

"Is he in Riverside?"

"Yes." Ramirez didn't ask how Drew knew that. "So, he should be here in about an hour and a half."

"Where's the meeting place?"

"We figured we needed a place that was open twenty-four hours with no danger of closing down any time soon."

"Which Denny's are you meeting at?" Drew knew that was the only answer.

"The Denny's in Pacific Beach, you know it?"

"Who hasn't slogged down Moons Over My Hammy after a night of PB drunkenness?"

"Yeah, well," Ramirez said, "I'm on my way there."

"Copy that." Drew brought the phone back to Trey.

SEVEN

Gerardo fired up the Ninja. The throaty whine and vibration felt like unbridled power beneath him. He slowly made his way out of the parking lot and onto the road. He knew what he had to do. The meeting spot was 120 miles south in Pacific Beach. Head straight there, he thought. But part of him needed to know for sure. There were a few things he needed from his apartment. Vestiges from his old life. Photos, notes, phone numbers . . . fuck, he hoped he'd not written down Drew's or Ramirez's numbers for someone to find in the apartment. What else was in there that could connect him to the others from that evening?

He was dressed in dark clothing, a dark helmet, and rode a dark motorcycle. This would be as unidentifiable as he would ever be. He had to try. As he drove down Martin Luther King toward the 215, he weighed the risk. He was moving on a fast vehicle. He could be gone before they even noticed him.

The sun had set, and the sky surrendered to a darker blue-black. A few stars sprinkled the sky. Speed away into the dark, he thought. He needed to make it to San Diego to plan his next move. The right thing to do was to contact his handler in the Witness Protection Program. United States Marshal Dennis Vance seemed like a nice enough guy, but Gerardo never completely trusted him. Now, if he was right, someone had penetrated the veil of the Witness Protection Program. The only ones who knew who he was or where he was were government agents. That means somebody inside had leaked information. In reality, there were only four people in this country whom he could trust. He needed to get to them because he needed their help and they needed to know their lives were in danger.

It was still gnawing at him. Who were they? Did he know them? *Puta madre,* he thought, he needed to know. Instead of heading straight to the freeway, he turned right down Chicago Avenue toward his apartment.

From a distance, everything looked normal. It was a newer complex, two stories, bright white with copper accents. Gerardo had the second-floor corner unit facing the street. He slowed the motorcycle as he approached the complex. The lights were off in his place. The activity in the complex appeared normal. A few lights on in other units. He could see one of his neighbors in a kitchen. The downstairs neighbor, a UC Riverside cop, was leaving to go to work. He was dressed in uniform. Even though he was a campus cop, keeping the peace among a bunch of college kids, his outward appearance looked like law enforcement to anyone watching.

This was good. A cop living below him might chase some criminals away. The thought quickly dissipated because he knew these were not common criminals looking for him. A uniform meant nothing to them.

He started to turn into the parking lot when he noticed the headlights from a parked vehicle illuminate to his left. He looked over at the instant he heard the engine turn over. Gerardo did not stop. He continued into the parking lot and turned to the left, away from his apartment. He could see that lights were coming from a car that started to move. He increased his speed in the parking lot and began to circle behind the complex. The rear of the complex had an exit to a residential street. As he turned left toward the exit, he saw a second vehicle parked on the street across from the rear exit.

Fuck. This is not good.

He could see the outlines of a driver and a passenger and that the vehicle was not running. He purchased the Ninja for acceleration and maneuverability. After he bought the bike, he practiced sudden bursts of acceleration and turning. He took the bike up into the mountains above Orange County and ran it at high speeds on the winding roads. He was ready for this.

He hit the throttle. The high-pitched whine of the motor pierced the silence in the parking lot. He heard the parked car's engine start. He passed the vehicle and saw movement inside. Behind him, Gerardo could hear the screech of the tires from the other vehicle.

Adrenaline supplanted any fear he might have had. Gerardo was confident he could outrun them. Unless these cars were Ferraris, which they were not, they would not be able to match the torque and acceleration of the Ninja. He turned right onto the residential street and headed right again down Chicago. Speeding past the orange groves attached to UC Riverside he tucked himself low on the bike and flew. He couldn't be sure, but he thought he heard the muffled crack of gunfire. He did not look behind him. He needed to get to the freeway and keep an eye out for other vehicles that they may have alerted. If they were smart, they would have someone waiting by the 215.

He could see the freeway rising above the road about a quarter mile away. The university was on his left, more orange groves on his right. He accelerated toward the on-ramp. The road T-ed against a hill under the 215. He realized the direction he took on the freeway might give away his destination. He decided to go the opposite way. He slowed to pass under the freeway and turn left onto the ramp to the 215 when he saw a car off to the side. The lights were illuminated, the windows tinted. The rear driver's side rear window was open. Then he saw it. It was unmistakable. A bright muzzle flash. He could not hear anything, most likely because of the whine of the motor and the helmet he was wearing. He leaned into the bike as low as he could and downshifted into the turn. The vehicle was now moving to his right trying to cut off his route to the ramp. Gerardo accelerated. The bike shot like a rocket. Another muzzle flash from the vehicle. He had not been hit, but now the car was on the move

He entered the freeway at about eighty miles per hour and immediately began to weave in and out of cars. He sped down the 215 away from San Diego. Increasing his speed to ninety miles per hour to get farther from his pursuers, Gerardo did not look back. He cut back on the 10 toward Los Angeles and then caught the 15 back toward San Diego. He figured he had been traveling at speeds between ninety and one hundred for about fifteen miles and was now clear of them.

Gerardo slowed and moved over to the slow lane. He glanced over his shoulder to check for any erratically moving vehicles. It all looked normal. When he was certain he was not being followed, he tucked into the bike and flew down the freeway at one hundred miles per hour plus for another ten miles just to make sure. He slowed again and checked behind him. It looked clear. Normal traffic. Normal drivers. Everyone except him. He doubted that anyone driving on this road was on the run from cartel *sicarios.*

He had a clear shot to San Diego. Another ninety minutes to think about what had happened in the desert five years ago and what shitstorm was coming his way.

EIGHT

Jimmy Connors was standing in the kitchen of his two-bedroom apartment in Clairemont. It wasn't so much of a kitchen as it was a place that had a small refrigerator and a two-burner stove. The refrigerator had an Oakland Raiders cheerleader calendar opened to August and held in place by a magnet clip. It was some generic blonde with lots of hair and ample cleavage, but Jimmy loved looking at it. Next to the calendar was a photo of his nephew, Chester, with his two business partners in front of the bar they opened. Jimmy never understood how his slouch of a nephew could be associated with what looked like straight-up, law-and-order Marines. Jimmy had spent ten years in the Navy never rising above an E-4, petty officer third class. He was last stationed on the USS Carl Vinson, an aircraft carrier homeported in San Diego Bay. After the Navy, he spent the better part of twenty miserable years working as civilian technician in the Naval Yards. He had lived in the scruffy Clairemont neighborhood of America's Finest City for twenty years with an angry ragdoll cat and no close friends. Jimmy was a drinker and a fighter. As a drinker, he was world class. As a fighter, he usually was not the winner. He always had a chip on his shoulder about Marines. They always thought they were better than Navy swabs. Whether they were or not, Jimmy ended up in plenty of fistfights over it.

He inherited Chester after his nephew was sent to juvie prison for punching the ticket of his no-good, wife-beating father. Jimmy knew the son of a bitch better than anyone because he was his brother. When Chester was released from the Youth Authority, his mother was nowhere to be found, and Jimmy was his only next of kin. He put a roof over Chester's head and food in the fridge, but Jimmy didn't know jack about being a father figure. He did his best, even through various deployments, and it never was good enough. Jimmy and Chester were more like roommates, but both knew they were the only family left.

Below the photo of Chester and his partners was a photo taken eighteen years ago on Chester's sixteenth birthday. The photo, taken at a Chargers-Raiders game, showed Jimmy in his black Raiders game jersey standing next to his nephew. When he looked at the picture, Jimmy could sense the onset of his own middle age. His perpetual crew cut, graying at the sides, the crow's feet etching themselves into the creases that he now possessed. Now at fifty-seven, he looked years older. His crew cut had become shock white. His once bright blue eyes had seemingly faded to hazy grey. The deep furrows across his forehead gave him the appearance of constant dismay and lack of patience. Living off skimpy retirement checks and part-time plumbing work gave Jimmy plenty of reasons to be upset.

Jimmy was on the phone, and he was angry. He leaned back against the sink. The small of his back contacted the edge of one of the many dirty plates that had been piling up the last two weeks. He had been on a call to his cell service provider for fifty minutes now and was becoming more and more upset. Now he was on hold, elevator music on the line. The apartment was small and cramped and hot. The recent heatwave pushed temperatures into the nineties, and the apartment had no air conditioning. The sliding windows in his living room were open, and the front door was open to let in some air.

There he stood. In the kitchen, in a pair of paint-stained, faded green cargo shorts and rumpled, blue-toned Hawaiian shirt, ten-year-old leather Top-siders molded into the shape of his feet. Sweating.

A voice came on the line.

"Good evening, sir," the voice said, "if I can please have your name and account number to verify the . . ."

"Connors," he interrupted. "James, Jimmy, like the tennis player."

The voice on the other end was silent.

"Jesus, don't you know who he is?"

The service representative continued with the script he was no doubt reading from.

"In order to fully assess the issues that you are having with your phone service, I will need to transfer . . ."

"Don't you do it . . ."

"transfer you to a technical . . ."

"Do not send me to . . ."

"a technical support representative."

"Listen to me," Jimmy yelled into the phone, "if you transfer me to some customer service room in Mumbai, I am going to walk over to the nearest Sprint store and shove this phone up the ass of the first employee I see. And it is all going to be your fault for transferring . . ."

The phone went to static for a second.

"This is Sprint customer service representative Tony," a voice said in a heavy Indian accent, "I am here to assist you with any problems that you may . . ."

"Jesus Fucking Christ!" Jimmy screamed into the phone.

"Sir," Tony sounded offended, "I would request that you refrain from using profanity during our conversation."

"Profanity?" Jimmy screamed into the phone. "Listen to me you curry-loving piece of shit . . ."

The phone line went silent.

"Fuck! Fuck!" Jimmy slapped his hand on the kitchen counter.

He turned from the counter and saw two men standing at his open front door. Two dark-skinned Mexican men. He assumed them to be Mexican, anyway. It didn't matter to him. He lumped them into the category he used for anyone who lived south of Chula Vista. They were both the same size. Not taller than himself, maybe five-nine or five-ten. One was wearing jeans and a tucked in western-style shirt. A big, shiny belt buckle drew Jimmy's attention. The other was also in jeans but wearing a blue *guayabera,* a beaner waiter's shirt, as he was fond of calling them. They stood there and said nothing. The one in the *guayabera* was holding an eight-by-eleven sheet of paper with a photo on it. He looked down and then looked up at Jimmy.

"You *pendejos* are in the wrong fucking place!" After living more than twenty years in San Diego, even an amateur racist like Jimmy knew how to swear in Spanish.

They said nothing.

"I told you that . . ."

They started walking toward him.

"Hold on, you wetbacks! Who the fuck do you think you . . ."

The one with the belt buckle reached behind his back and pulled out a gun. Jimmy stopped. They continued walking toward him. Jimmy did not have to time to consider why they were here or why they wanted him. He reached for a knife in the butcher block on the counter. The man in the *guayabera* rushed Jimmy and pushed him back against the refrigerator. The three bottles of liquor on top of the refrigerator bounced up into the air and crashed onto the kitchen floor. Jimmy struggled to push back when the one with the gun came in from the side. Jimmy felt the hard crack of steel against his skull. He was stunned. His torso had bent over with the blow, and he came up and couldn't see. His eyes could not focus. Another blow came across his side of his face and knocked him to the ground. The man who pushed him against the refrigerator was now on top of him and driving his knee into Jimmy's chest. He couldn't breathe and was able to make out a few of the man's features. Pockmarked cheeks, porn mustache. He tried to speak but couldn't get out any words. Neither of the two had uttered a word. He was trying to move when he looked over and saw a boot coming toward his face. He turned right before impact.

NINE

The Denny's in Pacific Beach is a never-closing, twenty-four-hour hub for surfers, drunks, and tourists. The restaurant stands on the corner of Garnet Avenue and Mission Boulevard across from the famed Crystal Pier. Garnet Avenue packs an extraordinary number of bars onto a short span of road. In less than a mile there are over twenty-five. The Denny's lies at the end of the avenue and has a constant flow of patrons at all hours. The bland, beige façade with red accents harkens to the 1960s, complete with faux stone walls and bright yellow sign. The busy corner is constantly occupied by pedestrians and bicyclists waiting to cross.

Drew and Chino arrived together at eight thirty in the evening. This was a Tuesday, so the madness of Pacific Beach partying was manageable. The interior was not unlike any other Denny's in the country. High-back, red vinyl booths, plastic-top tables with wooden chairs, pendant lights centered over the tables with just enough light to see what you were eating but not necessarily enough to examine it. On the walls were historical photos of older Denny's restaurants. Even at this hour, the aroma of coffee and maple syrup permeated the air.

Drew spotted Ramirez in back. He hadn't changed much from the last time he saw him, except for the large mustache that stretched across his face. Ramirez saw them coming his way, gave them a wave, and stood to greet them.

For a moment no one spoke. An unspoken bond existed between the men. They made it through battle, they killed men, and they had lived. Each owed his life to the other, and the reality of the bond was sobering. Drew spoke first.

"You are one person I hoped that I would never see again."

Ramirez smiled.

"No offense," Drew added quickly.

"None taken."

"I like the badass 'stache," Chino said.

"Yeah, well this is what you get when you sit around at a desk all day." Ramirez used his fingers to brush down the sides of the mustache.

"Any word from Gerardo?" Drew asked.

"Not yet," Ramirez said. "Still waiting for him to get here. How about your friend? I don't think I ever got his name."

"Chance," Chino said.

"But you called him something different."

Drew laughed. "Gordo."

"That's right."

"He's on his way," Drew said.

A waitress in her early twenties with blonde hair pulled back in a ponytail and wearing a mustard-colored dress with printed Denny's logos arrived at the table. She had the bright smile of someone not yet saddled by the realities of age. She handed them each a menu and left to get the coffee they ordered.

"Well," Ramirez said. "We know Gerardo's text meant that he has been found."

"How could they have found in him in witness protection?" Chino asked.

"Money can get you anything. As we all know, there are dirty feds everywhere. There is a whole line of people who could have leaked the info. US Marshals, US Attorney staff, even local law enforcement." Ramirez stopped to consider the situation.

"If you think about it," he continued, "the only names these *narcos* have are mine and Gerardo's since the original ROIs would have identified him as a material witness. The reports also would have my name all over them."

"They also know about Chance," Chino said.

"How's that?" Ramirez asked.

"He's the guy that put us into contact with Caritas in this first place."

"The feds don't know about him." Ramirez seemed confused.

"But Caritas certainly knows, and he could have said anything while he's been locked up," Drew said.

"Do they have any identifying information about you two?"

"Only that they called us' 'the Marines,'" said.

"I know that we got our driver's licenses back," Drew said.

"And crushed the phone and tossed the SIM card," Chino added.

"Well, it all doesn't matter right now since they got to Gerardo," Ramirez said.

"True that," Chino said. "If they can get to him, then they can get to us."

Just then Drew saw Chance walk in through the front door. He lifted his arm to get his attention. Chance nodded and walked over.

Ramirez looked up, hardly recognizing him. He stood up and extended his hand for a shake.

"The last time I saw you, your face looked like raw hamburger meat and you were wearing that dumb-ass Laker gear in the middle of the desert."

Chance laughed. "Not much of an improvement, huh?"

Chance took a glance around the restaurant and sat down.

"Has anyone heard from Gerardo yet?" he asked.

"Not yet," Drew said. "We're standing by. I might suggest the Lumberjack Slam. Two eggs, bacon, sausage, and ham. All the essential pork products."

Chino laughed but checked the menu to see if it was really there. He was hungry.

"So," Ramirez said to Chance, "we've been talking a bit, and from what we know, they already know who you are because you met Caritas before that night."

Chance nodded.

"They know my name because of the newspapers and television accounts of the shootout," Ramirez added.

"And they may know Gerardo," Chino added.

"Why do you think that?" Ramirez asked.

"At least one of those narcos called him *detective* before he got wasted," Drew said.

"Yeah," Chino said, "I definitely remember that motherfucker with the sunglasses saying that."

"And he was clearly a leader under Caritas,"Drew said.

"I think our boy is here," Ramirez said, craning his neck around Chance.

Gerardo entered the restaurant. Black clothes, black backpack, black motorcycle helmet.

He looked around and made eye contact with the group.

They all stood for Gerardo as he arrived at the table.

"*Órale, caballeros!*" Gerardo reached out, and Chance was first to shake his hand. "*Qué onda, Gordo!*"

"Nothing much," Chance answered, "unless you count the very real possibility that there is one angry drug lord out to murder our asses."

Gerardo was too tired to laugh. He finished shaking hands with everyone and slid down into a chair.

"Well," he said, "I think that they have finally started to figure things out."

"It might be a little worse than that," Ramirez said.

"Worse than a fuck ton of *sicarios* heading our way?" Chance said, looking down into his coffee cup.

"If they got to Gerardo, then it means that someone in the Department of Justice got them the information."

"Which means that we can't trust anyone," Drew said.

Chino said, "Except for everyone at this table."

The waitress came back to the table, and they stopped talking. They placed their orders. Chino did order the Lumberjack Slam, and the rest got burgers. Another smile from the waitress, oblivious of the dire circumstances, and she was off.

"Why don't you fill us in on what happened out there," Drew said to Gerardo.

Gerardo related the events of the night. His travel back to the apartment and the short chase that ensued.

"How sure are you that they made you?" Drew asked.

"Three cars and people shooting at me," Gerardo looked at each one of them. "I'm pretty sure they found me."

"So, what's our play?" Chino said, looking to Drew.

"For starters," Drew said as he pushed his coffee aside, "knowledge is power. We know that someone is coming so we can take precautions."

"But what the hell, they just want to kill us because we fucked them up a little bit a few years back," Chance said.

"That and pride," Gerardo said. "Caritas is in prison for who knows how long and—"

"There's the matter of the half million in cash," Chino said.

"Whatever it is," Drew said, "this is bad. We can't wait on this. We need to start thinking about a plan."

Chance was about to say something when he felt the vibration of his phone in the side leg pocket of his board shorts. He pulled the phone out and saw a text from an unknown number.

"Fuck!" Chance nearly yelled through his clenched mouth.

The others stopped talking and looked over at Chance. He was not talking. Chance stared at the image on his phone.

"What's up, Gordo?" Gerardo asked.

Chance said nothing. He slid the phone across the table. Drew picked it up. Chino and Gerardo moved closer to see the screen. The image depicted an older white man. He was shirtless with his arms behind his back. His right eye was swollen. Blood was visible around his mouth.

"What the fuck, Chance," Chino said. "Who is this dude?"

The Southern California summer tan had left his face. Chance was staring down at the table. He took a deep breath.

"That's Jimmy," Chance said. "He's my uncle. My only family. He's the mean, ornery son of a bitch that took me in after I was released from YA."

"Motherfucker!" Chino said.

The telephone on the table shook as a new message arrived.

Chance reached across and opened the message.

"What the fuck?"

The image was that of two children. A boy and girl. Dark haired, maybe twelve or thirteen. They were sitting on grass somewhere by the water. Both had on T-shirts that read "San Diego Junior Lifeguards."

He slid the phone across the across the table.

Ramirez didn't need to focus on the image.

"Shit!" he said. "Those are my kids!"

Drew sat silent. He thought of his own children and Katie at home. Were they safe now? Should he call Katie?

Taking a closer look at the photo, Ramirez was able to place the time.

"This was taken within the last few days," he said. "They are wearing the Junior Lifeguard shirts, and they started the camp a few days ago. They know where my kids are, goddammit."

"Okay," Drew tried to remain calm, "we know they can tie Chance, Gerardo, and Ramirez to this incident. Me and Chino are the unknowns."

Drew looked at Ramirez and could see the panic in his eyes. Drew knew that he would feel the same if this was a photo of his kids.

"We can use that to our advantage," he said.

Gerardo looked at the photo of the children, and an odd bit of solace grew from memories of his violent employment with Cicatriz. He placed the phone down on the table.

"If they wanted to kill us," he said calmly, "they would have done it. No threats through the phone. I know the way they operate. This is not like some movie where they tell someone that they are going to kill them before doing it."

He looked over to Ramirez.

"They would just kill us. No demands. No threats."

Drew began to understand.

"He's right," Drew said. "They want something. They need something from us."

The waitress passed by to ask if the table needed anything. Drew waved her off.

"Whatever it is," he continued, "it is important."

"Important enough to threaten a federal agent," Ramirez added.

"Right." Drew was thinking it through. "It can't be just about the money."

Gerardo was sure that was right. Victims didn't get warnings, and the crews didn't do much planning. Just pick up some *pobre pendejo*, drag him out to some dirt road and put two bullets in the back of his head. No, he thought, they needed something.

"What do we have?" Gerardo asked. "Something of value for them. They think we have something."

Gerardo looked to everyone at the table.

"Except for the bag of cash, nobody walked away with anything of value," Drew looked to the others. "Right?"

Nods of agreement.

The phone vibrated again. They all looked down at the phone. Chance reached out and picked it up. He opened the message.

VIERNES. 1700 HR. VISTA DEL MAR.

"I guess we were right," Chance slid the phone across the table. "They want to meet."

"Vista del Mar in Chula Vista on Friday," Chino said. "I know the place. Fairly busy most of the time. They make a mean *siete mares* soup."

"Five p.m.," Drew said. "The place shouldn't be too crowded."

Drew looked over to Ramirez.

"I think I know the answer," he said, "but is there any chance you might want to get the feds involved in this?"

"Well, for starters," Ramirez said as he slouched back in his seat, "that means my entire statement is perjury. A federal crime. But more importantly, it would mean that Caritas would probably walk since all of the evidence provided against him is from me and my co-conspirator."

Ramirez looked over to Gerardo.

"Of course," he continued, "this does not include the fact that you boys would be implicated in the deaths of nine narcos and two federal agents."

"In other words," Chino said, "we all go to jail."

"At the very least, we are all in custody pending trial which could be a year and a half from now," Ramirez said as he straightened up.

No one said anything for a few long seconds. The choices were limited, and they all knew it.

"Well, fuck it," Drew said. "We have two days to gather some intel about the meeting place. Chino and I will be eyes on the site. We can set up a tail and follow anyone who shows up at the meeting. Once we have their home base, we can decide on a plan of action."

Drew looked around the restaurant to see if other patrons were listening to the conversation.

"We are also going to need weapons," Drew said in a low voice.

Ramirez laughed.

"What could be so funny about that?" Drew asked.

"That's the one bit of good news." Ramirez smiled. "You know those guys who go to the dumb-ass gun shows, spout off about the Second Amendment and the NRA?"

"I know plenty of those types of assholes," Chino said.

"I am that asshole!" Ramirez laughed again. "I have enough weapons and ammo at home to arm a Marine rifle squad."

"Well then," Chance said. "Let's get ready to get my piece-of-shit uncle back."

"One question," Chino said and started to smile. "You got a sniper rifle?"

Ramirez turned to Drew.

"Abso-fucking-lutely!"

TEN

Jimmy Connors was mad as hell. These no good, border-crossing Mexicans had beaten him senseless and thrown him in the trunk of some piece-of-shit Toyota. His hands were zip tied behind his back. The right side of his face was bloody and swollen. He could barely see out of his right eye. He braced his legs against the wall of the trunk to keep himself from rolling every time the vehicle turned. He had seen this in movies a thousand times. He wasn't optimistic. His heart was racing. He was breathing hard. Mostly he was pissed.

The car had been moving for about an hour now. Were these assholes taking him to Mexico? Fuck. Dying on some shit street in TJ was not something he had planned for himself. Then again, he never did have a plan for himself. The big question that rattled around his brain was what the fuck had he done to someone that led to this? The truth, and Jimmy knew it, was he hadn't done anything with his life the past ten years except piss it away in shitty bars and watch Fox News.

Fucking Chester! It had to be. His wanna-be gangster phase was over, but he still talked a tough guy game. Still called himself "Chance." His Marine partners called him "Gordo." What type of wetback bullshit was that? Had to be something that fat, dumb fuck got himself into.

He heard the tires crossing over gravel. The car slowed and eventually stopped. He could hear the doors open and footsteps move toward him. At least two men were speaking in Spanish.

This is it, Jimmy thought.

The trunk opened and a flashlight beam burned into his vision. He pulled his head away from the light.

"*Despierta, pendejo,*" one man yelled.

Someone grabbed Jimmy by the back of his shirt and pulled his torso up from the trunk. Another man grabbed him by the feet and flung him out of the trunk and onto the ground. The impact caused the air to leave Jimmy's lungs. He gasped for breath but was kicked in the ribs before he could recover. He coughed up spit and blood.

"Levántate, puto!" Jimmy knew enough Spanish to know that he should get up or take another blow to the ribs.

"Okay, motherfuckers!" Jimmy yelled.

He rolled to his right side and tried to lift his torso. Jimmy was able to get one knee under him and was trying to get up when one of the men ripped him up using the back of his shirt.

"Fuck you, wetbacks!" His entire body was in pain. It hurt him to breathe.

Jimmy's vision was beginning to regain focus. He could see a single-level house. Nothing special about it. He couldn't make out the color in the dark, but he was sure it was some boring beige or off-white. He looked to his right and then to his left. There were no houses nearby. He caught the silhouette of a mountain or set of hills behind the house.

He tried to place where he was. They had driven for less than an hour, so he figured that they might have driven into Mexico, but he would have heard the noise associated with crossing the border. No, he thought, he had to be somewhere in East County. Definitely rural since no houses were nearby. He was trying to commit the visual details to memory when the man who was dragging him on his left side slipped his grip. Jimmy, hands tied behind his back, crashed face down into the sharp gravel walkway leading up to the front door.

"You stupid fucks!" he cried.

The man said nothing. He grabbed Jimmy by the crook of his arm and dragged him up and forward. They pulled him into the house. The lights were off, but he could make out a few pieces of furniture. Folding chairs next to a plastic table. A dark sofa against the far wall. A small flat-screen television sat on a low table in front of the couch. One of the men switched on a floor lamp, and he could see that no one lived here. The house was only used for things that were happening to him now.

What was happening?

"Listen," he tried to reason, "I think you got the wrong guy. I'm nobody. I don't know—"

The man who dropped Jimmy delivered a kick to his ribs. Pain radiated throughout his body. Jimmy was on the ground again, face up. He could now make out the features of the one who kicked him. Mexican, definitely Mexican. Slightly overweight. Weak attempt at a mustache. Looking up at the man, Jimmy thought he looked no different than any other Mexican he had seen making burritos at Los Dos Panchos or at the carwash. He would never be able to identify this guy to the police.

The thought quickly left his mind. The police. I'm not going to make it to the police. I'm not making it out of here.

They dragged him into a small bedroom and dropped him again on the floor. One of the men cut the zip ties and freed Jimmy's hands. The blood rushed to fill the veins that had been restricted, and the feeling of his arms in a normal position was, for an instant, euphoric. He looked up, and the second man was holding a gun.

"Look, *amigo*," Jimmy said. "I don't know who you think I am but —"

Before he could get another word out, Jimmy felt a blow to the side of his head. The crash of steel against his cheek made a dull thud that did not match the jolt of pain that drilled into his head. He stayed flat on the floor, trying to focus his bleary vision. The last he saw before he passed out was one of the men standing over him with a telephone. He saw the flash from the phone camera, and then everything went to black.

ELEVEN

Ramirez was in his office the next day when he got the call. Charles Winters was on the line. Winters was the director of the Regional Task Force for the Western states. The task force oversaw operations from California to Texas and interacted with multiple agencies. Ramirez couldn't even count how many levels Winters was above him on the organizational flow chart.

Ramirez, still shaken from seeing the photos of his children sent to the phone, took a deep breath and released the hold button.

Winters did not bother to introduce himself.

"I will be in your office today at thirteen hundred to discuss your involvement in the Corriente case."

Ramirez did not know how to respond. The timing of the call in relation to the events of the day before caused him to hesitate. He looked at his watch. Twelve forty-five. The guy would be in his office in fifteen minutes. *Thanks for the notice.* This seemed like an ambush. "Sir?" he said. "The ROIs for that case are all in the case file and pretty much lay out word for word my involvement."

"Well," Winters said in a quick, condescending tone, "they are insufficient. I have been working with Justice to assist in prosecution of the case, and there appear to be numerous gaps in your account."

"Sir, I believe that the timeline is fairly detailed and accurate, and it has been over five . . ."

"Ramirez!" Winters raised his voice. "Did I ask for your opinion?"

"No sir."

"Then be prepared to brief me when I arrive." The phone went silent.

What a douchebag. He got up from his desk and went to the metal filing cabinet against the wall. He opened the top drawer and reached to the back. A red accordion file was wedged into the last file holder. He took the file back to his desk and emptied the contents. As a witness, he was not entitled to the entire investigation file, but Ramirez did have copies of his ROIs and memorandums of investigation, "402 memos," from other government agencies. He leafed through photographs of the crime scene. The dirt road where their final shootout occurred. An SUV and a pickup truck riddled with bullet holes. Four men dead in the dusty dirt. He took particular note of the one he had killed. Ramirez never took the time before to study the photo. The man was lying face down. He was literally eating dirt. His arms were splayed out. The two shots he fired into the man's back were adjacent to each other and opened a hole about the size of a baseball.

He never saw it coming. *Fuck that guy*

In reality, Drew and Chino confronted the attackers and fired from different locations. In his account to Homeland Security Investigations, Ramirez claimed that the stress of his capture and escape had made his recall of exact details difficult. He told the HSI agents that he and Gerardo had escaped and taken three weapons with them after the flight from the ranch house. He told the investigators that Gerardo rushed them from the front and he swept in to flank the gunmen. He was never specific about how many shots he fired or details of the shootout. The dead federal agents in the ranch house were closely associated with wanted human traffickers, so investigators were more than willing to accept the hazy and heroic version of events from Ramirez. This would make for good press. Dead federal agents tied to cartel activity would not.

He read his statement. He read it again. He recommitted the details of his statement to memory and was ready to answer any question regarding his involvement except for the presence of Drew and Chino. Ramirez lost track of time and was surprised when his telephone buzzed. His secretary alerted him that Winters was on his way back to the office.

He placed the reports in a stack in front of him on the desk. Winters opened the door. He didn't knock.

"Director Winters, it's a pleasure . . ." Ramirez said as he stood up from behind his desk and extended his hand.

Winters stood behind the chair in front of the desk. He did not reach out to shake hands. Ramirez dropped his arm. Winters said nothing at first. He walked over to the wall with the framed newspaper article and was silent as he read through it.

Pompous ass, Ramirez thought. Typical management asshole right down to the standard gray suit, button-down white shirt, and red and blue striped tie. Of course, no management uniform would be complete without the American flag lapel pin on his jacket. Winters was in his mid-fifties. His ashen complexion faded into his gray-white crew cut.

He turned to Ramirez.

"Impressive, Agent Ramirez." He tapped the glass on the frame with two fingers.

Ramirez did not know how to respond.

"How much of this actually happened?"

"I'm sorry, sir," Ramirez stammered, but then recovered a bit. "I don't understand what you are asking."

Winters went to stand behind the chair again.

Ramirez knew he was standing to try to intimidate him. Fuck that, he thought. I have been kidnapped, bound, beaten, and nearly executed. I have killed a man. What the fuck have you done?

Ramirez sat down in his chair and leaned back. Winters's eyes widened at the show of confidence.

"What is that you want to know, sir?" Ramirez asked.

"I've seen the ROIs and the 402s," Winters said as he pulled the chair back to sit down. "What I am interested in is what is not in the reports."

"I don't understand."

"I want to know what evidence you discarded, looked at and hid or retained in some other manner," Winters said.

"Sir," Ramirez leaned forward. "Are you suggesting that I tampered with evidence or somehow obstructed justice?"

"No," Winters said as he looked around the office. "I just wanted to know if there was anything that you decided not to inform HSI about during the investigation."

The half-smile on Winter's face made Ramirez want to reach across and slam his face down on the desktop. Ramirez shifted in his seat and tried not to look nervous.

"Well, sir, it's like this," Ramirez said very slowly. "The entirety of my recollection of the events that night is contained in the investigation reports and recordings of my interview. I did my best to be as accurate and detailed as I could."

Winters pursed his lips and looked around the office as if he were bored.

"But like I have told you before," Ramirez continued, "until you have been beaten, tied up, and basically told that you are going to be murdered and then had to shoot and kill men in order to survive . . ."

He paused for a moment to let the words sink in to this pencil pusher who had never faced any significant danger, unless you count rounding up ten or so illegal aliens off a dirt road. Ramirez could see that Winters was uncomfortable.

"You will have to excuse me if I did not recall the exact words spoken or articles of clothing worn by the assholes that were going to sell those children to pedophiles and murder me."

Winters glared at Ramirez.

"What I want to know, Agent Ramirez, is whether you saw or *heard*," Winters put the emphasis on heard, "anything of evidentiary value which was not accounted for in the discovery."

"Like what?"

"Like names of people, intended locations of the drop-off for the children, who they were being delivered to."

"Like I said before, Director, things were moving pretty fast in that house, and near-death experiences tend to distort your recollection of minutiae."

"You sure about that Agent Ramirez?" Winters had an accusatory tone.

"I don't know what you are implying."

"I don't need to tell you about the things law enforcement selectively ignores or buries because an agent is too lazy to document it in writing or because it creates problems for the investigation."

Fuck this dickhead.

"Well, Director," Ramirez said as he pushed the file toward the center of his desk, "I can tell you that everything of evidentiary value that I was a party to is accounted for in these reports."

Winters seemed to become upset. He bit down on his lower lip. What did he know? What was he after?

"That's fine, Agent Ramirez." Winters stood up from the chair and put two fingers on top of the files. "But you had better hope that nothing comes to light that you should have alerted us to which ends up thoroughly fucking up this investigation."

Ramirez thought about the last statement for a second. "You mean prosecution."

"What was that?"

"You said investigation." Ramirez could sense he was moving into need-to-know information. "The investigation in this case has been over for a number of years. The case is before the District Court and pending trial. There are no active investigation requests or follow-ups that I am aware of."

Winters was silent for a second as if he were taking in his verbal miscue.

"You better just be goddamned sure that you are not holding onto some piece of evidence or document that should have been turned over to HSI," Winters said, his voice rising.

Documents? What the fuck was he talking about?

"Director Winters," Ramirez said, trying hard to keep his tone measured, "I am very much aware of my duties as a federal agent as well as my ethical obligations regarding evidence. If I happen to remember where I hid the delivery manifest that the smugglers were using that evening, you will be the first person that I will call."

Winters did not respond. He turned away from the desk and headed toward the door. He paused for a second to look at the newspaper article again and then continued out the door.

Ramirez thought he heard Winters laugh as left.

Ramirez sat back in his chair. What the fuck just happened? Five years and not a peep out of administration except for what an all-American hero he was. Now, out of nowhere, the regional director comes into his office and outright accuses him of concealing evidence. All this on the heels of Gerardo's cover being blown by someone on the inside, and Chance's uncle being kidnapped.

Something was most definitely up.

TWELVE

Drew couldn't do it any longer. He couldn't lie to Katie. His family meant the world to him. Little Jake and Drew were twelve and thirteen now. His weekends revolved around travel baseball clubs and soccer. His boys had grown into rambunctious but obedient kids who were quick to jump on the chance to do anything with their father. Hunting, fishing, monster truck rallies, even helping him around the house on renovation projects. Katie was always there for support. Whatever he needed, she provided. No questions asked.

Drew had the perfect family, but his secrets made him the not-so-perfect dad.

Before they left the Denny's, Drew told Chino that he was going to tell Katie everything.

"You think that's a good idea, boss?" Chino asked.

"They are coming after family now," Drew said. "I think she has a right to know."

Chino pondered the revelation. "Dude, she is going to be pissed beyond belief!"

"That's putting it mildly."

"Do you think I should talk to Sonya?"

"That's your call, partner. But if they have any information on us, then they know about her."

* * *

Drew sat at the kitchen table peeling at the label of the cold Pacifico. He had only taken a small sip from the bottle when he asked Katie to sit down. She knew something was up by the way he drank his beer. Drew's first sip of a newly opened beer was usually an aggressive swallow. Katie used to joke that half the beer was gone after the first sip.

"What's wrong, Drew?"

"I don't," Drew spun the bottle between his hands, unable to look up at her. "I don't know where to begin."

"Honey," Katie said, "you're starting to scare me."

Drew looked up and pushed the beer aside with one hand and began to talk. At first, he slowly tried to justify his actions. The economy, the mortgage three months behind, the loss of their savings in the medical fraud investment. Chino had proposed that they meet his friend, Chance, who had a contact for a job that would bring in fast money.

"Oh, God," Katie said. "What did you do?"

"It was supposed to be just a one-time thing, something to get us out from under all the debt and the bullshit."

"What did you do, Drew?"

He explained the deal. He, Chino, and Chance were to transport undocumented people after they had crossed the border in the desert to a drop-off somewhere in San Diego. No guns, no drugs, he assured her. He told her that he wanted to back out of the job, but they had met the leader, Caritas, who now was in possession of their identifications and threatened them.

"He basically told us that we were in or we were dead."

Katie could sense where the conversation was headed.

Drew explained to her that after they picked up the truck and trailer, he decided that he needed to see what they were carrying.

"I didn't want to be transporting drugs, a nuke, or some group of terrorists."

"What did you find?"

Drew could feel the weight of his secret begin to lift as he started to tell her the story. He told her they discovered children between the ages of six and eight, bound and drugged. They were trying to help them when the smugglers came upon them with weapons. The smugglers dragged the kids out the trailer and savagely beat Chance. Drew, Chino, and Chance were outside the trailer about to be executed when a man came out of the brush firing at the smugglers.

"Who was he and where did he come from?"

"His name was Gerardo Rios," Drew answered. "And I am alive today because of him."

Drew explained that Gerardo was a former federal police officer from Culiacan, Sinaloa. Gerardo was escaping his own cartel-connected life and was trying to cross into the United States. Along the way, he noticed the children being led, bound at the wrists and in pairs, through the desert. He knew that wasn't normal, and these children were being transported for reasons other than just safe entry into the country.

"What do you mean?" Katie asked, already knowing the answer as the words left her lips.

"Abuse, Katie. Some sort of pedophile ring."

"Jesus, Drew." Katie thought of her own children.

"Yeah, and we were all dead until Gerardo showed up."

Drew reached over for his beer and took a long, deep draw from the bottle. Katie noticed that he was acting more normal as he was finally telling her this story.

"We all made the decision right at that time to help the children."

"Wait," Katie said, holding her open hand up to stop Drew. "What happened to the guys that were holding you hostage?"

"Katie." Drew leaned back in his chair. "They weren't holding us hostage. They were going to execute us. Bullets to the head, face down in the dirt. Gerardo took one of the guys out, and I got to one of the others. Chance," Drew thought about it for a second, "Chance took out the one in charge."

Katie couldn't say anything.

"These guys got what they deserved, darling. We were already in this shit, and we needed to get the kids to safety."

"So what happened?" she asked.

Drew told her about the GPS tracker they discovered on the trailer. He decided to leave the children with the trailer, and that they would use the GPS locator in the truck to follow the trailer and then attempt to rescue the children. They located the final destination at a ranch in a box canyon in the backcountry desert of East County and planned an assault with the weapons they recovered from the truck of the *narcos* they had killed.

"I made my way down the hillside in a makeshift ghillie and got to a place of concealment under the house."

Katie had heard Drew describe his missions in Iraq and Afghanistan, and the tone and pacing of this story were no different.

"The others were to rush the house when I started firing, but Chance was discovered and captured before I could start."

"Oh God, Drew. What did you do?"

"They brought him into the house." He shook his head at the memory. "They had him tied to a chair and were torturing him. He had been shot through the shoulder. They continued to beat and pistol whip him. The leader, Caritas, drove a knife into the open gunshot wound."

"Oh my God." Katie could not reconcile the image of Chance with the laid-back business partner that she knew.

"The worst thing was watching it from beneath the house."

Drew told her how he positioned himself under the leader and fired a round straight through his foot. He then fired more rounds through the floor. Once the firing started, Chino and Gerardo came storming in and took out the remaining gunmen.

"There was a bit of a problem," Drew said.

"You mean separate and apart from a bunch of dead men in a ranch house and kidnapped children on their way to Neverland Ranch?"

"Well, it turns out that the smuggling organization had two federal agents working with them." He paused because he knew that what followed would be difficult for her to understand. "They started firing at us, and we had to take them out."

"You killed two federal agents!" She started to tear up.

"Dirty agents, Katie." Drew was adamant.

Drew explained that the traffickers had also had another agent captive. The agent had stumbled upon the operation, and his partners turned on him.

"Is this that thing that happened in the desert four or five years ago. It was all over the news."

"Yes, that was us."

"They reported that some hero Border Patrol agent fought off the traffickers and saved the kids."

"Ramirez, Agent Victor Ramirez," Drew said. "Well, he is the guy we saved, and he did help us out in the end."

Drew described the desperate final confrontation with the smugglers. The only one left alive after the shootout at the ranch house was Caritas. He had a badly mangled foot, so they dragged him along with them. Drew left out the argument they had on whether to execute him. He told her about the escape and the trailer stalling in the dirt road.

"We couldn't leave the kids," Drew explained.

"I guess, knowing you," Katie reached over and put her hand over Drew's, "it doesn't surprise me."

"So, there we were, Chino and me, standing in the middle of some shitty, no-name dirt road outside of Jacumba." Drew choked up a bit. "All I could think of was how badly I had fucked things up and just wanted to get back to you and the kids."

Katie couldn't say anything.

"But we couldn't leave these kids. Jesus, Katie! They were the same ages as our boys at the time."

Katie nodded and grasped Drew's hand tighter.

Drew described the final confrontation in the desert. Four armed men standing in front of them in the roadway. He and Chino with limited ammunition. They knew that Ramirez was behind them attempting to flank the gunmen.

Drew laughed.

"What could be so funny?" Katie asked.

"They wanted their boss back," Drew said. "We said not until we were safely away from the area."

"That's not funny," Katie said.

"One of them said something to the effect of what made us think that we were getting out of there alive."

Drew smiled at the memory.

"And Chino started laughing. I still remember it because it was such a loud laugh. In the silence of the desert backcountry, it sounded like he was on a megaphone."

"Why was he laughing?"

"Chino told the guy that we were thinking the same thing. What made them think that *they* were going to make it out alive."

Katie shuddered at the thought of her husband, the father of her two sons, standing on a desert road facing off with four gunmen.

"Not funny. Definitely not funny."

"When the firing started, it was over in less than a minute. Chino and I took out three of them, and Ramirez saved my life when I couldn't get a shot off at one of the *sicarios* who had me dead in his sights."

He paused remembering the scene.

"Ramirez came out of nowhere and punched the dude's ticket."

"Oh my God!" Katie leaned back away from Drew, unsure of what to make of what he had told her. "But what about the story? That's not the way the news reported it."

"Ramirez came up with the cover story. He told us that our involvement would be very difficult to explain. He was going to tell the investigators that Gerardo saved him and assisted Ramirez in the rescue of the children. He figured that the feds would probably not look closely into the case since they had the very negative fact that two US Border Patrol agents were involved with a human-trafficking ring."

Drew could feel the weight of his secret being lifted as he finished the story. He leaned back in his chair and took another long drink from the beer.

"And it worked." Drew perked up. "Gerardo went into witness protection, and Ramirez got promoted and was a hero."

Drew hesitated. Katie knew her husband well.

"But what?" she asked.

"Well." Drew looked around the room and then back at Katie. "We didn't know this at the time all of this was going on, but it turned out that these traffickers were doing an exchange at the site for the children."

"What does that mean?" Katie asked.

"It means that there was this duffel bag with half a million in cash."

"Holy shit, Drew!"

Of course. Katie remembered Drew coming back from the "security job" in Mexico. He told her that he had been paid thirty-five thousand in cash. They used the money to pay the back mortgage and to open the cantina with Chino and Chance.

"You guys walked away with half a million of cartel money!" Katie didn't even try to hide her anger.

"It was already a done deal. We couldn't leave it there, and Ramirez was going to keep our names out of it. He sold it to the feds as a rip-off by rival drug gangs and no one was going to be listening to Caritas because he was facing a life sentence."

Katie took a few seconds to take in Drew's explanation.

"You are such an asshole, Drew!" Katie was near tears. "You put this family in danger."

"I know, darlin', I know." Drew put a soft hand on Katie's shoulder. "But I don't know how to explain it. It was like a hole that I had already fallen deep into. It was done. Part of me hoped it would be over."

"I feel so stupid." Katie brushed Drew's hand off. "I should have known that pile of cash you brought back from the job in Mexico was dirty."

"But we put it to good use."

"So, you're telling me that we money laundered your narco cash into starting the restaurant that is our only source of income?

"Well, money laundering sounds a bit harsh." Drew knew he was digging a deeper hole.

"You know that I'm pissed at you for lying to me." Katie reached over for Drew's beer and took a hard swallow. "But why are you telling me now?"

Katie knew something bad had happened. She should have asked more questions back then but, given their dire financial state, she chose to look the other way. She chose to believe Drew.

"Before we parted company, it was decided if something happened in the future that might expose us, whoever had negative contact would send out a code to the others." Drew could see Katie starting to look concerned.

"Code?"

"Alamo. We made sure that we all had each other's phone numbers. We even practiced running an alert sequence. Whoever was contacted would text out ALAMO to the others so that we could be ready to defend ourselves."

"Oh, great." Katie was exasperated. "Alamo. You mean where everyone died."

"More like a rallying cry."

Drew explained that Gerardo's identity, location, and relative safety in witness protection had been compromised from inside the federal law enforcement system. Whoever it was could only know about Ramirez and Gerardo, so Drew and his friends had a slight advantage. He told her about the meeting at Denny's and that someone had kidnapped Chance's uncle. Drew also told her that whoever it was had demanded a meeting at a Mexican restaurant in Chula Vista.

He did not tell her about the photos of Ramirez's children.

"Jesus Christ, Drew." Katie started to tear up. "What are we going to do?"

Drew grabbed Katie's hands with both of his own. He looked into her eyes and tried to calm her. He spoke slowly.

"I will do whatever it takes to protect you and the kids. Do you understand me?"

Katie couldn't speak.

"Do you understand me?"

"So, this is why you had me take those crazy Filipino self-defense classes?"

Drew nodded.

"And shooting at the gun range?"

"I just needed to know that you would be ready," Drew said as he clasped his hands around Katie's, "just in case."

Katie felt incredible rage at Drew for subjecting the family to danger. And as she considered it, Katie was swept away by pure, unadulterated fear of legendary border cartel violence. She did her best to compose herself. She sat back, closed her eyes, and took in a long, deep breath, the same way she had seen her husband do a thousand times. A cleansing breath to clear her mind and get ready for the task at hand.

Katie opened her eyes and looked directly at Drew.

"I'm going with you."

THIRTEEN

Regional Director Winters sat in his white, government-issued Chevy Tahoe outside the Customs and Border Protection office in San Diego. The air conditioning was cranked to maximum, but the car was still a hot box after sitting in the ninety-plus August heat. People who think it's always seventy-two degrees in San Diego have never ventured very far from the beach. Still, Winters had not removed his suit jacket. He was distracted. Having left Ramirez's office, he was certain that information was being withheld.

Winters flipped open the enormous center console and pulled out one of three cellphones stored inside. He checked his watch. One twenty-seven in the afternoon. He was to receive the call at one thirty sharp. The air conditioning unit was beginning to blow cold air furiously throughout the cabin. He reached over and opened the glove compartment to retrieve a thick, dark brown file. The cover of the file was marked, "United States Homeland Security Investigations: Classified Contents." He opened the file and began leafing through it.

Winters went directly to the section with crime-scene photographs. A labeled diagram outlined the location of each item depicted in the photographs. The photographs showed standard yellow numbered evidence placards placed next to evidentiary items, including all the bodies. He stopped when he got to the photographs of the interior of the ranch house. Multiple bodies lay sprawled on the floor in dark pools of maroon-colored blood. What stood out most were the bodies of two uniformed Border Patrol officers. One was leaning against the wall. A gaping hole was visible in his chest. The other lay face down, blood pooling from under his stomach area. Both had their guns out of the holsters. The room was a mess of blood, bodies, splintered wood, and propped up yellow evidence tags.

Winters stopped at a photograph of a body of an unknown gunman. He was sprawled near a desk against the living room wall. This area had most of the carnage. What interested Winters most was not the image of the body but of the desk. The photograph showed the main drawer open and empty. Protocol would be to take photographs of the scene undisturbed once it was secured. No search of the premises would have begun before the photographs were taken. Winters knew that something was in the desk drawer and someone had removed it. He kept staring at the photograph looking for anything that might reveal the movement of evidence. Winters knew exactly what he was looking for, and it was not there.

Just then his phone vibrated. Winters checked his watch. One thirty on the dot.

"He is not giving any information," Winters said immediately upon answering.

"We do not need to impress upon you the need to find the item that we seek."

"I understand. I am on it. A collateral source may prove beneficial."

"Then do it." The voice on the other end of the phone terminated the call.

Winters placed the cellphone back into the center console. The air conditioning had turned the hot interior into a cool zone, so he adjusted the fan to a normal level. Winters reached back down into the console and retrieved a different cellphone. He activated the call screen. The phone had no stored contacts and only one number listed in recent calls. He scrolled to the number and called. A voice answered on the other end.

"Proceed as planned," Winters said.

There was no reply. The phone went dead.

FOURTEEN

Jimmy Connors woke up in a dark room, lying on a hardwood floor. His hands were bound tight in front of him with duct tape at the wrists. He felt like his brain was swelling out of his skull. He lifted his upper torso and scooted across the floor and put his back against the wall and tried to get his bearings. Let his eyes adjust to the dark. He tried to focus, but the pain in his head was overwhelming. He looked around the room. There was a small window, maybe three feet by three feet, on the wall facing him. He could see from the distance there was a thick, metal security grate bolted over the window from the inside. In the corner was a single twin mattress. No bedding or pillows. A ratty looking blanket was crumpled up to the side of the bed. There was a liter-sized water bottle lying on the floor in the middle of the room. There was no other furniture. It was clear to Jimmy that this room was outfitted to hold someone hostage.

His head continued to throb, and he did his best to search his memory for some indiscretion, fight, or other insult he may have drunkenly hurled at someone that would account for his present situation. The truth was, and Jimmy knew it, that he was a nobody. He was a guy getting by on a retirement check and blowing what little was left on alcohol. There would be no reason for anyone to beat and kidnap him.

Fucking Chester! He knew that dough boy was up to something. There was no way that he was a successful restaurant owner. Likewise, there was no way that he would have these stand-up former Marines as his partners and best friends. What the fuck!

Jimmy was getting more and more pissed at the thought of his involvement in one of his nephew's schemes. He took a deep breath. Calm down, he told himself. They have him for a reason, otherwise he would be dead. Jimmy knew he was a nobody so they must need him to get to someone else. He realized he had some time.

Jimmy got up and walked around the room. He picked up the water bottle on the floor. No telling how long he would be stuck in this dungeon, so he took a measured sip. Just enough to wet his dry throat. The water felt like a healing medicine sliding down through his body. He could feel the sweet-tasting water circulating in his veins. His head throb even began to subside. He moved toward the window and inspected the security grate. The heads of the screws holding the grate in place had been stripped to keep anyone from trying to remove them. He reached up to the grate and pulled. No movement. It was dark, but there was some light from a streetlight a distance away. He looked out the window. There was a one-level, slate-roof house about one hundred yards away and he could see the outline of another house an equal distance beyond that. From what he remembered when they dragged him into the house and from what he could see now, Jimmy figured he was somewhere outside the city in the rural area of San Diego County. He held on to some hope that there were people nearby.

Nothing in the room stood out as a potential weapon or tool. In his present state, he was thinking more along the line of a tool because he didn't know if he could wield any sort of weapon. Jimmy ran his palms along the walls. Standard drywall over two by four construction. He had worked for several years after the Navy installing drywall during the construction boom in San Diego. He was well acquainted with the strengths and weaknesses of drywall. Sometimes installers were less than careful when installing the sheets and reinforcing the seams. This was particularly the case in lower-end houses. He thought maybe the ceiling in the closet could be one of those weak spots. Through the ceiling, into the crawl space and maybe, just maybe . . .

He moved to the closet. It looked like a standard, eight-foot ceiling. He also noticed a vent. Jimmy knew that a vent in the closet meant the room was an addition. No builder would put a vent or run ducting into a closet. This was careless. Careless work would mean weak construction and possibilities.

Still, Jimmy thought as he looked around the room, there was no way to access the ceiling. There was no chair or desk in the room. No way to get to the vent. He walked over to the door. He lightly tried to turn the knob, but it wasn't moving. Jimmy placed his ear against the door. He could hear the faint noise of a television. He heard muffled voices. He listened for a few more minutes trying to make out any of the words they were saying, although Jimmy knew they were most likely speaking in Spanish and he would probably have no idea what the hell they were talking about.

Motherfucking Mexicans run this state! Jimmy thought.

As he moved away from the door, he heard the distinct sound of an exterior door opening. The voices responded immediately. The sound of the voices grew louder. Now Jimmy could discern they were speaking in Spanish. He heard heavy footsteps and the sound of furniture moving. The sounds were now coming toward the door. Jimmy backed away to the far wall.

The door opened. Three men. The two who attacked him in his apartment and a new man. Another dark-skinned Mexican. He was short, maybe five seven. A thick head of hair was tucked under an Oakland Raiders ball cap. In one hand he was dragging a chair. He had something in his other hand that Jimmy could not make out. One of the other men was holding a thick roll of silver duct tape. None of them said a word. They entered the room, the man with the chair first. The other two followed and moved to his side. They were now standing five feet away from Jimmy.

"What the fuck do you fucking *cholos* want from me?" Jimmy figured that something bad was going to happen to him so an insult wouldn't make any difference.

Still, none of the men spoke. All three of them moved toward Jimmy. As they approached, Jimmy could make out what the man had in his hand.

Garden shears.

FIFTEEN

Vista del Mar was a Mexican seafood restaurant off Palomar Street at the south end of Chula Vista. Despite the name, there was no vista of the ocean. The restaurant occupied the corner of a strip mall, the only view from the windows was of traffic moving north and south on busy Third Avenue. The side of the restaurant formed part of an alley to the rear parking lot, which was bordered on the other side by a chain link fence with overgrown oleander shrubs.

The place was a classic Southern California Mexican restaurant. This was not part of a chain with oversized margarita glasses, children's menus or twelve-inch-high piles of multicolored corn chips covered in thick yellow cheese and mild red sauce. This was a restaurant for Mexicans or, at least, those who knew the difference between real Mexican food and taco salads. Margaritas were never blended. They were served cold and strong. The Tecates were served in the can, no glass, with a slice of lime and shaker of salt. The Pacificos served cold, dripping with condensation, and a slice of Mexican *limón*. The interior was filled with Mexican memorabilia. It was as if the owners bought every item from vendors who walked the line of cars and trucks waiting to cross the border into the United States. Figurines of surfing monkeys, ceramic cacti, hanging rugs depicting Our Lady of Guadalupe and the random Tecate or Corona beer poster with bikini-clad models made up the interior design. The dining area was set in a cavernous open space. Twenty of so plastic-topped tables with wooden chairs painted different shades of green and red were spread out throughout the room. The bar, with a palm frond overhang and old wooden top, took up the entire back wall.

It was a quarter to five in the afternoon, and the only patrons in the restaurant were a family of four—husband, wife, and two small children—and two young women occupying a table near the window.

Katie and Sonya had been there now for twenty minutes waiting for the others to arrive. Chino had explained everything to Sonya. At first, Sonya was angry at him for putting himself at risk in such a stupid venture. Then she became frightened about what could happen to him. She circled back to anger when she realized that these were men who trafficked in and victimized children. She was in this thing, no matter what Chino said.

The sight of two attractive females in the bar did stand out, but it was not out of the ordinary. Sonya, with her natural olive complexion and dark hair, was definitely Latina. In this part of California, the sight of multi-ethnic friend groups was natural. If anything, it would make sense that two such pretty women would be friends.

Katie was wearing a San Diego State Aztecs tank top and jeans. Sonya was in a light blue sundress. The window they were near faced the parking lot. Katie spun a margarita on the rocks between her hands and Sonya was nursing a michelada. They both tried to appear natural, but it was difficult to maintain the façade since they knew that the people soon to be entering were associated with kidnapping and violence. Their job was simple. They were to keep watch on the vehicles in the parking lot. When they determined which vehicles the traffickers arrived in, Katie would text the make, model, and license plate of the vehicle to Drew. She would also text the descriptions of the men. If possible, Katie might try to get a photo of the men and send it to Drew.

There were only two roads that led to the restaurant. Third Avenue ran south to north. Chino was posted up about five hundred yards up the street ready to follow the vehicle if it went that way. Drew decided they should rent standard sedans that would blend into the traffic. They selected two gray Nissans. Chino joked that they were the color of wet concrete and would blend into the pavement. Third Avenue crossed Palomar Street, which ran east-west and had an entrance ramp to the Interstate 5 freeway. Drew took his chances that these guys would most likely be headed to the freeway, so he positioned himself about a half mile west on Palomar.

Drew figured it would difficult to transport and keep hostages in the more populated areas of San Diego. His guess was that they were using a place somewhere in the rural part of San Diego County. This would mean the vehicles would most likely use the I-5 to get to the 8 or 94 and head east. Gerardo was positioned off the 125 in Drew's pickup. The 125 intersected both the 94 and the 8. If everything went as planned, they would be able to follow the vehicle to where Chance's uncle was being held. Of course, if they turned into Mexico, the entire plan would go to shit, and Drew would be left alone driving through unfamiliar Tijuana in a rental car with California plates.

They all met earlier in the parking lot of the Del Sol shopping mall. Drew rented a forgettable white Hyundai sedan for Katie to drive to the restaurant. The late August afternoon was building in heat. The temperature hovered around ninety degrees, and the heat off the black tar pavement bounced it right back in their faces. Chino was in his rented Nissan with the windows up and air conditioning on. There was nothing left for him to say to Sonya. He had begged her to stay home, but she would have none of it. Chino sat gripping the wheel and mentally preparing himself for the mission ahead.

Ramirez was in his Suburban with Chance in the passenger seat. The plan was for them to make the meet. Ramirez was known to them through media accounts and Chance had been associated with the traffickers before the shoot-out in the desert. Drew walked over to the Hyundai and got in the back seat to talk to Katie before she and Sonya went to the Vista del Mar. Katie looked at him through the rear-view mirror. Drew's view was of her bright blue eyes staring back at him.

"I don't want you taking any chances," Drew said.

"I don't see myself being any sort of hero," Katie replied.

"I also don't see you sitting back and doing nothing if the shit hits the fan."

"Well, partner," she said, turning back to look at Drew. "Let's see just how valuable that Kali training you dragged me to turns out to be."

Drew was relentless in encouraging her to take the self-defense training. He had a bit of training in this style of fighting in the Marines

79

and knew it entailed close quarter, hand-to-hand combat. Quick, trained, directed strikes from a lighter weight female could do more damage than long-range blows. He watched her at the training sessions and was impressed at how quickly she picked up the basic moves and evasive footwork. Drew would also test her skills from time to time by grabbing her from behind to judge her reflexive moves. Katie thought it was all in fun. Drew knew otherwise. He hoped she would never have to rely on it, but he felt the slightest bit of relief to know she had some basic knowledge in self-defense.

"Just remember that running hard and fast is always the best defense," Drew said in a slow and serious tone.

"That is something I am certainly capable of doing."

"I love you, darlin'."

"I know that cowboy."

Drew exited the vehicle, looked around at the other cars and made a sweeping motion with his arm.

Time to saddle up.

* * *

It was now ten to five, and Katie saw a pickup truck pulling into the parking lot. It was a maroon Ford with tinted windows. The truck made a sweeping arc and backed into a space in the empty lot. She immediately texted Drew the make and model of the pickup and the first three letters of the license plate. The rest of the plate was blocked from her view.

"Looks like it's showtime," Katie said to Sonya.

Just then the waitress arrived with the food. Katie and Sonya were preoccupied with the activity in the parking lot as the server placed the orders in front of them. Sonya eyed the steaming bowl of *siete mares*, the house specialty. A red chile broth seafood soup piled high with shellfish would require concentration to consume, none of which she had now. Katie had acted the *gringa* and ordered the more manageable plate of fish tacos.

The waitress noticed their distraction and looked out at the men getting out of the pickup.

Two men, dressed in dark jeans. They appeared to be in their mid-thirties. The one exiting the driver's side was slightly overweight. The buttons of his white, western-style shirt strained in the stomach area with spillover flesh on the sides. The other was in an untucked, long-sleeve, black dress shirt. He was tall and lean, just under six feet. They were both Latino and, aside from the almost all white goatee on the heavier man, did not stand out at all in this part of San Diego County.

The waitress gave them a once over to see if she knew them and walked away.

The men entered and made their way to the opposite side of the restaurant near the family that was already mid-meal. Sonya glanced over at the two men as they sat down. She made eye contact with the younger one and gave a quick smile. He did not return the smile.

"So much for womanly charm," she said to Katie.

"Let's keep this tight. No improv. Stick to the plan," Katie said.

They went back to a preplanned conversation. Loud enough to let everyone know that they were just two female friends sharing food and a few drinks. Katie was basically retelling the plot of *The Notebook*, Drew's least favorite movie, to Sonya with a few laughs thrown in. At one point, Katie placed a FaceTime call to Drew. Once connected, she leaned across the table, as planned, and pretended to be taking a selfie with Sonya. She used the camera to show Drew the interior of the restaurant and the two men seated opposite them. She then quickly disconnected the call and went back to her food and staged conversation.

Drew called Chino after Katie disconnected.

"Looks like two of them just showed up," he said.

"Could you get a description?" Chino asked.

"Standard issue *narco* henchmen. Katie texted me a partial license plate of the truck they came in. Brick red Ford, nothing out of the ordinary. I will text you the plate."

"Copy that, boss. Have to say, this is the first time that I have ever trailed someone in a vehicle."

"Just stay close, maybe ten car lengths back."

"Let's hope they don't take a turn toward Mexico."

The Palomar Street exit off the Interstate 5 was three miles from the international border. Following them into Mexico would present a unique set of problems. Unfamiliarity with the roads, spotty communication, and potentially hostile law enforcement would make it difficult for Drew or Chino to follow.

Fucking Mexico, Drew thought. Might as well be Kandahar.

* * *

Ramirez and Chance were sitting in Ramirez's Suburban in a strip mall parking lot off Third Avenue. They pulled into the lot to wait for notification that the men had arrived. When Drew texted the descriptions of the vehicle and the men, they knew it was go time.

"Remember," Ramirez said, "we are gathering information. They wouldn't be holding anyone hostage unless they wanted something from us."

"Yeah, I know," Chance said. "But these fuckers are all the same. We dealt with them last time. Mexican cowboys with guns. Take the guns away, and they are just like any other Mexican walking the streets here."

"Yes, but some of these *vatos* are stone cold killers."

"I can say that I do have some experience with those types," Chance said unconsciously touching the three-inch scar under his right eye.

Ramirez looked over at Chance. He was wearing khaki colored Dickies, a long-sleeve polo shirt, and steel-tipped work boots. No ball cap. No jewelry.

"I noticed that you have changed your wardrobe since the last time we spent any time together," Ramirez said.

"Yeah, well . . . I learned my lesson last time belly crawling through desert cactus and shrub in a pair of shorts and a basketball tank."

"Well, let's hope we don't have to do anything like that anytime soon."

Chance looked at Ramirez and let out a long breath.

"I think we all know where this is all going to end up," he said.

"Well," Ramirez said as he fired up the ignition, "let's keep our cool and try not to get killed."

"Copy fuckin' that, *migra* boy."

SIXTEEN

Director Winters was leaving a federal task force budgeting meeting when he received a text on his backup phone. The meeting was being held in the Edward J. Schwartz Federal Building in downtown San Diego. The brownish-maroon building with smoke-tinted windows sprawled over Front Street and took up two city blocks. The complex was attached to the United States District Court for the Southern District of California. The interior of the building was a maze of hallways stretching over six floors. He was walking down a long, gray-carpeted hall with the regional director for Homeland Security Investigations when he felt the vibration from the burner phone tucked away in his blazer pocket.

Winters waited until he made it back to his vehicle to read the text message.

GREEN LIGHT TEN MINUTES

Winters scrolled down his phone for contacts. There were only three numbers stored. He placed a call.

"You have news?" a voice asked.

"Green light in ten minutes," Winters said.

"No mistakes," the voice said. It was a command, not a statement.

"There will be none."

"That's what you said last time."

"Understood, sir," Winters answered. The line went dead.

Winters cleared the screen and slid the phone back into the breast pocket of his blazer. He continued making his way out of the building, fuming at the thought of blame being foisted on him for unforeseen events. He performed as directed and the previous transfers had gone off without a hitch. It was not his fault. He was a perfectionist, and these loose ends had been hanging around for the last five years. Now this amateur with money and power wants to blame him for the foul-up.

Not my problem, he thought. But, being a professional meant cleaning up the mess, and that is precisely what he was going to do. No loose ends. No witnesses.

SEVENTEEN

Ramirez pulled the Suburban into the parking lot and backed into a space. He turned the ignition off, and he and Chance sat silent for a moment.

"Looking for the quick getaway?" Chance asked.

"I know, huh?" Ramirez said. "Not too obvious."

"I think that I should do most of the talking," he added after a pause. "We know they think we have something of theirs. I have spent hundreds of hours in interrogation rooms extracting information from detainees, and these guys are basically the same."

"They're not some poor fuck illegal aliens," Chance said.

"But they are criminals, and I have experience with that."

"It's your show, boss," Chance said as he reached under the seat to pull out two Glock nine-millimeter handguns.

Before arriving, Ramirez provided the group with weapons from his home safe. They had gone to Ramirez's home while his wife was at work and his children were at school. Chula Vista's Eastlake section was a modern community with high-end tract and semi-custom homes and top performing schools. As a result, the neighborhood had many affluent Tijuana families looking for a safer place to live and school their children, as well as law enforcement families. Ramirez lived in a newer two-story, five-bedroom house. The house was beige stucco with clay-tiled roof. The Mediterranean style façade blended in with the neighborhood. Drew was impressed as they walked into his impeccably clean three-car garage.

"Dude, this makes me think my garage should be on that hoarders show," Drew said.

"Definitely," Chino added. "Gives me garage envy."

Ramirez had always been a gun collector. His ten-foot-tall garage gun safe had over twenty handguns, two hunting rifles, one shotgun and one sniper rifle equipped with a digital scope.

Ramirez reached into the safe and pulled out the rifle. He gave Drew the grin of a proud father and handed the weapon over to him like it was a piece of art.

"Jesus Christ, Ramirez!" Drew said. "You looking to shoot deer from a mile away?"

"I told you guys that I was a collector."

"Check it out, Chino, bolt action repeater, twenty-four-inch barrel." Drew handed the rifle over to Chino. "Weighs maybe nine pounds."

"Nice piece, Ramirez! What are the specs on this scope?" Chino ran his fingers down the length of the sleek bit of optics attached to the rifle. The scope was fluted narrow to wide at the end with adjustment knobs at the base.

"Five to twenty-five by fifty millimeters. They say it's good in the thousand yard-plus range."

Chino handed the rifle back to Drew.

"We sure could have used this beauty a few years back," Chino said.

"Well, let's hope we don't have to use it this time," Drew said.

Drew and Chino each removed a handgun, and Drew put the rifle in the canvas carry bag along with ammunition. No one else was around to give a second thought to the sight of five men leaving a garage with duffel bags and what was clearly a rifle.

In Ramirez's Suburban in the parking lot, he and Chance both looked down at the weapons on the floorboard.

"We already checked those," Ramirez said. "They're good to go."

"Just need to see them for the security."

"You know about the safety on these Glocks?" Ramirez asked.

"You mean that there is none," Chance responded. "Yeah, I learned a little bit about that the last time."

"Well, since the guns are staying in the car, they are not going to be any help when we are in the restaurant," Ramirez said.

"I know, but we may have to get them pretty quick."

"Let's hope not. Let's go in and gather as much intel as possible. We find out what these fucks want, and we let Drew and Chino do their magic. Then . . ." Ramirez turned toward Chino.

"Then we get my piece-of-shit uncle."

"Roger that, Gordo."

EIGHTEEN

They made their way into the restaurant. Chance did his best to calm his nerves. Ramirez looked through the glass door and gave Chance a nod. He pulled the door open wide for Chance to enter. It was obvious who they were supposed to meet. They sat off to the far right of the restaurant. Katie and Sonya were off to the far left. Ramirez did his best not to look in their direction. Toward the back of the restaurant was a Latino family. Two young boys, age six or seven, with a mother and father. They did not turn to look at the new customers.

Ramirez turned to walk to the table where the two men were seated. Chance said nothing and followed. The men were seated, each drinking a Corona. Chance and Ramirez sat down in the two empty chairs.

"I take it you wanted to talk to us?" Ramirez did his best to commit the description of the two men to his memory. In the academy, he had been trained in memory clues and methodology relating to description. The taller one was in his mid-thirties. He was lean and strong. He could see the muscle striation leading up his forearms because of his rolled-up sleeves. No facial hair, and sharp, angular features. Dark eyes and short cropped dark hair. A faint but noticeable scar ran down the left side of his face starting right next to his ear. The other man was slightly older. He was heavier set. His short gray hair was offset by a shock-white goatee.

"You have something that belongs to us," the lean one said.

"What makes you think . . ." Ramirez started to say.

"*Mira, Migra, no jodas!*" Even Chance understood enough Spanish to understand that he was telling them to quit fucking around.

"What is that you fuckers want?" Chance asked in a defiant tone.

"*Tú sabes, Gordo,*" the man said as he took a long draw off the bottle of beer. He placed the beer back on the table and looked at the parking lot and then to Chance.

"And I can tell you it's not the *pinche lana.*"

The statement raced through Ramirez's mind. They weren't after the money. What did they want? He hadn't been part of the division of the money and had not even seen the insides of the bag.

Chance was seething but said nothing. Instead, he watched the heavier man with the goatee. He noticed that, even though the man was silent, he was watching every movement on their side of the table.

"I can tell you that . . ." Ramirez said as he leaned forward.

"You *pendejos* fucked up," the lean one said. "You thought we wouldn't catch up to you."

Chance had reached his limit.

"Where the fuck is my uncle, you wetback piece of shit!" Chance raised his voice. Everyone in the restaurant looked over.

The men said nothing. The man with the goatee smiled and removed a small manila envelope and placed it on the table in front of him. The other man reached into his shirt pocket and pulled out a folded piece of paper and flipped it over to Ramirez.

"Two days," he said, "this address, and you know the rules."

The men got up from their seats. The larger one with the goatee looked over to Chance.

"Quieres ver a tu tío?" he asked.

"If you fuckers have . . ." Chino started to say.

The man slid the envelope over to Chance and walked away.

The envelop had a small bulge visible, and it was clearly not paper. Chance picked the envelope up and opened it. He emptied the contents onto the tabletop. A half-inch ball of paper towel, dark red stains. Chance knew before he even opened the paper. He said nothing and slid the paper over to Ramirez. He looked inside. A mass of dark fleshy tissue was crunched into a ball, caked with what looked like dried blood. He spread the paper out for a better look. What he saw was mangled but unmistakably the top half of a human ear.

"These fuckers are going to die," Chance said.

NINETEEN

Katie and Sonya watched the exchange from their table. Katie did her best not to noticeably look in their direction, but it was difficult to do. She felt a strange surge of energy rushing up from her stomach. She could feel it pulsating through her veins. Her heartbeat was racing. This is what Drew would describe when he talked about the adrenaline rush of his operations. She felt fear and curiosity toward the men who had kidnapped Chance's uncle. It was like a car accident. She couldn't look away.

"Katie!" Sonya said with her mouth clenched.

Katie snapped out of her daze.

"You're being too obvious" Sonya said.

"I know, I know," Katie said and took a deep breath.

She reached for her purse and pulled out her day planner and a pen.

"Okay," she said to Sonya. "Let's act like some stupid MILFs out day drinking."

Sonya nodded in agreement and gave a forced laugh.

"Let's commit these descriptions to memory," Katie said as she opened the planner.

"Okay, I got you," Sonya said. "First guy. Tall, maybe five foot eleven. Dark hair, dark eyes. No facial hair."

"Looks like?" Katie said, using a prompt from a game they often played together on strangers. Katie and Sonya would pick out someone and try to come up with a celebrity look-alike.

"Kind of a dark-skinned James Franco?"

Katie took a quick look over.

"Okay. Okay. I can see that," she said as she wrote in the day planner.

"Second guy. Maybe mid-forties. Five seven, five eight max." Sonya looked over again at the table across the restaurant. "A little chubby, I'm thinking maybe 190 pounds. Salt and pepper hair and white goatee."

Katie looked up from the planner.

"He looks like . . . like a chubby version of that guy in the beer commercials," Sonya said.

"The Most Interesting Man in the World?" Katie asked.

"Yeah, I know I'm giving him an upgrade, but it's pretty close."

Katie took a glance and wrote Dos Equis.

Katie could tell that the men were talking to Chance and Ramirez. She could not hear them but could see the conversation was terse and direct. The body posture of Latino James Franco and Dos Equis was intimidating. She saw Dos Equis stand up and slide something across the table to Chance. The two men walked across the restaurant toward the door. Katie made eye contact with both of them and quickly looked away.

"Shit! Shit!" Katie said. "They saw me looking at them."

"Relax, just start smiling. Remember we're just two friends having lunch."

"Right, out here in a Mexican restaurant spitting distance from Tijuana." Katie knew they looked out of place. She tried to keep it out of her mind, but she knew the man had noticed her. It was definitely not a typical man checking out a woman sort of look. She got the distinct impression that he suspected something.

Chance and Ramirez both got up from their table and made their way toward the door. Katie could tell that Chance was angry. Neither of the men looked over at them before exiting. Katie looked out the window to the parking lot and watched Dos Equis and his partner get into their truck. She quickly picked up her phone and called Drew.

Drew answered.

"They're leaving now. It looks like they are heading toward you, east on Palomar."

"Okay, got it," Drew said. "Listen to me, Katie, this is very important. Finish your meal. Don't rush. Don't do anything out of the ordinary. Pay your bill and tip well. Leave the restaurant. Don't look around. Don't call anyone. Just get into your car and drive home. Do you understand?"

"Yeah, Drew. I think I can manage that."

Katie ended the call and put the phone into her handbag.

"I think that we are done here," she said to Sonya.

"Let's hope this all works. It seems so, so . . ." Sonya was looking for the word.

"Fucking dangerous?"

Sonya said nothing but nodded in agreement. They closed out their tab and got up from the table. As Katie was leaving, she gave a once over to the almost empty restaurant. It looked pretty much the same as when they arrived. The same family was eating in the far corner. She noticed that the man who was most likely the father was no longer sitting in his chair. Katie didn't think much of it and figured he had gone to the restroom. As she reached the door, Katie remembered she had never really looked at the man. No description, no idea what he looked like other than he was with a family.

She was about to say something when Sonya said she had to use the restroom before they left.

"I'll meet you at the car," Katie said, looking down at her phone as she walked. She was trying to compose a text to Drew as she opened the car door. She was about to slide into the driver's seat when she felt her head violently pulled back by her hair. She tried to scream, but for some reason she was focused on retrieving the phone that jumped out of her hand and was now on the center console. Before she could make sense of anything, Katie felt a blow to the side of her head. The impact made her vision blur and her body go limp. She felt herself being dragged. She tried to scream but couldn't form any words. It was over so quick, she thought. In a matter of seconds, she was off her feet and thrown hard, face down into what she surmised was the trunk of a car. Before she could let out a word, the trunk lid closed.

TWENTY

Drew waited in the parking lot of a Chevron gas station on Palomar just short of the onramp to the Interstate 5. He had the engine running and the air conditioning up full blast to keep him alert. Drew felt the familiar rush of adrenaline pulsing through his forearms as he tightly gripped the steering wheel. Although he was never tasked to drive on missions in Afghanistan, there were several combat situations that found him behind the wheel of a Humvee or transport. On those occasions, he found that his sniper training took over his actions. Time slowed for him while driving as he scoured the road for potential hazards and targets.

This was an entirely different operation. He would need to follow a vehicle and avoid detection in an urban environment. It helped that Drew was familiar with the area and there were only two directions that the vehicle could travel. That is, if it didn't go into Tijuana, in which case the mission would go FUBAR. Ramirez was the only one with any real investigative training and had given Drew, Chino, and Gerardo the basics. No sudden movements, keep in communication with partners, stay two car lengths back, behind passenger side if possible, on the freeway.

"One more thing," Ramirez said to the group. "Most of my agents get made because of what they are wearing. Tactical boots. Obvious T-shirts. I don't know how many of my agents think they blend into the scenery with a Harley Davidson black T. And for God's sake, don't wear aviator sunglasses."

Drew had his aviators in the car and Chino had his hanging from the collar of his Padres T.

Drew had driven the distance between the restaurant and the on-ramp to the Interstate 5 on four trial runs. He averaged seven minutes to get there from where he was waiting. He planned to get on Palomar in front of the truck and then back off and trail them on the freeway. He looked down at his watch. An Omega Speedmaster, 007 version, a gift from Katie on his birthday last year. While he still preferred the military feel of his Luminox, he wore the watch as much as he could for Katie. Now the watch stood out like a neon sign and made him feel miserable. His stupid decision to try to make quick money transporting border crossers led to multiple dead bodies and the dread of looking over his shoulder for some narco *sicario.* Now he was sitting in a rented car ready to tail gunmen to locate the kidnapped uncle of one of his friends.

FUBAR. I fucked this all up, he thought.

The surreal image of dropping his two boys off at their grandparents for a three-day weekend was seared in his mind. Now he had dragged his wife into a dangerous situation. They had come within seconds of execution five years ago, and now he was heading back into the snake pit.

Six minutes had elapsed since he received the call from Katie.

Drew entered the roadway. Traffic was light, and he could see two vehicles approaching. One appeared to be the truck Katie described. He slowed a bit to let the truck catch up. The freeway was about five hundred yards ahead. Drew moved over to the far right as he approached the onramp. The truck tucked in behind Drew. He breathed a sigh of relief because it was clear they were heading north and not into Mexico. He could now see two men inside the truck. They matched the description given to him by Katie. Drew accelerated onto the freeway.

Drew once again felt the adrenaline of the hunt coursing through his body. He forced himself to control his breathing. He found it difficult to concentrate on the road ahead of him with the truck behind him. They were driving in the lows fifties in the slow lane, so there was nowhere for Drew to go. The usual Southern California traffic flew by making Drew wonder if the driver was consciously moving slow to check for a tail. He made a conscious effort to avoid looking in the rearview mirror. He was able to keep a bead on the truck through his sideview mirror.

The traffic was light for midafternoon. He was doing about 60 miles per hour in the slow lane when he saw a tractor-trailer coming up in the middle lane. When the semi passed him, Drew changed lanes and came up behind it. The semi slowed for traffic ahead, and Drew could see that the target truck was now moving past him on the right. He let the vehicle pull out of range, and then he passed the semi by changing into the fast lane. With the semi behind him, he ducked into the middle lane and was able to sight the target truck that had now also moved into the middle lane. He maintained a distance of about seventy-five yards. Drew reached over for his cell phone and called Chino.

"We are in route, North 5, coming up on the 54," he said.

Chino was waiting near the 805 until Drew could tell him which of the intersecting freeways their targets would take to go east. The choices were state routes 54 and 94 and Interstate 8. He sat in the parking lot of a strip mall off J Street ready to move.

"I'm ready, boss, just let me know when they turn."

Drew kept the truck within sight as it approached the 54. The turn signal flashed. Drew laughed to himself at the thought of two hired guns taking the time to obey the traffic laws. He was about to call Chino when he noticed something out of place to his left as he changed lanes to follow the truck. A white sedan. American. Maybe a Ford or Chevy. Two men in the vehicle. Black T-shirts and aviator sunglasses.

No fucking way. Drew reached for the phone and put it on speaker.

"Chino! They are heading your way, and I think we have some new players in the game."

"Fuck! You sure?"

"I've got two white guys wearing Ray-Bans in what looks like a government vehicle."

"Wait, wait. You sure about this?" Chino said. "These guys look like law enforcement or narcos?"

Drew hadn't thought about it. He caught a glance back at them in his rearview mirror. No mistake. Two men, dark shirts. High and tight haircut in civilian wear, always a dead giveaway. Even more obvious, the two men were not talking to each other. They looked straight ahead. He remembered Ramirez told them that two grown men do not drive in a car together and not say a word to each other.

"Fuck! Fuck!" Drew kept his eye on the vehicle. "Definitely law or at least ex-military."

"What the hell . . ." Chino started to say.

"All right, buddy, this changes the game plan. We are going to need to adjust."

"That means they were following them from the restaurant," Chino said.

Just then Drew remembered Katie. He hadn't heard from her in over ten minutes.

"Listen, partner," Drew said. "I'm going to exit and circle back to the restaurant to check on the girls."

"Holy shit, Drew! You don't think anything happened to them?"

"Don't know, Chino. You stay focused and let Gerardo know that we have a tail. I'll take care of the girls."

"Copy that, boss."

Drew activated his turn signal as he approached an exit. He tried to keep looking straight ahead so he would not attract their attention. As he began to exit, the sedan slowed but stayed on the freeway. The vehicle passed Drew as the exit lane curved away. Through his sideview mirror, he saw the passenger turn his head to look at him.

TWENTY-ONE

Sonya came out of the restroom looking down at her phone. The restaurant was empty except for the same family in the corner. She gave her table a once-over on the way out in case they left anything. They had been in the restaurant for over an hour and a half, and she was not prepared for the brightness of the afternoon sun. As she stepped into the light, she squinted and looked down into her purse for sunglasses. As she was pulling them out, Sonya looked up and saw her car. Katie was not inside. She scanned the parking lot but could not find her. Sonya was about to turn to go back into the restaurant when her head was yanked back and down by her ponytail. Her arms flew out and up and her purse shot out from her hand. Sonya hit the ground hard. The hot asphalt singed her skin. She tried to scream but the shock of the moment caused her to let out only a whimper. She was now on her back, the bright sun blinding her eyes. She saw the outline of two men. The one closest to her had not released his grip of her hair. With the other hand, the man gripped her upper arm and started to drag her on the ground. The hot, loose black asphalt ground against her skin. She started to scream.

"*No grites, puta!*" the man yelled as he backhanded her across the face.

The pain made it hard to see, and for a few seconds, she could not breathe as the man continued dragging her. He pulled her to the side of the restaurant and stood her up against the wall behind a trash bin. With the sun behind her, Sonya was no longer blinded. The man dragging and beating her was the man who had been inside the restaurant with what she thought was his family.

He had been watching them the whole time.

"You don't think we were watching you and *la guerra?* You think we are that stupid?" he whispered forcefully into her ear. His warm spit slid down her neck.

Fuck, Sonya thought. What did they do to Katie?

The man delivered a powerful blow to her stomach. All the air in her lungs left her body. She tried to cough, but nothing happened. She bent over and started to spit up briny tasting bile. The man yanked her up by the ponytail again and pushed her up hard against the wall. His hand grasped her neck tightly. He put his face up to her ear. Sonya could feel the stubble of his unshaven face and smell avocado and salsa and the faint odor of beer.

"*Oye, puta,* tell your men that they better deliver, or your friends will be taken out to the desert."

Sonya could not speak. Pain-induced tears poured down her cheeks.

"You *pendejos* fuck this up, I'm coming back for you, *chica.*" The man ran his other hand up Sonya's thigh and under her dress. He pushed his hand hard against her crotch.

Sonya closed her eyes and nodded that she understood.

The man released his grip from her throat, and Sonya crumpled to the ground. Sonya closed her eyes for a few seconds to gather her senses. When she opened them again, she was on all fours. Her knees were bleeding from the impact on the concrete. She looked over and saw her purse and its contents spread out into a bush against the walkway to the restaurant. She slowly got up and looked around. It seemed strange that a parking lot could be so empty anywhere in Southern California. She made her way over to her purse.

Katie, she thought. Oh my God, they have Katie! She got up and hurried over the purse and found her phone. She scrolled through her contacts and found Drew.

TWENTY-TWO

Chino was pulled over to the side of the onramp to the 54. The ramp was elevated so he could easily see the vehicles pass below him. He had Gerardo on the phone speaker.

"Drew says that someone besides us is tailing these guys," he told Gerardo.

"Do we know who they are?"

"No, he couldn't give me much info. Two dudes in dark glasses, white sedan."

Just then Chino noticed the maroon truck pass under him.

"I see the pickup. I'm on the move!"

Chino entered the freeway and accelerated in the middle lane until he came within a hundred yards of the truck. He stayed back, looking for the other vehicle. After about three miles, he saw it. A white sedan with two men inside. The vehicle was traveling to the truck's right side about fifty yards back. They were coming up to the 125 interchange. They could go north and head toward Interstate 8 or south to the border.

Chino gambled that they were headed north to the 8.

"We'll be at the 125 in about one minute. You can get on in forty-five seconds and hang back in the number two lane."

"*Qué pinche* two lane?" Gerardo asked.

"Second from the far right."

They had started to exit onto the interchange.

"I'm going to stay back about a half a mile. You let me know when and where they exit."

"Okay," Gerardo said. "I think I see them now."

Gerardo timed his entry to the freeway almost perfectly. There was only one car separating him from the maroon pickup and its tail. As he merged into traffic, Gerardo did his best not to look back at the

100

vehicles. He was driving Drew's now ten-year-old blue pickup. There was nothing flashy about the vehicle. His motorcycle was strapped down in the bed of the truck covered by a black tarp. You never knew, he told others, when you might need a rocket.

Gerardo was dressed as inconspicuously as possible. Jeans, gray T-shirt and a San Diego Padres ball cap. With his three-day beard, Gerardo looked just like any other nondescript Latino male driving a pickup in East County San Diego.

Gerardo dropped behind a recreational vehicle hauling a set of ATVs and let the truck pass him on the right. He waited for the tail. He still had Chino on the speaker.

"What type of car was the tail?"

"He said white sedan driven by . . ."

"*Puta madre!*" Gerardo spotted it coming up fast on his left. He let the car pass. No question they were the tail. Ramirez was right, there was no reason for these two grown men to be traveling together in silence. Gerardo could make out their general appearance. He got the impression that they might be law enforcement. From the outline of their haircuts, they looked like ex-military.

"Are they in your sight?"

"*Oye, carnal,*" Gerardo dragged his fingers across the stubble on his face. "We have a problem."

"You mean besides the *narcos* kidnapping Chance's uncle and posing an immediate threat to our lives?"

Gerardo considered the thought and suppressed the desire to laugh.

"*Pues,*" he moved in behind the trail car, "it looks to me like we have two ex-military or law enforcement *gueros* trailing the *pendejos* who have Gordo's *tío.*"

Chino was back on the freeway heading in Gerardo's direction. He considered the thought.

"Either they are trailing them for a criminal investigation or . . ."

"They are trailing them to protect them," Gerardo finished.

Gerardo could now make out the make and model of the vehicle. A newer white Chevy Impala. Not a very likely law enforcement vehicle, Gerardo thought.

"Chino," Gerardo said as he accelerated and moved to the left of the trail vehicle to stay in its blind spot, "I am going to need both hands. Call Ramirez and Drew and merge the calls. We all need to talk."

"Copy that." Chino slowed and moved to the slow lane. He called Ramirez and Drew and merged the calls. Gerardo gave a detailed description of the trail vehicle and the men driving.

"The government sometimes uses that model Chevy," Ramirez said.

"You think they are investigating these assholes?" Drew asked.

Ramirez thought about it for a second.

"The problem I see is that you wouldn't just have one vehicle in an investigation like this. You would expect to see multiple vehicles and, just like we did, they would coordinate the tail. One car would drop off, and another would pick up."

"So the other explanation would be . . ." Chino started to say.

"They are protecting the truck," Drew said.

"They just exited off the 125 and are headed east on the 94," Gerardo reported.

"They're heading toward Tecate," Chino said.

"Would make sense," Ramirez said, "plenty of open space and right next to the border."

"Okay. I am heading in that direction and will . . ." Drew was distracted by an incoming call. The caller ID read Sonya.

"Hold on," he said. "I just got a call from Sonya."

Drew switched the call. He heard Sonya crying.

"Drew! Drew!" She was sobbing. "They've got Katie!"

TWENTY-THREE

When she woke, all Katie could see was the dim light from the back side of the taillights. She knew that she was in the trunk of a moving vehicle. The back of her head was throbbing with a dull pain.

The trunk of a car. How the fuck did this happen? She thought for a brief second about how she was going to lay into Drew about getting everyone involved in this shit storm until the reality of the situation came back to her. She was in the trunk of a car.

What to do? Don't panic. Don't fucking panic.

She closed her eyes and took in a deep breath. The hot air inside the trunk had the taste of metal. She let the breath out slowly trying to calm her heart rate. What was it Drew had told her? Visualize your heart beating and will it to slow down. She opened her eyes. Her hands were not bound so she desperately ran her hands on the floor of the trunk looking for anything she could use as a weapon.

She picked up a roll of duct tape. There was also a slick, plastic container of motor oil. One roller ball ink pen was wedged against the carpet lining. A lone leather work boot lay near her head.

Think. Think. They need something from Drew, and that's why they have me and Chance's uncle. They are not going to kill me. They need me. Fighting coming out of the trunk will get me nowhere. I will be in unfamiliar terrain against an unknown number of assailants. What was it the Kali instructor always said? You must have a center of gravity and know the number of attackers.

She thought it through. Come out fighting, kicking, biting, and scratching. She would be ineffective from a prone position in the trunk. If she resisted, they would beat her, and maybe she would sustain injuries that would limit her ability to fight back later.

Better to play the weak female and wait for the right time to make a move.

The air in the trunk became thick and stifled her senses. Sweat stung her eyes and caused tears to flow. Pull it together. Stop crying! Katie looked around again for anything that might be of use. The tan, high ankle work boot had a long leather lace. She pulled the lace off and stuffed into her pants pocket. She grabbed the pen and shoved it down the front of her jeans.

Katie could sense the car slow down. She felt the tires leave smooth pavement and heard the crushing of gravel underneath her. This was it, she thought. Get ready.

TWENTY-FOUR

Drew pulled the car over to the side of the street. He couldn't breathe. In an instant, all the fear and adrenaline of that night in the desert five years ago came rushing back. The decision he made in that low-rate diner in the desert to engage in criminal behavior to save his home now pounded straight through the center of his brain. How could he be so stupid to let his wife be part of this dangerous operation?

What the fuck was I thinking?

Drew pounded the steering wheel with his open palms.

His heart was hammering so hard he thought could feel the skin on his chest rising to meet his shirt. Breathe, he told himself. Think! What could they want? The only thing Drew and the others left with that evening was the duffel bag of money. The bag was stuffed with wrapped bundles of hundred-dollar bills. Out of fear, maybe partly shame, they never really took it out and counted it. He assumed that there was only cash in the bag, and they had all agreed to lay low with the money for a few years until things died down. Drew peeled off twenty thousand for each of them. Six months later, they took out an extra fifty to start the restaurant. But no one had emptied the bag. Drew realized he needed to get to the bag and see what was inside that was worth kidnapping and, he tried not to consider it, killing someone.

He called back Chino and told him about Sonya's call.

"These fuckers are going to die!" Chino yelled into the phone.

"Listen, partner." Drew paused to gather himself. "I need you to reconnoiter these fucks. Make sure that Gerardo doesn't lose them."

Drew was silent for a few seconds.

"Chino," he said in a calm tone. "We need to find the location and then get my wife."

"Copy that, boss."

"I'm heading back to the bag and see if I can figure out what the fuck is so important for these assholes."

"Hey, Drew, Gerardo got a good look at the tail."

"And?" Drew already knew.

"He said they weren't *narco* types."

"Military?"

"That or law enforcement."

"Well, we've been here before. If they are law enforcement, you can bet they're dirty."

"And one more thing."

Drew said nothing.

"If they have Katie, they are going to know who we are."

"I'm pretty sure they didn't have any intel on us," Drew was somber in his tone. "It seems pretty simple. They've got her purse, her ID. If they know who she is, they're going to find us."

"We need to seriously consider our situation here, boss," Chino said.

"I screwed up when I let Katie get involved in this."

"Well, Drew," Chino said, "no use crying over it now. We need a plan."

Drew did not answer and thought the situation through for a few seconds.

"There's only one thing we need to do," he said.

"What's that?" Chino knew the answer the moment the words left his lips.

"Find my wife and make these cowboys pay for fucking with us," Drew said in a slow and deliberate tone.

"We're going to find her, boss. You can count on that."

Drew ended the call and fired up the engine. He raced onto to the freeway toward his home in Santee.

TWENTY-FIVE

Historic California State Route 94 became a winding two-lane road after it veered southeast from Jamul. The urban sprawl gradually gave way to larger Mediterranean-style homes on large lots and then to open space marked by chaparral and cacti. Oak and mesquite trees dotted the brown hillsides. As he passed through Jamul, Gerardo got a sense of the ranch lifestyle of the area. There were two grain and feed supply stores and some other businesses that looked like they had been frozen in the 1960s. The road moved out of the tiny commercial center and opened up to the low, boulder-pocked mountains. The road tacked right and passed the Jamul Casino, which stood out like an uninvited guest in the rugged-looking terrain. The giant, dull brown building seemed to incorporate none of the bling and eye pop of most Indian casinos in California. It looked more like an afterthought than a master-planned resort.

The road opened up again after passing the casino. The parched sienna and ochre fields were broken up by rolling hills with scattered, burned out oak trees and occasional low green brush. Gerardo remembered the area from his previous encounter with the smuggling organization.

He had two cars between him and the white sedan. There was another car between the sedan and the pickup. It was lucky for him that this was a relatively well-traveled route to the Tecate border crossing. The other cars and the fact he was in Drew's truck gave him confidence he had not been made.

On this road, everyone was following someone.

The road wound through the dry foothills toward Dulzura. The August heat baked the landscape. He could see the steam rising off the road in the distance, and even the bone-dry tall grass off the side of the road seemed to wilt. There was no breeze. He passed a field with thirty or forty cows. A few lay almost lifeless in the open sun, the rest gathered in the shade of a lone giant oak.

Pobre pinche vacas, he thought.

Gerardo was about a hundred yards behind the sedan they thought was tagging along with the pickup, and he was in contact with Chino and Ramirez.

"You know," Gerardo said with a laugh, "this looks like the same place we dealt with these *pendejos* the last time."

"Yeah, I know," said Ramirez. "I was thinking that also."

"But then again," Gerardo said, "it all looks the same out here."

"Hot, dry . . ." Ramirez started to say.

Gerardo looked out over the scrubby hillsides. Amber boulders the size of houses with cactus spread between them stood watch over the road.

"And deadly," he said to finish Ramirez's thought.

Ramirez did not respond. He was silent for a few seconds concentrating on the road ahead of him and remembering countless patrols he had been on in the area as a line Border Patrol agent.

"Where are you now?" Chino asked.

"We just drove through Dulzura."

"Ranches, dirt roads, and a lot of empty space," Ramirez said.

"*Tú sabes, Migra.*" Gerardo couldn't help but needle the Border Patrol officer.

"That I do. We're about ten minutes behind you so keep us posted."

Just then Gerardo drove past a federal immigration checkpoint on the westbound side of the road. The roving checkpoints were common in Southern California. They also weren't really roving since everyone knew where they were. This checkpoint slowed cars to a stop sign for Border Patrol agents to decide whether to wave the vehicle through, question the driver and occupants, or refer the vehicle to the side of the road for a secondary inspection. Gerardo thought it was strange that kidnapper narcos would take the risk of being anywhere near an immigration checkpoint.

"Oye, Migra," Gerardo said to Ramirez, "you know that there is a *migra* checkpoint out here?"

"Yeah, I was just thinking that."

"Why would these *vatos* take the risk of running into *migra?*"

"I don't know, but there are plenty of back roads out here."

Chino was listening in the conversation.

"You know," he said, "it's kind of a roundabout way these assholes are going."

"What do you mean?" Ramirez asked.

"I mean these guys could have taken Otay Lakes Road and cut out the back way from Chula and hooked up to the 94. That cuts about fifteen miles off the trip."

Ramirez thought about this for a second.

"You're right. The only reason to go the long route they are on now would be to make sure they weren't being tailed."

"Still," Chino said, "Gerardo's right. Why would these guys run the risk of contact with Border Patrol when they are up to gangster kidnapping shit?"

Ramirez had an uneasy feeling.

"Maybe they aren't afraid of contact with CBP," he said.

Ramirez knew this was something to think about. There would be no reason to risk law enforcement contact if you could avoid it. There were a thousand other places they could have holed up short of the checkpoint. It did not make sense.

Gerardo kept one vehicle between him and the trailing car. He could barely make out the lead vehicle, but he was willing to gamble that the tail car was part of the whole operation. He knew they were also gambling with Katie's life.

As he drove, he ran through scenarios. He knew that Cicatriz was angry at the incarceration of his nephew, Caritas. They were all part of the operation. He also knew Cicatriz was most likely murderously upset that they had relieved him of five hundred thousand dollars in cash. Even so, he thought, Cicatriz would not be going through all this hostage taking to exact revenge.

But that's just it, Gerardo thought. He knew Cicatriz. He knew the way the cartel operated. If this were about the money, things would be different. He had seen Cicatriz burn ten thousand dollars cash in a Weber barbeque just to show he could do it. If it were just the money, there would be no warning. No kidnapping. No meetings or hostage demands. They would find them and kill them. No long movie speech about how they had crossed the line and now would have to pay. In real life, and he knew because he had been part of it, they would kill them on the spot or, if they were bored, take them out to the fields and put a bullet in the back of their head.

What was it about that night five years ago that has these *pinche narcos* acting like TV gangsters? It had to be about the children. Everyone knew that the children were being trafficked for criminal reasons. *They were being peddled to child abusers.* He tried to remember the details of the night. The gun battle in the ranch house was over in less than two minutes. The only items taken from the house were the weapons they picked up off the floor. None of them searched any of the rooms. In fact, nothing was taken from the house or from the vehicles at the final shootout. The only thing they walked away with that evening was . . ."The bag!" he said out loud to no one in the truck.

The bag had to have something inside that identified the traffickers. No, he corrected himself. Not the traffickers. There would be no reason to list their names or identities. It had to be the buyers.

Puta madre! Not only do they think we know about their customers but there is someone, or more than one person, that is important enough to hunt us down.

Gerardo reached for his phone to call Drew.

TWENTY-SIX

Drew was almost in his driveway when he got the call from Gerardo. He skidded to a stop in the driveway of his picture-perfect cottage. Drew had used some of the money they liberated from the traffickers to update the place. Over the garage, he built a granny flat with a gabled roof that matched the original part of the house. The large space served as a playroom for the boys and guest house. He replaced the living room window with a large atrium style window complete with bench seat. The exterior of the house was renovated with new paint and energy-efficient windows. The aging picket fence had been repaired board by board and now was painted bright white. The perfect house for the perfect family.

Except for the blood money stored at his house and the fact that his wife was now being held hostage. Not quite so storybook.

His phone vibrated. Drew saw the caller ID from Gerardo's phone number.

"It's the customers," Gerardo nearly yelled.

"Huh?"

"The customers," he continued. "They think that we have a list of the *putos* that these kids were being sold to."

Drew considered the thought.

"You know," he said, "part of me wanted to believe it was just about the money. I didn't want to think about those kids. It sure makes a lot of sense now."

"*Sabes que,* Drew," Gerardo said. "I don't think the money in the bag was payment for the children."

"Then what was it for?"

"I think Caritas was demanding the money for the names."

It made sense to Drew. Whoever was behind this needed something, and it wasn't just the cash.

"Caritas somehow got the names of the customers and was running his own side game for the cash," Drew said as he opened his truck door.

"Did you ever go through the bag?" Gerardo asked.

"No. "The duffel was pretty small, and the cash was vacuum sealed in plastic. I just cut it open with a knife and peeled off the cash we needed."

"It's the only thing they could be after."

"Right, otherwise we would all be dead."

"*Pues, amigo,* I suggest you find what they are looking for."

"Copy that and don't lose those assholes."

"*No te preocupes,*" Gerardo said in a slow and deliberate tone. "I will not lose them and believe me, I will find your wife."

"Thanks, Gerardo."

Drew ended the call and took a moment in his car to compose himself. He didn't want to think about the possibility that nothing was in the bag. He didn't want to think about his wife being roughed up or held at gunpoint. He didn't want to think about the mistakes he had made five years ago that brought him to this point. There was no escaping it. This was his mess. He had to clean this up. Drew knew , like the last time, people were going to die. If someone hurt his wife, then he would make sure that everyone responsible would die.

Drew got out of the truck and made his way into the garage. The granny flat over the garage had an exterior entry and stairway and a trap door entry to the garage with a skeleton stairway. The boys loved this entrance because the room felt more like a clubhouse to them. When the room was being constructed, Drew consulted with the contractor to build a storage compartment under the interior stairs. He instructed the contractor to build a panel with hidden releases not visible to anyone looking at the stairs. Drew found it interesting that the contractor never asked why he needed a hidden storage area. It was apparently not unusual for people to make such requests.

He moved a stepladder under the stairs and climbed up to the panel covering the storage compartment. The panel was three by three feet square. A four-inch trim piece framed the panel. Each corner of the trim piece was secured by a wooden dowel. The dowels were spring loaded so that when pushed, the dowel would release. Drew pushed in the dowels and released the trim pieces. He removed the panel. Sitting in the center of the space was the canvas duffel. Cobwebs had formed on the handles of the bag. It had been over three years since Drew last touched it.

Chino and Chance had both been equally as hesitant about circulating large quantities of narco cash so close to the border. After the initial dispersal of cash, it sat unused for almost a year. It was only the decision to start the cantina that had them going back to the bag for cash.

Drew reached in and pulled out the bag. He came back down the ladder and threw the bag onto the workbench. A cloud of dust escaped the bag as it hit the surface. This was it, he thought, whatever these people wanted was in this bag. If it wasn't, they would have nothing to bargain with or, since bargaining was probably out of the question, there would be nothing to use as insurance. He unzipped the bag and turned it over.

Five years ago, when Drew first opened it, he found the entire bundle of cash had been plastic wrapped. Drew used his tactical knife to slice through the top of the plastic. The cash was bundled in twenty-thousand-dollar units. Each bundle had five thousand-dollar packs, all hundred-dollar bills, wrapped in separate plastic. He always thought it strange that such a large sum of cash occupied such a small space.

Drew emptied the contents onto the workbench. The still wrapped bundle made a heavy thump as it contacted the wood surface. He looked back into the bag to see if he missed anything. The bag was empty. The wrapped bundles of cash lay on the table, the hundred-dollar labels visible through the thick plastic. He unwrapped the plastic and fanned through each bundle to make sure he did not miss anything. He found nothing.

Fuck! Fuck! Drew dropped his head onto the surface of the workbench. The bag, he thought. He needed to check the bag again.

He reached for the bag and turned it over again. The bag was a green canvas. Nothing fancy. No interior pockets. Drew shook it hard, and nothing came out. He flipped it upright and pulled it wide open. There was nothing visible inside. He ran his fingers along the bottom of the bag. Nothing. He started to panic. His heart was racing as he took a step back from the bag. He moved closer again. There were no external pockets, but the handles were wrapped in Velcro padding. The handle padding had a zipper pouch on the inside grip. The pouch was just big enough for a set of keys. It was the only place Drew had not searched. He ran his fingers over each wrapped handle. Nothing on the first one. Moving slowly over the second handle he could feel something under the wrap and in the pouch. He unfastened the Velcro closure and carefully unzipped the pouch.

A small thumb drive was taped to the side lining of the padding.

This had to be it. After pulling the thumb drive out and sticking it in his pocket, he ran into the house to grab his laptop. As he was leaving, he caught a glimpse of himself in the mirror in the hallway. Jeans, T-shirt, and high-top sneakers. Fuck that, Drew thought, not this time. He ran down the hall to his bedroom. He changed into a pair of camo cargo pants, a black long sleeve T, and tactical boots. Drew went to the nightstand and picked up his Luminox and took the Omega off his wrist. He buckled the Luminox to his wrist as he scanned the bedroom once more. The closet. Of course. Drew had made an over-the-top hunting knife purchase last year. He saw it at a gun show in Arizona while visiting a friend in Phoenix. The knife was matte black, including the ten-inch blade. The blade was aggressively serrated, and the blade bowed out toward a sharp point. XDEFENDERX was stamped across the blade. The knife screamed violence.

If this is what they wanted, Drew thought, then this is what they were going to get.

TWENTY-SEVEN

Katie was taking slow, deep breaths to keep from hyperventilating. She could hear at least two male voices. She heard the gravel crush under the heavy footsteps of the men. She was scared. Katie tried not to think of what might happen to her when the trunk was opened. The chemical taste of the hot air in the trunk started to make her gag, but she did her best to keep under control. Don't panic, she told herself. There was nothing she could do inside the trunk that could change her circumstances. She knew Drew would tell her that she should wait to assess the threat before she tried anything.

The voices were speaking in Spanish. She could not make out what they were saying. She heard other footsteps coming toward the car. The voice called out something to the men . . . in English. She couldn't make out anything except that it was an order of some sort. The two men immediately stopped talking.

She heard someone walk to the front passenger side door and open it. She could hear him moving articles inside the car. The man then made his way back to the trunk area.

This was it, she thought. In these brief seconds, Katie tried not to let fear consume her, but she couldn't shake it . . . she was scared for her life. She thought of her children and how stupid she was for being out here instead of at home with them. She thought of how angry she was at Drew for getting his family involved in all of this. As quickly as she ran through those thoughts, she realized it made no difference. She was in the trunk of a car. Men were outside discussing her fate. She knew that she had to stay alive. She knew she might have to fight. Katie knew, in every ounce of the blood coursing through her veins, Drew would find and kill these men. She just needed to stay alive.

The man speaking in English continued to order the others in a muffled but forceful tone. The muscles in Katie's legs and arms flexed in anticipation of the trunk opening. The men were silent for a few seconds. Katie was breathing hard. The saline taste of tears reached the corners of her mouth. She heard one of the men jingling keys near the trunk latch and heard the key enter the lock.

This was it. This was it. Be ready.

The trunk lid opened. Bright daylight pierced the stifling dark of the trunk. Katie only saw the outline of someone leaning over her. She closed her eyes for a second to adjust to the light. She opened them again just as the man's fist was inches from her face. The crushing blow to her nose caused her entire body to jerk. Her vision went completely black, and she felt someone grabbing her by the shoulders. One of the men placed a hood over her head and rapidly secured it with duct tape at the neck. Katie could feel the blood pouring from her nose, but she could not move her arms. She felt her body being extracted from the trunk and thrown on the loose gravel. Her face made the first impact. One of the men was laughing.

Katie was in too much pain to scream out. She felt her arms being ripped behind her and one of the men binding her wrists with duct tape. Fucking Mexicans and duct tape, Drew always used to say that to her. Now she knew why. Her nose was still pulsing blood, and she could taste the warm flow as she tried to gasp for air. The men dragged her across the gravel and up a set of wooden stairs. Katie felt the tops of her feet slam against the steps. She felt the temperature change. She was inside a home or a building of some sort. The men kept speaking to each other in Spanish as they dragged her across the floor. She knew details might matter later, so Katie tried to count the seconds that she was being dragged from the front door. When the men stopped, she heard one of them jingling keys. Katie heard a door open. At that moment, one of the men grabbed the back of her hair and her bound wrists. He flung her to the floor. Katie's face again made first impact, and a new round of pain assaulted her. She didn't move, hoping the men would leave. One of them grabbed the top of the bag over her head and pulled up. Katie did not cry out. She tried to steady her breathing. The man grabbed a portion of the tape around her neck and ripped it off. He pulled the bag off over her head and shoved her face down into the wood floor. More pain. Her vision was blurry, but out of the corner of her eye, she could make out another pair of feet. The last thing she registered in her mind was the duct tape around the ankles.

TWENTY-EIGHT

Gerardo kept his eyes steady on the lead vehicle. The winding, two-lane road made it relatively easy to keep the truck in sight. As the road started to make the climb up the steep hills outside of Tecate, he began to worry the truck might be headed into Mexico. That would be the last place he wanted to be. Even though the Department of Justice provided him with legal permanent residency under a new name, Gerardo knew that would mean nothing if he were recognized by the wrong people in Mexico. Regardless of how small the town, the cartels controlled the border and had their people set up everywhere. Any gas station, *llantería*, or cantina might have an associate monitoring new faces. Anybody in *la vida* would recognize another player. Word would spread quickly to those who trafficked information.

He remembered when he was instructed by Cicatriz to monitor traffic at the port in Topolobampo, Sinaloa, just outside of Los Mochis. They were looking for a nephew of a competitor who had been trying to get back to his home state after incarceration and deportation from the United States. A source informed Cicatriz that the man, known as Cachito, made it from Tijuana to La Paz. Sources in La Paz confirmed he was there with two *sicarios* awaiting transport by boat across the Gulf of California to Topolobampo. From there, he could travel at night on the highway until he made it out of Sinaloa and into Nayarit.

Cicatriz's reason for wanting to kill Cachito was a daily truth of narcotics trafficking. The man, a nephew of a rival, had been apprehended and prosecuted in San Diego for the distribution of more than five hundred kilos of cocaine. The southwest region of California belonged to Cicatriz, and for someone to presume he could muscle in was an insult. Cachito used one of Cicatriz's distributors in Orange County and brought down law enforcement scrutiny on his organization. It was public record that Cachito had been sentenced to seven years in federal prison. Anyone entrenched in the drug trade knew the quantity Cachito was moving carried a mandatory minimum of ten years in prison. The only way to do less would be for Cachito to cooperate and rat out others in the distribution chain. This gave Cicatriz the moral high ground for eliminating the *rata,* not that he felt he needed it. He waited patiently for Cachito to complete his prison sentence. He retained an attorney to chart Cachito's transfers in the Federal Bureau of Prisons. He reached out to his sources in US Immigration to be advised of the precise date of deportation. Cicatriz then alerted his network of informants and government officials to keep him apprised of Cachito's travel through Mexico.

That was the reason Gerardo was in a dusty pickup with another *sicario,* "El Mono," waiting for Cachito to arrive. El Mono was dressed in typical *Sinaloense* ranchero attire. Western-style shirt, tight-fitting boot-cut jeans, and weather-beaten snakeskin boots. He was wearing a white cowboy hat with a broad black band across the brim, and silver mirrored aviator sunglasses. Mono was manipulating a toothpick between his teeth, slowly chewing on one end. The radio was turned to a local *ranchera música* station playing old school stuff. Vicente Fernandez was belting out a traditional version of *Volver, Volver* while Mono sat silently watching the activity at the port. Gerardo had been sent out with Mono on a previous occasion and was always unnerved by his silence and cold demeanor. El Mono had no conscience that impeded his ability to kill people on command. Gerardo knew today would end with blood on the streets.

Topolobampo was one of the last underdeveloped ports in Sinaloa. For years there had been talk of building a mega-port in the village that would boost the city of Los Mochis and the state to major-player status in import and export. The mega port never materialized and, for now, the town remained a small-time fishing village replete with poverty and unemployment. The ferry, however, continued its daily crossings to and from the Baja California peninsula.

The ferry arrived one hour late. Mono said nothing to Gerardo and got out of the pickup as the crowds started to debark. Gerardo knew what was going to happen. He knew Mono would not speak to Cachito. He would not tell him that he should have never cooperated with American law enforcement. It was simple, he would find Cachito and execute him where he stood. Just another day for El Mono.

Gerardo trailed behind him as they parted their way through the crowd of passengers. Families, working men engaged in familiar conversation. He noticed a woman in her late sixties pushing a luggage cart, her back bent over an odd angle. Gerardo considered moving over to help her until he remembered why he was there. Mono was oblivious to the crowd and continued his laser-like trajectory. From behind, Gerardo knew he had seen the target because Mono reached behind his back and pulled out his firearm. Gerardo moved to the right of him and rested his own hand on the Glock in the front of his waistband. Gerardo scanned the crowd for gunmen who may have been traveling with Cachito as protection. Then he saw him. Criminals in *la vida* could spot another player a mile away and, like it or not, Gerardo was in the life. Cachito was about thirty feet away. He held the hand of an attractive female who could have been no more than twenty. She was dressed in skintight designer black jeans and high heels. Lugging an enormous bag, she looked annoyed that she had to walk on the uneven asphalt street. She stood out among the simple, working-class people around her. Gerardo noticed two men trailing Cachito and the girl.

As they made their way through the crowd, Gerardo saw a few people in the crowd eyeing El Mono and the handgun held low in his right hand. A few walked quickly to the side to make way for him. Cachito and his girlfriend were walking side by side, each looking down at a cellphone.

Mono began firing from about ten feet. He was holding a Glock nine-millimeter out in front of him. The first shots hit Cachito in the chest and throat. The arterial spray exploded in all directions as he went limp to the ground. The gunmen behind Cachito moved out to both sides of their dying boss. Gerardo did not remember pulling his weapon out, but he instinctively fired at the man moving to his right.

Two shots and he was down. Mono continued walking forward and firing at the other man. Five quick rounds took the man down.

The crowd dispersed. People disappeared. This was Mexico. There were no crying women, no bystanders calling 911. Cachito's girlfriend stood motionless. She dropped her phone and stared, open-mouthed. Mono said nothing and walked over to Cachito, who was on his back staring up into space with a hand holding the gaping wound in the front of his throat. Gerardo could see the flap of tissue hanging over Cachito's hand. It was over for him.

Gerardo did not have to get any nearer to determine the two gunmen were also dead. Mono turned back to Gerardo. He took his sunglasses off and wiped off the residue from the chemical vapor of the gunfire on his shirt.

"*Bueno, pues,*" he said as he put his sunglasses back on, "*ya está quebrado este cabrón.*"

Gerardo did not respond. Mono was right, this fucker was absolutely dead. He looked over Mono's shoulder and saw the girlfriend still standing in the same place. Three dead bodies on the ground around her and her shoulder bag open and sprawled at her feet. Standing in the street on her five-inch heels, she stood out like a telephone pole. She was whimpering.

As Mono walked away, he stopped as if he had suddenly remembered something. Gerardo knew what it was. Without saying a word, Mono turned and took three quick steps back to the girlfriend. She was still wearing sunglasses so Gerardo could not make out the expression in her eyes as she came to the realization that her short life was over.

El Mono fired three quick shots into her face. He stood over the girl, the top half of her face was now a pulpy mess, and seemed to be examining his handiwork. He then turned to Gerardo.

"*Tienes hambre?*" he asked.

Food was the last thing that Gerardo could think about, but he could not show any weakness or compassion in front of this *sicario* because it would get back to his boss. Gerardo shrugged.

"*Te gustan tacos estilo Los Mochis?*" Gerardo asked.

El Mono gave a grunt of approval and made his way back to the truck.

This is what would happen if Gerardo were to set foot back in Mexico. Word would spread quickly down the *narco* line, through the *plazas*, and directly to Cicatriz. The only thing waiting for him in Mexico was a bullet from someone exactly like El Mono.

TWENTY-NINE

Katie was lying face down on a wooden floor when she regained consciousness. Her hands were bound behind her back. She knew it was duct tape by the sticky feel on her wrists. She could hear someone talking loudly but was having trouble making out the words for a few seconds.

"Fuck you, shithead, motherfucker, greaser pieces of shit!" the voice yelled. "Get your asses in here and fight me like a man, you pussy dirtbags."

The voice was coming from behind Katie. Her head was throbbing, and she could feel dried blood caked on her upper lip. She gathered her senses and turned over toward the voice. A man was sitting with his back up against the wall. His hands were also bound behind him. His right eye was swollen, and blood smeared the front of his rumpled blue Hawaiian shirt. He looked out of place in his tattered green cargo shorts. The thought quickly left her mind when she realized there was no normal in this place. When Katie rolled over, he stopped shouting and looked at her.

"You okay?" he asked her.

Katie pulled herself up to a sitting position.

"Looks like it. At least for now."

"Who are you and what the fuck are you doing here?

Katie tried to smile. "I could ask you the same thing."

"Yeah, right. Connors. Jimmy Connors. Like the—"

"Like the tennis player."

"Well, thank you. At least you have made my otherwise fucking, shitty day." Jimmy was out of breath.

"My name is Katie, and I have a pretty good idea why I'm here."

"Well, maybe you can shed some light on my current predicament, besides the obvious fact that I'm totally screwed."

123

"To tell you the truth, I am a bit new to the whole thing, but it all started about five years ago."

Katie described a few of the events in the desert involving Drew and Chino. She told him about the stupid idea to get involved with Caritas and alien smuggling. Katie did her best to describe the children and the decision of Drew and the rest to go back and save them.

"Wait a minute, is your husband a Marine?"

"Yes, he is."

"Well, fuck me," he said, "don't tell me that this has anything to do with my tub of lard, slacker nephew?"

Katie looked blankly at him.

"Chester. Chester Connors."

Same blank look.

"Took to calling himself Chance. Now for some dumb shit reason he calls himself Gordo."

Katie's eyes lit up.

She told him what she knew about Chance's involvement in saving the children from the traffickers including the shooting and torturing.

"I remember that now. He told me that he got his ass kicked in a bar. I totally believed that his wise-ass, fake gangster attitude would have resulted in a beating somewhere. Shit, I would have beat the crap out of him if he wasn't my nephew."

"That's not the guy I know. Chance, I like Gordo better, is a wiz at marketing and keeps a pretty low profile."

"Not low enough, since I'm sitting here tied up by a bunch of Mexicans and missing the top half of my ear."

Katie noticed for the first time the purple clot of blood over his ear.

"They," she hesitated, "they did that to you here?"

"Yeah, the bandido in charge ripped it off with a pair of gardening shears. Hurt like a motherfucker. They put a paper towel over it and wrapped duct tape around it but . . . ."

Jimmy nodded his head at the clump of duct tape and bloody paper on the ground.

"It fell off while I was trying to sleep."

Jimmy laughed.

"Fucking Mexicans and duct tape."

Katie smiled. "Yeah, I hear that's a thing."

"Well," Jimmy straightened his back up against the wall. "I have checked every inch of the place for a way out. Nothing. The window screen is bolted in, the floor is solid, and I have no tools. Some fat fuck Mexican comes in about two o'clock each day and gives me a plate of food and a water bottle, and that's it. I've been here two days now."

Katie looked around the room.

"Okay, listen," she said. "We need to get out of here. These assholes are not going to make some nice exchange for whatever it is that they want from Drew and the guys."

"Yeah, I have been thinking that for a day or so now."

"We need to figure out a way to fight our way out."

"Hogtied like this?" Jimmy rotated his shoulders to show his wrists.

"Well," Katie said as she rolled onto her back. "Let's take care of that right now."

She squirmed on her back for a second and then pulled her wrists under her waist. She then slid them under the back of her legs, knees and then around her feet. She sat up with her wrists in front of her.

Jimmy looked at her as if she had performed a magic act.

"Ten years of hot yoga finally pays off," she said.

Katie made her way over to Jimmy and started to work on the tape around his wrists.

"I know one thing," she said as she peeled back some of the tape, "these guys are not going to let us go. We're screwed if we don't try to make a run for it."

"We don't know how many men they have out there or what type of firepower they have." Jimmy kept his voice low.

"I'm sure Drew is posting up outside. I know he is pissed. I know that he and Chino and Chance are getting ready to come for us. We need to make it easier for them by causing any sort of disruption we can."

Katie pulled the last bit of tape off from Jimmy's wrists and held her hands out toward him to so that he could take the tape off her wrists.

"Still," he said, "we don't have any weapons."

"We have surprise and the fact that we know we are going to die if we do nothing."

"You are one tough woman," Jimmy said as he finished taking off the tape.

"No, Jimmy," she said standing up, "I am one tough bitch who is going to get home to her kids."

Jimmy yanked down hard on the last bit of tape binding Katie's wrists. She pulled her wrists apart and began shaking them to get some circulation back.

Jimmy watched as Katie pulled a pen out of her pants and a leather boot lace from a pocket. She held the pen in the palm of her hand and started to secure it to her palm by wrapping the lace over the pen and through her fingers. She tied it off using her mouth.

"You planning on writing shit all over them?"

Katie smiled.

"This is a Kubotan, a palm stick. I learned this in Kali training. It extends the distance of my hand strike. All of my force is concentrated in the tip at the point of impact."

Jimmy nodded as if understanding what she was doing.

"Kali is Filipino self-defense," he said.

"You know it?"

"I was stationed in the Philippines, Subic Bay, when I was in the Navy. Watched some tiny Filipinos kick the shit out many a drunk sailor during my time there."

"Well, the first fucker that comes through that door is going to get his eyes gouged by the point of this Bic pen. Once the commotion starts, we run to the door and keep moving."

Katie got up and moved toward the grated window. She could see steep hills and a rough green and brown landscape. High ground, she thought. Drew always talked about the best defensive position was high ground. He also said it was the best position from which to stage an attack. Although the window was looking south, she could make out the waning rays of the sun to her right. The dark, she thought. Drew's mantra. I am the Silence, I am the Dark, I am the Weapon, I am Death.

He would wait until dark.

Katie quickly moved back to Jimmy.

"We need to retie our hands."

"Wait," Jimmy said. "We just got out of these and . . ."

"Drew and the boys won't make a move until it gets dark. I know him. I know he will bank on me remembering all of this. We have to sit tight until it gets dark, so we need to look like good, tied-up prisoners. I can wrap the tape so it looks like you are still restrained."

Katie moved over and pulled Jimmy's hands behind him and started to wrap the tape around his wrists.

"They are loose enough for you to pull out of them quickly, but they look secure."

Katie started wrapping the loose ends of the tape around her wrists using her mouth. When she had done her best job of recreating the binds, she sat back down on the floor and pulled her legs up under her wrists and then under her rear. She sat back up and moved against the wall.

"So, we just sit here and wait?"

"Well," Katie said with a muffled laugh, "it's kind of a wait and see. We hope they don't come in here until after nightfall. If they do, we need to act like we're scared and still bound by the tape."

Katie thought about it for a second.

"I mean I'll act scared. You act like the same crazy-ass old man that you have been all the time."

Jimmy laughed.

"That, sweetie, is something that I can most definitely do."

"We need to stay alive and in the game until we can make our move."

"Sounds like a plan that can't fail," he said with a tinge of sarcasm. "An angry woman with a twenty-five-cent pen and a fifty-seven-year-old Navy sailor with half an ear."

"Better than sitting here and waiting for them to shoot us."

Jimmy nodded in agreement.

"You really are one tough bitch."

THIRTY

Agent Winters sat in the study waiting for Henry Harrison. Winters arrived at the mansion in Point Loma fifteen minutes early knowing Harrison's disdain for tardiness. Winters was seething. He could not believe he had to sit in this dark-green-carpeted room. It felt like he was being punished. The walls were lined with floor-to-ceiling wooden shelves stuffed with books and small sculptures. The head of a Greek goddess, several globes, and mounted firearms broke up some of the lines of books. Winters sat there like a child waiting for a scolding from his father. He was furious things had deteriorated to this level. Winters knew better than to leave the operation in the hands of a sociopath. Corriente, or Caritas as he called himself, should never have been trusted with such a delicate operation. Add to that Caritas's amateurish attempt at extortion, and you had the makings of a disaster. Now it was his burden to deal with the mess and answer to Henry Harrison.

Henry "Hank" Harrison was a direct descendant of Jackson Haynes Harrison, owner of some of oldest land holdings in Southern California. After the Mexican-American War, Jackson Harrison used a combination of fraud and luck to become one of the wealthiest Californians of the era. After Mexico gained its independence from Spain, the government of Mexico rewarded loyal "friends" with massive private land grants called "ranchos." The system worked well for the wealthy friends of the governor of Alta California, enriching a few families while nearly enslaving the local population working for them. After the war, the Treaty of Guadalupe Hidalgo in 1848 recognized the existing land grants. The problem was proof of the grants, which required grant holders to engage an array of surveyors, lawyers, and historians to maintain possession of the valuable land. Jackson Harrison made his way west from Baltimore to seek his fortune in the fur trade only to change careers when he discovered his Jesuit education had bestowed upon him a useful commodity in the rugged Western states: the ability to read and write in Latin. He realized that most legal documents, while written in English, had arcane Latin phrases that made up the important parts of most writs and filings. When he finally arrived in San Diego in 1849, Harrison told anyone who would listen that he was a successful real estate attorney from Chicago. He also routinely mentioned that he was a member of the Harrison family, descended from one of the founders of the nation, Benjamin Harrison V, and from the man who had died a few years earlier while serving as president of the United States, William Henry Harrison. Given the distance from the East Coast and the lack of a means of discrediting his fabrication, Jackson Harrison was able to capitalize on his alleged family name and successfully edge into the local real estate and business communities.

Harrison researched the land grants and approached Juan Diego del Castillo, the owner of the largest rancho south of Los Angeles. He quickly endeared himself to Castillo and his family and offered to assist him in the processing of his land grant in exchange for a portion of the property. While Harrison did do the work necessary to achieve legal recognition of the land grant, he maneuvered a particularly large plot for himself as compensation. Jackson Harrison was now the owner of 150,000 acres of prime farming area in the rolling hills that reached the coast of what is now North County San Diego.

Harrison was able to profit enormously from his real estate concerns and he and his four sons became business giants in the rapidly growing city of San Diego. He and his scions built the thirty-thousand-square-foot Harrison Mansion on three rolling hillside acres in Point Loma with an unobstructed view of San Diego Bay and the growing city. The mansion was built to replicate the old money mansions of Newport, Rhode Island. Lush, manicured gardens gave way to sweeping steps that led up to the wide, deep, and blazingly white two-story mansion. Replicating the old money existence of influential families of the East Coast is exactly what Jackson Harrison sought to accomplish. He bought up as much land as he could in the port district of San Diego and vigorously entered the world of politics. Fearing the discovery of fraudulent family history, Harrison never ran for office. Instead, Harrison became a wealthy donor and influencer of local politics. Over the years, he inserted his voice into national politics as the importance of resource-rich California could not be ignored. Harrison's money grew as did his family's influence and power. His sons and grandsons continued to entrench the family position in all aspects of the Southern California economy. For this reason, Hank Harrison had the ear of every Republican member of the US Congress and every political mover and shaker in the state. The Harrison Family Trust was well positioned to maintain that wealth.

All of this meant nothing to Winters as he sat waiting for the tongue lashing from Harrison. He knew the situation had deteriorated to a point where people would need to be eliminated in order to cover tracks leading to Harrison and other influential people. Those tracks also ran directly over Winters.

Winters heard the footsteps behind him and started to rise before Harrison entered the room. He did not look back. He waited for Harrison to come around him and move behind the enormous wooden desk in front of Winters. The carved, leather-topped piece of furniture created a good four feet of distance between the two men. Harrison was in his late seventies. Almost six-four, he towered over the barely five-eight Winters. He was dressed in a neatly pressed, charcoal black suit, white shirt, and slate gray tie. His full head of white hair was combed back and severely parted to the side. The dull gray, darting eyes were unnerving to Winters. Harrison did not greet Winters. Instead, he pulled the leather partner's chair from behind the desk and stood for a second looking at Winters. Agent Winters sat back down in his chair and waited for Harrison to speak.

"I think that it is unnecessary for me to state the obvious nature of the problem we have in the situation you created." Harrison's voice was stern with a nasal tone.

Winters started to talk, but Harrison held his hand out for him to remain silent.

"There are several parties concerned here that will go to any extreme to ensure their interests are protected."

"I understand the gravity of the situation, sir." Winters shifted in his seat. "I don't need to remind you that my position is extremely compromised as well."

Harrison shifted in his large leather chair.

"I take it you have had no luck in locating the information that we need returned?"

"We are taking measures at this time to secure that information," Winters responded.

"Have you identified all of the parties involved in the transaction?"

"We have, sir, but . . ." Winters paused.

"But what?"

"We have discovered one of the parties is the daughter of a relatively prominent financial planner. I think you might know him."

"What's her name?"

"Katie Archer. That is her married name. She is married to a former Marine—"

"Not former, once a Marine always a Marine."

Over Harrison's shoulder, Winters caught a glimpse of the shadow box holding an American flag and mounted, crossed swords. He did not want to ask.

"Understood. She is married to a Marine named Drew Archer. Decorated sniper, two combat tours. Her father is Cameron Stratton."

"I know him," Harrison said as he turned his gaze toward the window. "He is a name. Not a major mover and shaker. It is something we will need to handle, but it is not a problem."

"Well," Winters continued, "at present we have positioned ourselves to use leverage to obtain the information within days."

Harrison did not ask about the leverage. He continued to look out at the window.

"I don't need to impress upon you the importance of the situation at hand."

Winters did not respond.

"I want this taken care of. I don't want any loose ends."

Harrison looked back at Winters and leaned across the desk.

"No loose ends. No witnesses." Harrison's low tone seemed almost comical to Winters.

He held in the urge to laugh but did not respond.

"Is that clear?"

Winters stood up and fastened the top button of his blue blazer.

"Crystal, sir. Crystal clear."

Winters turned to leave and then stopped and turned back to Harrison.

"If you care to know," he was defiant in his tone, "we are set to eliminate a loose end shortly. And rest assured, Mr. Harrison, it was solely through my efforts were we able to accomplish this task."

Harrison gave a quick snort.

"We will see how effective you really are and whether or not I need to bring in outside actors."

Winters didn't wait for any additional derisive comments. He turned and walked out of the room.

THIRTY-ONE

Vicente Corriente-Torres sat waiting in a cell at the Metropolitan Correctional Center in downtown San Diego. The MCC was directly across from the John Rhoades Federal Judicial Center that housed the offices of the United States Attorney's Office for the Southern District of California. The MCC was also across the street from the United States District Court where his case had been pending for five years. Corriente-Torres was in the Solitary Housing Unit, the SHU, awaiting his transfer to court for yet another lengthy continuance of his trial date and then to a debriefing session with Kerry Williams, the assistant US Attorney prosecuting his case and head of an investigation of the Corriente-Torres drug-trafficking organization.

Over the past five years, Corriente-Torres had been cooperating, providing information to government agents and the US Attorney regarding the activities of the organization and related groups operating out of Sinaloa and Tijuana. In reality, however, he offered only selective information his uncle passed to him through his lawyer. The individuals selected by his uncle, El Cicatriz, were essentially fall guys whose arrests would help Corriente-Torres get a reduced sentence. Cicatriz ordered members of his organization to assume "name only" roles in the organization and arranged for them to be fortuitously apprehended by Mexican authorities working with the DEA. Of course, these men had no opportunity to refuse Cicatriz's orders, and their families were well provided for during any period of incarceration.

Facing a thirty-year sentence under a drug-kingpin statute, Corriente-Torres reached out to his uncle for help. The sophisticated false network of narcotics trafficking cost Cicatriz at least two million dollars in seized narcotics and the arrest of fourteen men. For all his preening and ridiculous nickname, this was still the only child of his deceased brother. Cicatriz promised his brother to always look out for family members, and the thought of his twenty-nine-year-old nephew spending the better part of his adult life in prison was too much to bear.

Caritas was always nervous when he had to go to the MCC. The US Attorney arranged for him to be housed during his pretrial proceedings at a privately run facility on contract with the Bureau of Prisons. The facility held mostly nonviolent people who would be deported. The danger of reprisal from other drug organizations was minimal at the facility. The MCC, however, was different. It housed all types of inmates facing a variety of drug and violence charges. The SHU housed dangerous and "high profile" inmates. Even though he was kept separate from other inmates, there was no avoiding his "parade route" through the MCC and into the court building. His lawyer assured him that his transportation to the facility was kept confidential until the date of his court appearance, which would then become public record. This was not especially reassuring to him since he knew his uncle routinely was provided with such information on other inmates and snitches. The leaks at the Bureau of Prisons, the US Marshals and even in the US Attorney's Office ran deep. Anyone was exploitable for the right amount of money or the right threat.

In his twelve-by-twelve cell, Caritas was left to his own to ponder his predicament and worry about what might happen. The cell was painted a drab, institutional gray with a stainless-steel toilet and water basin in the corner. The sleeping space was a concrete bench with a two-inch mattress. Above the water basin, a thin sheet of metal served as a wavy mirror. He moved toward the basin to drink some water. Caritas paused at his reflection. The last five years had aged him. The boyish good looks that had given him his nickname had faded. The face in the mirror had dark circles under his eyes and paunchy cheeks. Institutional food and a steady diet of junk food and Top Ramen available to a prisoner with resources put at least twenty-five pounds on him. It had to be over soon, he thought. He could get back to the world and his life of money and power. His lawyer told him this would be his last debriefing with the prosecutors and agents, and the government would allow him to plead to a ten-year minimum mandatory charge.

With the time he had already served and the sentencing reduction for substantial cooperation, he hoped he would be out soon.

It was so close he could barely stand it. He had it all planned, including his ace in the hole if they wanted more. The information he possessed about the trafficking event from five years ago was worth a get-out-of-jail ticket. What he knew would bring the downfall of government officials and prove to be an embarrassment to federal law enforcement. At his last debriefing session with the government, he teased the information that there was a way of identifying others involved. It was something they missed in the investigation of the crime scene. Everyone at table knew what that meant. The customers. The buyers of children. They seemed to be extremely interested in the proposition that there might be a way of establishing the identities of unindicted co-conspirators.

Caritas hoped the agents from the various agencies—the DEA, FBI and HSI—would fall over each other trying to get a piece of the action. Independent corroboration was always better than the word of a rat trying to save himself years in prison. Caritas could tell they were interested, and his suspicions were confirmed when he was called back to talk within weeks of his last meeting. He knew it was dangerous, but his uncle's efforts were not enough, and he wanted out. He wanted out now! It was a bombshell, but he would keep it to himself until the last moment.

He heard the clang of the metal door opening at the end of the hallway. The footsteps heading his way were unmistakably those of MCC guards marching toward his cell. The screaming from the individual cells as the guards headed his way was deafening in the confined space. Caritas moved toward the cell doors and rested his hands between the bars.

"Corriente 549!" The guard shouted the last three numbers of his inmate registration number.

Caritas took a step back from the doors and waited for them to open. The thick steel doors made the distinct sound of incarceration.

Two guards stepped in. While one stood watch, the other attached leg shackles with twenty-four inches of chain between his feet.

"Hands in your waist!" the guard standing watch shouted.

The movement had become routine after five years. Both hands stuffed into the front waistband of his bright orange jail suit. He shuffled out the door and followed his escort to the elevators. Along the way, occupants of the other cells shouted curses at the guards and at him for no other reason than to have something to do. The elevator made it down to the basement, and they entered the tunnel connecting the jail to the Federal Building. Along the way, the guards remained silent. They turned a corner and arrived at the entry to the US Marshal holding cells. In "holding," all inmates awaiting transport up to courtrooms were placed together in a large open cell.

The doors opened, and Caritas was prodded to enter the cell. He learned over the past five years that whoever he was on the outside meant nothing inside the jails. He learned to show respect, keep his mouth shut, and above all, show no fear of other inmates. As he entered, Caritas noticed that something was different this time. While normally he could count on ninety percent of the inmates in holding to be harmless deported aliens and drug couriers, he noticed immediately that there were twenty or so *soldados.* "Soldiers" were street gang members in the service of various narcotics cartels. Over the years, Mexican cartels relied upon Latino street gangs in American cities to provide protection for drug loads, extortion of street-level dealers and, most notably, to carry out assassinations.

No! No! No! This was no coincidence these men were all here. He scanned the room and made eye contact with a man, not much older than eighteen, across the room. A large SD in the form of the San Diego Padres logo was tattooed across his right cheek. It did not take an expert to see that he was not a season-ticket holder. The partially blocked tattoo across his neck was visible enough to make out the word LOGAN. He knew from past dealings his uncle utilized Logan gang members for a variety of illicit duties. He also knew they were for sale to the highest bidder. In addition, if any of the *cholos* were heading to prison for a decade or more, their allegiance to any employers on the street ceased to have any meaning to them. The prison gangs ran a completely different show.

Fuck! He moved quickly to the far right of the cell and found a seat next to some poor sap from Michoacan facing charges for illegal reentry. The Logan boys had no beef with the *Mexicanito* who walks hundreds of miles so that he can dig ditches for ten dollars an hour. They did have a beef with someone like him. Still, this was no coincidence. His attorney and the government had undertaken great effort to make sure something like this would not happen. Someone leaked his transport and court dates. Someone manipulated his placement in a cell with twenty gang members. He knew the system by now. There were never this many street gang members together in a cell at one time. He glanced back up at the one with the tattoo across his face. He was now standing, speaking with two other tatted-up gangsters. Caritas watched as two other men now came out in front of tattoo face to shield him from view. He was able to see one of the men starting to reach behind himself. During his time in custody, Caritas had become acquainted with the various ways inmates conceal items, and they always involved storing them in their asses. "Hooping" involved secreting a prison-made shank deep into the anal cavity so that only a small loop, usually a string tied around the shank, was accessible. The unwritten rule was to insert the shank far enough in that the loop was at least one inch into the cavity. The person could then insert his finger into his anus and "hoop" the shank out.

That was happening now in the corner of the holding cell. The chances they were going to kill someone in the cell other than him were minimal. No, he was the target, and he was not going out of this world at the end of a shit-coated shank.

Caritas figured he had one chance. He could rush the gangster and make as much noise as possible. He would have to hold them off for at least thirty seconds before the guards could make it into the cell. No time to think it out, just go! At the instant before he flew off the bench, he promised himself that he would fire his fucking lawyer if he got out alive.

It was twenty feet across the cell and his legs were still shackled, but so were the gangsters'. He was moving as fast as he could, head bent down and screaming at the top of his lungs. He slammed into the group of now four inmates and flailed at them with his arms while continuing to scream. Caritas could feel blows raining down on his back. He caught a knee deep into his solar plexus that sent him to the ground. He could not breathe or talk but kept his arms out in front of him. A few more seconds.

In that instant, he saw it. The Padre fan was holding it. It was about five inches long and made of plastic. How it was constructed made no difference. He saw the shank come down at him. He tried to block it with his right hand but felt himself being held down by the others. The first stab did not cause much pain as it entered right below his left armpit. Another came down in the same area. He was still trying to scream, but nothing came out. He could sense that others in the cell were shouting, but he could not make out any words. Now the pain started to register as the shank pierced his lung. One of the men drove his knew hard on his right shoulder.

The last blow he felt was to the left side of his neck. The man drove the shank hard and twisted it before pulling it out and dropping it to the floor. Everyone moved away from him. Caritas was on his back staring at the ceiling. He could feel the warm pool of blood under the back of his neck. The last sound he heard in his time on earth was the squeaking of the guards' rubber-soled boots as they ran down the hall.

THIRTY-TWO

Gerardo was getting nervous. The international border crossing at Tecate was a few miles away, and it looked like they were heading that way. The lead car was a good quarter mile in front of him. The follow car was about five hundred feet out. Two cars separated him from the trailing vehicle. Gerardo could see the lead vehicle as it made its way through the winding curves in the road as it began to ascend the final set of hills before the border. Gerardo was still on the line with Drew and Chino. He pulled up the microphone piece on the cord from the phone.

"*Estoy preocupado,*" he said before remembering Drew could not speak Spanish.

"I'm worried," he shouted into the microphone, "that these *vatos* are heading into Mexico."

Drew knew this would not be good for them. Drew passed the casino on his right.

"I'm still about twenty minutes behind you. Chino what's your position?'

"I'm about five minutes behind Gerardo."

Just then, Gerardo could see the brake lights on the lead vehicle. The vehicle was beginning to make a right turn.

"They're getting off!" Gerardo shouted over the whine of the engine.

"Just note the name of the street, you keep going past and circle back later. Chino can pick up the tail," Drew said.

Gerardo watched the trail car turn onto the same side road that led to a few ranch-style properties scattered between two large hills. The road looked to be the only way in and out of the small valley. As he neared the turnoff, Gerardo could see both vehicles slowing near a single-level home surrounded by a low metal fence. The home was at the base of a hill parallel to the highway. Gerardo came within view of the road. A large real estate sign advertising the sale of 170 acres of land with water partially blocked the name of the road as he got closer. As he passed the sign, he could only glimpse the street name.

"Dulzura Rancho Road!" he shouted into the microphone.

"Copy that," Chino responded.

"I'm on my way," Drew said.

Drew passed a slow RV and felt his heart beginning to race. Calm down, he told himself. Drew started to engage his combat mode. There was no margin for failure. They had Katie. He made a mistake by involving her in trying to remedy the situation—unfuck the FUBAR, Chino used to say.

But their decision to grab her was a monumental mistake.

* * *

Chino could see the right turn off the highway. He pulled off to the right and parked the car. He reached down under the seat to retrieve a pair of high-powered binoculars. This would not be like the last time. They were prepared. Chino wore slate gray military-style cargo pants, steel-toe tactical boots, and a black stretch workout shirt. He still had Drew on the speaker phone as he focused the binoculars on the road ahead of him.

"They're definitely reaching home base," he said watching both vehicles slowing near a single-story house. "Looks like the home is secured by an iron fence, three, maybe four feet high. The rear of the house faces west with foothills rising a couple hundred feet."

Chino trained the binoculars on the rugged hills. Thick, dark brush was interspersed with ochre boulders.

"You know, boss," Chino said while still surveying the scene, "these hills are perfect for you. Elevation, natural cover, and the proximity of the other hills will dampen the sound of any round being fired."

Drew was silent as he took in the description. He could feel his senses tingling.

Chino saw the vehicles they had been following stop beside two other vehicles. One gray SUV and a tan American-make sedan. Two men got out of each of the vehicles that had just arrived. The two men exiting the truck matched the descriptions of the men in the restaurant Sonya relayed to him. The other two were completely different. White males, mid-forties, one was wearing a khaki jacket, the other in a red windbreaker. This stood out to Chino not only because the weather was a stifling ninety degrees, but the jackets appeared to be a lame attempt to look civilian. The haircuts. You can't hide it no matter what you do. After so many years, it becomes part of your DNA. They were definitely ex-military, maybe even law enforcement. Two *ranchero narco* types and two straight-laced gringo military. This did not look right. Then again, he thought, he had seen this five years ago.

"Looks like two plus two," Chino said to Drew.

"Same ones from the restaurant plus two more?"

"Affirmative. But it looks like the follow car had two ex-military or law enforcement."

"So we have four, two with possible military training. We don't know how many are inside and we don't know if they have Katie or Jimmy Connors inside."

"You know these guys took the long route to get out here," Chino said. "They were making sure they weren't being tailed, but the quickest route out here would have been the back way out of Chula using Otay Lakes Road. That would cut a good twenty-five minutes off the trip."

"Plenty of time to get Katie here," Drew said.

"My guess is they have both of them there."

Chino could see Gerardo coming back down the road toward him. Chino flashed his high beams for a second. Gerardo passed Chino and made a short U-turn behind him. He pulled off to the far side of the shoulder and got into the car with Chino. Drew was still on the phone and merged Chance and Ramirez onto the call.

"All right," Drew said, "I'm coming up on the Dulzura General Store. That's the rally point. It's a little before seven, we've got to wait it out until after sunset. Everyone meet me there."

* * *

The Dulzura General Store was a log-cabin-style building with a plain lettered sign in black letters on a white background. A shade structure

142

jutted out in front and covered enough space for two picnic tables. A large, open fire cooking grill was set off to the side. A sign for carne asada and adobada tacos was prominently displayed in the window. Two road cyclists were sitting at one table eating tacos and drinking from Aquafina bottles. Their bikes looked to be very light and expensive. Drew knew absolutely nothing about road cycling but concluded that these two were borderline stupid for riding on these winding and narrow-shoulder roads. As if to reinforce the notion, Drew caught a glimpse of a makeshift shrine across the street, a routine sight in Southern California. A Mexican votive candle, a small photograph of some poor sap who died at that spot in a horrific automobile accident, a vase with wilting flowers and a short, white, wooden crucifix.

Death was never very far away out here.

Drew walked into the store, a general-purpose market with all the basics. A cooler in the back was stocked with soft drinks and beer. The place had once served up drinks, as evidenced by the long bartop off to the side now stacked high with canned goods. He went to grab a liter of water and made it back to the cash register. The sign at the register advertised the simple beef and pork tacos. The description underneath read: "Mesquite grilled, no fish, no chicken, no quesadillas, no Bullshit!" Drew was under too much stress to be hungry, but he had no idea how long the next course of action might take. It might be better to load up on protein to fuel him through the next several hours. He ordered three tacos and waited at the counter for them to come off the grill out back.

The clerk made little small talk with him and returned a minute later with the plate of still steaming tacos. The salsa cruda was dolloped thick over the marinated beef, and Drew's stomach growled instinctively at the sight. He thanked the clerk and headed out to an empty picnic table set out in front of the store. Biting into the taco, he couldn't help but appreciate the quality of the meat. Succulent and spicy, wrapped in handmade tortillas. If they made it out of this alive, he thought, he was coming back to ask them about their asada marinade.

If they made it out alive.

143

He plowed through the tacos in minutes and went through a mental checklist of the gear in the trunk of the car. He had the rifle from Ramirez's locker. One Glock nine-millimeter with a box of ammunition. One roll of silver duct tape. Seems to always come in handy. One penlight. One torch lighter. As always, he carried his folding tactical knife. He also had the large hunting knife, which might be too large to crawl around with in the backcountry. He knew that Chino and Chance were carrying handguns. They grabbed the Glocks and a box of rounds. Gerardo picked out a .380 Sig Sauer. He told Ramirez it was his service weapon while he was with the Mexican federal police.

This time around they were armed and uninjured. What they were missing was the element of surprise. There was also a different mindset when hostages were involved. Precautions were taken. The guys in the house would be expecting some sort of rescue operation and be prepared for it. The presence of the military or law enforcement gunmen was a wildcard. It was clear to him and Gerardo these were American gunmen. Their general appearance led to the conclusion they were trained. This would require all of them to act quickly and efficiently.

In the back of his mind, Drew had to contend with the unknown physical condition of Katie and Jimmy Connors. He knew if Katie had the chance, she would try something. She knew enough about Drew to know he would be more lethal in the dark. He hoped she would wait until they started the assault. Then again, he didn't know whether she was in any condition to fight back. In his years in combat, Drew had come to the defense of fellow warriors who were bound by service and honor, and who had signed up for the very real possibility of death. Katie was a mother of two and never envisioned herself kidnapped and held captive. This fact weighed heavily on Drew, and he took time to try to separate himself from the emotion and bring himself back to combat mode.

I am the weapon. I am the dark. I am the silence. I am death, he repeated to himself.

THIRTY-THREE

A prison murder rarely makes the news. Unless the victim is famous, there is generally no interest in a low-life criminal who got what he deserved. A murder in the federal courthouse was something completely different. The courthouse went into immediate lockdown. US marshals ran through the halls to emergency positions around all exits. Spectators, lawyers, and staff were not allowed to exit. In the age of instant information, texts and Facebook alerts went out immediately from hundreds of people. With US marshal and federal police vehicles surrounding the courthouse, the media presence swelled within minutes. News reporters with longstanding relationships with court personnel and lawyers quickly started processing available information.

The first news stories circulated reports of a high-level Mexican cartel leader being assaulted during his transportation to the federal courthouse. Within an hour, cable news reported that Vicente Corriente-Torres, aka Caritas, American-born leader of a notorious drug and human-trafficking organization, had been killed while awaiting a court appearance. The news piece rehashed the incident from five years ago, which detailed his arrest and the death of two Border Patrol officers during a bloody shootout related to the transportation of children in a sex-trafficking operation. The reports also stated that Corriente-Torres was the nephew and last remaining family member of Arturo Corriente-Torres, aka El Cicatriz, alleged leader of a Sinaloa narcotics cartel.

Ramirez caught the news alert on his cell phone. As part of his job at the border, Ramirez needed to be aware of any activity that might impact his job duties. He had most of the major news sites bookmarked and set to alert on his phone. He also had Univision and both Tijuana news stations linked to his messages.

Ramirez was in the passenger seat with Chance. He read through the news alert.

"Fuck!" Ramirez said at a near shout and then went silent pondering the significance of the news.

"What's up?" Chance asked.

"Somebody just punched Caritas's ticket."

Chance pulled his foot off the accelerator, and the car coasted for a hundred feet before he started to accelerate again.

"How could that happen?

"Any number of ways. The news is saying that he was killed in the federal courthouse while being transported to his court appearance. No information regarding who or how it was done."

"This kind of stuff happen very often?" Chance asked.

"Not in the downtown federal fucking courthouse with prisoners in leg chains with US marshals watching their every move. Not to mention the fact they would make sure that someone high power like Caritas, who is either a prime street cred target or a snitch, would not be left in a cell with anyone capable of producing a shank or killing someone with their bare hands."

"So how does something like this happen?"

"Somebody leaked the transportation information or," Ramirez paused to consider his thought. "Someone arranged for Caritas to be placed in the same cell as the killers."

"How could they do that?"

"It's not so much how," Ramirez was beginning to see the significance, "with the access to the transportation schedule and courthouse criminal calendar someone could figure out how to place potential killers near Caritas. It's more of a question of who. Someone would need to know that Caritas would be transported to the courthouse for a hearing and then make sure to schedule the potential killers for a court date on the same day. This would require someone with some juice to influence lawyers and maybe even court staff. They would then need to be able to contact the killers and arrange the murder."

"Sounds like a lot of work," Chance said.

"Not a lot if you have something that needs to be put to rest."

They were both silent for a few moments as Chance continued down the road.

"Sounds like—" Chance said

"Sounds like someone is trying to clean up loose ends."

THIRTY-FOUR

Drew waited at the Dulzura General Store for ten minutes before Chino arrived. He sat at a picnic table in front of the store and had a six-pack of Pacificos sitting on the table. He finished his tacos and tossed the paper plate into the wastebasket. Drew was spinning the open beer bottle between the palms of his hands when Chino came over and sat down.

"A beer, boss?" he asked.

"Given the situation," Drew took a deep draw from the beer and swallowed. "I don't think one watered-down Mexican beer is going to make much of a difference."

Chino reached across and grabbed one of the beers from the six-pack. Drew pushed his church key opener over to him with the back of his fist.

"True that, man," Chino said as he drank from the bottle.

Chance and Ramirez arrived a few minutes later and Gerardo a minute after that. Ramirez related the information regarding the murder of Caritas and the degree of sophistication necessary for it to be carried out.

"Well," Drew leaned back and strummed his fingers across the tabletop, "the way I see it, whoever ordered the murder are the same people who want the information from us."

"What information?" Chance asked.

"I emptied the bag with the money. In one of the interior pockets was a thumb drive."

"Did you open it?"

"No, I didn't have time to fuck around, so I grabbed an iPad and threw it in the truck. We can try to open it later. Either way, these fuckers aren't going to get it, so we'll have time."

"It doesn't take a rocket scientist to figure out that the thumb drive has the names of the customers." Ramirez paused to think about it. "The people buying these kids."

"These *putos* have got to be some pretty important people," Gerardo said.

"Important enough to orchestrate the murder of the nephew of a cartel kingpin," Ramirez added.

"Whoever these fuckers are doesn't matter right now," Drew interjected. "We need to get my wife and Chance's uncle."

"Well, it actually does make a difference," Ramirez said.

"How so?"

"Look, we know that dirty law enforcement was involved in the transport of these children. Now we know someone with enough juice to be able to orchestrate the first murder of an inmate in the federal courthouse in San Diego is willing to go to war with the cartel if they are exposed. You can guarantee the men in that house are military trained, probably live combat experience."

"So are we," Drew said.

"That may be," Gerardo said, "but we need to take into account they are most likely expecting some sort of rescue attempt, which means they will be on the lookout."

"And most likely trained to do so," Chino said.

Ramirez said, "The surprise you cowboys pulled off last time is not to going to happen."

"Since they whacked the last living family member of a cartel boss, from the most badass narco state in Mexico, I guess we can assume this has nothing to do with Cicatriz or his group," Chance said as he nervously scratched at the scar across his cheek.

"We need to make sure we execute a plan," Drew said.

Gerardo slid his phone across the table to Drew. "I took photos of the road and the houses around the hill"

Chino got up and to look over Drew's shoulder at the photos.

"That's the house," he said pointing at the ranch home nestled next to a steep hill. "The cars stopped out in front of this one."

"Nice," Drew said looking at the steep hill to the west of the home. "You were right, Chino. High ground with plenty of cover. I can post up and have a direct line of sight to three sides. The front will have to covered by someone else."

Chino pointed to the hill in the photo. "My guess is they will have someone up there already."

"I know that I would put someone up there," Drew said.

"Most likely with the right equipment," Chino added.

"Right, we can expect someone up there with at least a night vision scope."

"I take it that is not a good thing for us," Gerardo said, a question in his voice.

"A trained shooter from an elevated and concealed position is never a good thing." Drew looked around the table. "Anyone have a pen and paper?"

"Hold on. I'll go check inside." Ramirez left the table and walked into the store. He came back with a pen and an empty brown paper bag, which he slid over to Drew.

Drew took the phone with the photos of the road and houses against the hill. He began to sketch an outline of the area.

"The play has to be this." Drew placed an X where the house was located. "The rear of the house is oriented west. The top of the adjacent hill has a clear view." He thought for a second, "And a clear shot at anyone coming from the rear."

He tapped the point of the pen in the area west of the house.

"We need a rabbit," Drew said.

"What the fuck is a rabbit?" Chance asked.

"A *conejo, mi amigo*, is someone to draw their attention," Gerardo said with a smile.

"He's right," Drew said. "I can come in from the extreme west but need to see some sort of movement from this guy in order to get to him. A rabbit can come down the road, and any shooter will follow the rabbit with his scope. If I have a clear view, I may be able to catch a glimpse of movement."

"We have spent hours," Chino thought about it for a second, "shit, even days waiting to spy some sort of movement in the scrub on some shit-colored mountain in Afghanistan. If anyone can spot them, Drew can."

"I will be the rabbit," Gerardo said.

"We should think about this for a . . ." Ramirez started to say.

"No. No. I already have the motorcycle." Gerardo motioned to the sizable lump under the tarp in the bed of the truck. "And dark clothing. I can drive down the road and pass the house." He traced a route with his finger. "I can then turn back around and pass the house again and try to draw at least one of the vehicles out to follow me."

"You would be on your own if they took the chase," Drew said.

"I have spent the last five years training on the *pinche* road rocket," Gerardo said with a grin. "Believe me. They will not catch me."

"Then that's the plan." Drew continued to draw on the bag. "Gerardo is the runner. Ramirez and Chance come in from the north side of the road. You guys are coming in low and slow. Chino comes in from the east. I will make my way to the base of the hill and wait for Gerardo to make his move. Once I locate the shooter, I will take him out and signal."

"What's the signal?" Chance asked.

Drew thought about it for a second.

"I will give two quick flashes from my cellphone flashlight." Drew simulated the flash by running his open hand across the face of the phone.

"Not one flash. Only two flashes. Copy?"

Everyone nodded in agreement.

"What if something happens to you?" Ramirez asked.

"You'll know because of the gunfire before any signal from me."

"And if that happens?" Chance asked.

"If that happens, Gordo," Gerardo said as he motioned toward the scene diagram on the table. "You need to come at the house with guns blazing."

"Like he said, Chance, we need to move like lightning." Drew adjusted the drawing toward him. "Look, this isn't like the last time. We are not out in the middle of nowhere. Although this is relatively rural, there are still houses nearby and a road with cars regularly passing by."

"Not to mention border checkpoints within a few miles," Ramirez added.

"Right. The point is that they can't afford to be in a prolonged shootout. It would attract too much attention. They are either going to bolt with the hostages or . . ." Drew paused considering the alternative.

"Or without them," Chino finished.

"And they won't leave any witness," Drew said.

The group was silent for a few seconds. The cars from the road continued to fly by stirring up dust in the parking lot.

"Well, boss," Chino stood up. "That's not happening on my watch."

Gerardo laughed.

"And don't forget," he said. "Gordo has some unfinished business with these *pendejos.*"

"Copy that shit." Chance smiled.

THIRTY-FIVE

Winters received the news about the killing of Caritas while he was in a task force meeting relating to drug interdiction along the border. The killing had been meticulously planned and took months to execute. The most difficult part was determining the transport dates for Caritas. As regional director, Winters had access to the ROIs of the debriefing, snitch sessions between Caritas and the government. Divulging the names of the end customers was intolerable. Winters knew that although no specific threats had been made, his life was in jeopardy if things did not come to a quick resolution. The murder of Corriente-Torres was only the start. He still needed to eliminate his points of contact with the planners of the attack and distance himself from the operation.

Sitting in the sterile, gray conference room, Winters did his best to seem engaged in target apprehension numbers of narcotics smugglers. He listened to the drone of department supervisors as they made incessant pitches about the need for additional funds and manpower. The reality was the war on drugs at the border had become an economic machine that was enriching private entities and justifying the existence of a bloated and ineffective government law enforcement apparatus. Early in his career as a supervisor, Winters's boss told him they were like therapists. There was no financial incentive to cure a patient. There was every financial incentive to tell their patient they were still fucked up but getting better. See you next week.

Winters was now caught in a minefield of his own making. Every step he made to cover up the disaster from five years ago led to a new set of problems. He tried to compartmentalize his problems and deal with them one at a time, but he couldn't shake the feeling it was all crashing down. There was no denying he had a huge problem. He had taken civilians as hostages. They were civilians with lives and contacts that could not be brushed aside. As sure as Winters was that they could not be left as witnesses, he was equally sure there would be inquiries as to their deaths or disappearances.

Winters tallied those who would become casualties. One decorated Marine hero and his wife, an attractive mother of two young boys and daughter of an influential businessman. Another decorated Marine and owner of a successful business. A civilian business partner of the two Marines and his former Navy uncle. A hero Border Patrol supervisor. A high-value witness purportedly protected by the federal government. The thought of the planning he would need to do to keep himself alive made his stomach seize. He caught the salty taste of vomit in the back of his throat but suppressed the urge to spit.

All of this, he thought, and a very irate Sinaloa cartel leader who would be making inquiries into the murder of his only nephew. But he was a survivor. He had lied and manipulated to get to his position of power, but he had an even loftier goal—the United States Congress. He had no other reason to involve himself with that dickhead Harrison. The dirty work he was doing for Harrison and his deviant friends would eventually pay off. He was not about to let a bunch of civilians get in the way of his rise to glory.

Winters continued to feign interest in the meeting. The room was divided between true-blue law enforcement veterans and bureaucratic appointees desperate to maintain their positions despite any real-world experience. The thought of decades in rooms like this with blowhards discussing the newest, most efficient way to plug a finger in the dike holding back the ocean of drugs heading to the United States was unbearable. This was it, he thought. Once he cleaned up this mess, Harrison would owe him more than just a little influence. Harrison would owe him for the rest of his life.

A smile started to stretch across his face when he felt the buzz of his personal cellphone in his inside blazer pocket. He pulled the phone out and quickly checked the message.

All parties accounted for and awaiting final action.

Winters closed the screen. He was close now. He could feel it. Years of planning were coming to fruition. He slipped the phone back into his blazer pocket and let the smile wash back over him.

THIRTY-SIX

The late August orange sun was making its descent as Drew and the men made final preparations. Chino made a run through the store to find supplies that might be useful. He returned with two bottles of wine, a lighter, one set of four steak knives, a serrated bread knife, one roll of nylon cord and a roll of silver duct tape.

"Wine?" Chance asked.

"It's not the wine," Drew said. "The cork. Toss the wine and use the end of the cork as lampblack."

"Huh?"

"You never played high school football?" Chino asked.

Chance shook his head.

"You light the end of the cork, and the burnt end can be used to black your face," Chino said.

Chance got the picture.

"Just diagonal lines to break up the face," Drew added.

"The steak knives I get," Ramirez said, "but what's up with the bread knife?

"I figured all of us ex-military have had training in hand-to-hand with knives, but Chance has not," Chino answered.

"Oh, so I get to slice up a loaf of bread?" Chance laughed.

"No, Gordo," Gerardo said as he reached over and held the knife in his hand. "This is the most effective weapon to inflict maximum damage. Every contact you make with the blade edge of this thing will open up huge wounds. Catch someone across the neck," he made a quick slash motion, "and you will open him up like a . . ."

Gerardo could not find the word.

"Like a," he looked over to Ramirez, "*cómo se dice esos dulces*, the ones with the handle?"

"A Pez dispenser," Drew answered.

156

Chance got the idea.

"The duct tape?" he asked.

"It's fucking duct tape, and you never know when you are going to need fucking duct tape," Drew said.

"It's the Mexican way," Gerardo said.

"That's right, *amigo.*"

He laid out the hand-drawn sketch of the scene again on the table. He traced the positions from which they were to begin the assault. He studied the sketch and thumbed through the photos from the cellphone again.

"Okay," he said looking up at the rest of the men. "Remember, wait for my signal from the hill. I need to take that shooter out, or we don't stand a chance. If you hear any gunfire then something has gone to shit, so start moving toward the house."

Chance spun the sketch toward him.

"Where is the Alamo this time?" he asked.

"No Alamo here," Drew said. "This time *we are* the Mexican army."

"*Órale!*" Gerardo said. "It's about *pinche* time we embrace some winners."

Everyone joined in a nervous laugh. Drew turned to look over his shoulder at the glow now burnishing the hills in crimson. Night was coming. The darkness was coming. Death was coming.

"We good to go?" he asked.

"Let's end this shit," Chino said.

They were silent for a second or two until Drew stood up. He looked at all them and gave a silent nod. It was time.

THIRTY-SEVEN

Katie looked out the window through the heavy security grate. She could see the last rays of the setting sun skimming the top of the hills in the distance. It would soon be dark. Drew would have to be planning something. She tried to think it through. He would wait at least thirty minutes after the last light of the sun died away. Once it was dark enough, he would move into position. She figured someone, probably Drew, would get up to the high ground with a rifle while the others came in from the street. From the voices she could hear, it appeared there were at least seven men inside the house. Jimmy told her at least three different men had come into the room to either feed him or, as he put it, break his fucking ear off. That much she knew. What she did not know was how many men were posted up outside. She also did not know the layout of the house she was in or where it was in relation to a main road. If she started to run, Katie wanted to at least be heading in the right direction.

Katie turned back to Jimmy.

"Listen," she said in a low voice. "We can't do anything until it gets dark."

"How do you know your husband and friends are out there?"

"Because I know him. I know how he thinks. I know how he would handle this."

"Then what's our plan?" Jimmy knew the answer.

"When we start to fight, we fight. We fight like caged animals. We bite, we kick, we bash our way toward the door. As much as a commotion that we can cause will be able to divert some attention from the boys moving in from the outside."

"All this is based on you believing they were able to follow these greasers to this house and have not been killed off themselves."

"They wouldn't be holding us if they had killed Drew and the rest."

"I guess these assholes do need something from them."

"Whatever happens," Katie said as she looked out the window again, "we need to buy another twenty minutes or so before making a move."

The door opened, and two men appeared. One was Latino, heavyset with a goatee. The other was Anglo. Katie had been around the military for most of her adult life and had no trouble identifying him as ex-military. Sandy blond hair cut short on the sides and near crew at the top. Khaki slacks with a black, short-sleeve polo. He went directly to Jimmy and pulled him by the collar of his shirt. Jimmy started to swear, but the man cuffed him hard with the back of his hand.

Katie kept her mouth shut despite her urge to curse them out at the top of her lungs. She nervously looked out the window, gauging the darkness. *Hold on Jimmy.*

The military man pulled Jimmy across the floor and out of the room. The other one stood at the door and looked around the room as if to make sure they had not been trying to escape. He gave one last look at Katie and shut the door.

Shit, Katie thought. This is it. We still need some time.

She pulled the tape back from her wrists. Fuck it. This was close enough to dark, so when someone came back in, she was going to rush him. Katie repositioned the pen in her hand. The point was facing out of the backside of her right palm. She tied the pen secure again by looping the leather boot lace around the pen and between her fingers. She took a few practice strikes. Just like the dojo, she thought. She moved around the room practicing the footwork she had learned. Constant motion, never stand square or flat-footed. Keep the strikes short and quick. She had been trained to use the hammer strikes from close-in positions, which meant she would have to move quickly and forward. She was not combat efficient from a distance and, therefore, knew she would have to inflict maximum damage within seconds to overcome her captor.

Katie knew the moves, but it's one thing to do them on a cushy training mat in a strip mall in El Cajon and another thing to do them in real life with men who have been hired to hurt you. Adrenaline was doing its work, and she felt herself starting to hyperventilate. *Calm yourself down.* Katie took in a deep breath and closed her eyes. Focus on the task.

Katie moved to the center of the room about four feet from the door and sat down, cross-legged on the floor. She continued to take in deep breaths and slowly release them while she tried to clear her mind. Her plan was clear: Move quickly, hard, surprise these fuckers, and get outside.

* * *

Jimmy Connors was still reeling from the backhand he received from the ex-military fuck who dragged him into what looked like a living room. An overstuffed, faux leather black couch was pushed up against a bare wall. Two chairs propped up against the other bare wall. In the middle of the room was a chair, standing alone, in front of a camera tripod with a phone attached to the top.

Shit! He knew what was going to happen. They were going to film him getting fucked up by these guys to put the pressure on the others to deliver whatever it was they wanted. All these years of being an asshole and looking for trouble had come back to smack him across the face. As they pulled him onto the chair, Jimmy looked around the room. He could count six, maybe seven, men walking around the room. None of them were talking. Two stood next to him by the chair as they started to wrap duct tape around his arms and chest.

"Fuck you wetbacks. Don't you guys own any rope?" He had to let it out even though one of the men wrapping him up was as gringo as he was.

The Mexican with the goatee gave him a smirk and delivered a closed-fist punch to the side of the head. His head bounced back like a punching dummy. As his vision came back into focus, he could sense the dull throbbing of nearly every nerve ending on the side of his face. He felt like throwing up.

He hoped that Katie was right. Twenty minutes. Maybe he could hold on for that long, but who was he kidding. He wasn't some twenty-year-old sailor. He was an alcoholic, out of shape fifty-seven-year-old with half an ear. Well, he thought, this might be the last time he got to act like a man.

Fuck them. Jimmy Connors, like the goddamned tennis player, wasn't going down without a fight.

THIRTY-EIGHT

Drew parked his vehicle about three hundred yards from the turnoff to the house where they believed Katie and Jimmy were being held. He checked himself for mission readiness. He pulled his dark blue Chargers cap on and spread his supplies on the passenger seat. His six-inch folding tactical knife was in a brown leather case with a snap cover. He ran the leather holder through his belt loop and secured the knife. He grabbed a dark blue backpack from the back seat. He placed the nine-millimeter Glock and one extra clip inside and dropped the roll of duct tape and nylon cord into the pack. Pulling out the penlight from the glove compartment, Dre turned it on and off to make sure it was working and put it in his back pocket. He pulled the zipper down on the rifle bag to inspect the weapon he had taken from Ramirez's safe. He ran his hand across the barrel and stock. It was a thing of beauty. A bolt-action repeater with a high-powered scope and twenty-four-inch barrel. Drew knew he should hope he did not have to use it, but his training and lizard brain reaction almost had him salivating. He checked the ammo and zipped up the bag.

Drew studied the photos Gerardo had snapped of the area on the fly. As the skies began to darken, Drew tried to associate orientation points from the photos to the actual terrain and remember them. In the photos, Drew could see the hill adjacent to the house rose a gentle two hundred feet or so. He could also see it was densely covered in low brush, most likely mesquite and spiny manzanita, and scattered boulders. The boulders, some looking to be twenty or thirty feet high, increased in number toward the apex of the hill. That is where he would be as a sniper. Plenty of places to conceal a shooter. That is where he was headed. He also knew the shooter would have his scope scanning the house and the area around the perimeter. Drew would

162

come in from the back side of the hill, which added time. He would have to move fast.

Drew directed the others to get into position at the top of the hour. With the summer sun setting near 8:00 p.m., Drew needed enough darkness to move undetected. The darkness would mean the shooter would only be able to spot their movement if it fell within range of the night-vision scope Drew was sure the guy would have. He checked his cellphone to determine the position of the moon. Out in the backcountry, the lack of city lights meant the moon would be providing significant illumination once it reached its peak. He noted the moon was at about eighty-five percent full and would be rising at nine twenty-one p.m. out to the northeast. That meant it would rise directly in front of the hill overlooking the house. The others needed to be moving before the moon rose, or he had to take out the shooter before then.

Given the timing, Drew knew the others would hang back at the store for another twenty minutes to allow him to get into position. In the car, he finished his preparation. After dumping the wine, Drew lit the dry end of a cork and let it burn for a few seconds. Pulling the visor down to use the mirror, he drew thick zigzagging lines across this face. He was deliberate and detailed in drawing the lines, employing the same method he used in all combat missions. Each dark line brought unique memories of combat. Now complete, looking at himself in the mirror, Drew felt the familiar comfort and sheer terror of impending violence.

Fuck it, he thought, time to go get my wife.

He took in a deep breath of air, the scent of his own perspiration and charred cork filled his lungs. He closed his eyes and let the air slowly out. Clearing his mind to a dark, blank space, he spoke the words that had seen him through battle, danger, and death.

I am the Weapon. I am the Dark. I am the Silence. I am Death.

"Okay, motherfuckers, here comes the pain."

He got out of the car and looked over the open field he would have to cross before he got to the base of the hill. Three hundred to four hundred yards. He would have to move quickly. There was at least one barbed-wire fence he would need to get past, and he would have to hope that none of the fields adjoined properties with dogs. Loud barking or a fight with a dog in the brush would be fatal to the mission.

Nothing to do about it now.

Drew shouldered the rifle strap across his chest so that the rifle was stretched diagonally across his back. He cinched up the strap to make sure the rifle would not move. Drew stepped off the road and into the brush. He crouched and plotted his route across the field. The grass to his far right seemed to be about two feet high. It was a longer route, but he could use the grass as cover. He made his way to the grass and dropped to his stomach. Drew looked up at the hill. The slope of the face descending to the back of the house looked like a giant cat resting her head on the ground. He charted out a spot fifty yards or so out and prepared to move.

He closed his eyes momentarily, cleared his mind, got up into a crouch, and broke into a low sprint.

THIRTY-NINE

Ramirez, Chino, and Chance drove together down the highway to a turnout about a quarter mile past the road to the house. Gerardo trailed behind them on his motorcycle. As they passed the road to the target, Chino noted the position of the trees. The access road was not divided by any lines and undulated over the uneven terrain for about a half of mile before it turned into the hill. Tall California oak trees lined both sides of the road with thick, twisted trunks, and hanging, leafy branches.

The turnout was on the westbound side and below the main part of the road. Traffic was light in the area. They gathered at the trunk of the car. Ramirez popped the trunk, and each man reached for the weapon he previously selected. Chino, Chance, and Ramirez picked up Glocks. Gerardo reached in for the Sig Sauer.

"Ammo check," Ramirez said.

They examined the clips, and each grabbed an extra.

"I know this might not be the best time to bring this up," Ramirez said. "But these weapons are legally owned and registered to me. So, it would be very cool if none of you tossed these things in the field or—"

"Or got killed with one in our hands," Chino said.

"Well," Ramirez thought it through for a moment, "something like that."

"If one of us gets killed then the whole thing is FUBAR, and it really won't matter," Chino said.

"Let's just try not to get ourselves killed."

"We should be able to move pretty well hidden down the southern side of the road behind the trees." Chino pointed out the line of trees.

"All of us?" Chance asked. "Shouldn't we split up?"

"Isn't that the way everyone gets killed in the movies?" Ramirez said with a laugh.

"In a perfect world, Gordo, we would all be trained together in the same sniper unit. We would know the way each other moves." Chino looked back over the terrain from the passenger seat. "Given the current situation, we are probably better staying together to limit the possibility of discovery."

Chino looked around at the others. Gerardo was dressed in the same black jeans, gray T-shirt and dark leather jacket. Ramirez was in dark green military cargos and a dark green T-shirt. Chance was still in the khaki colored Dickies and dark, long-sleeved polo. The all had applied the black from burnt cork to their faces.

"I would have like to see you in darker pants, but it sure beats that dumb-ass Lakers gear you used to wear," he said to Chance.

Gerardo laughed. He moved over to Chance and darkened some of the lines on his face.

"Gordo becomes *el pinche tigre Bengali!*" he said as he stepped away.

"How do you feel, Chance?" Chino asked.

"Like a mean motherfucker."

"Because you are one badass motherfucker," Chino said as he slapped him across the shoulder.

"*Eres el más chingón!*" Gerardo added.

"If you boys are finished with your high school football pre-game, we have some serious shit to do," Ramirez said.

Chino looked at the others. Blackened faces, dressed in dark colors, holding handguns.

"Considering that we are all strapped and look like we are going to kidnap or murder someone," Chino said, "not to mention the Border Patrol station about three miles away, we had better get the fuck off this road and away from the car."

"You've got a point there," Ramirez said.

Chino looked at his watch. A Luminox Black Ops. He and Drew purchased them at the base store before shipping out on their last deployment. The black face with bright white numbers was easy to read and illuminated when necessary in the dark. He knew Drew was probably looking at his right now.

"We move in ten minutes," Chino said looking up at the darkened skies. The moon had not yet risen, and the cloudless sky revealed a vast expense of bright, twinkling stars.

Beautiful night, he thought. He hoped it would not be the last one he ever saw.

FORTY

Drew was running hard. In the silence, he could hear the dry grass swish across the lower part of his pants. He ran for a twenty-second count and then hit the ground. He took a five count. Lifting his head slowly, Drew scanned the hillside for any sign of movement or light. After another twenty-five-second count, Drew rose and bolted again through the field. He kept his strides short and fast and kept his sight on a point one hundred yards out.

Twenty-five seconds and back down into the grass. He was breathing hard now. Drew buried his face into his crooked arm and stayed motionless for a twenty count. He slowly lifted his head and brought his left hand under him to check his watch. He was able to use his body to block the illumination from the watch. Three minutes in. He had seventeen minutes to get up the hill, locate the shooter and neutralize him.

Neutralize, he thought. A holdover from his days as a Marine. A mission euphemism for kill the fucker.

Drew could see he was a still one hundred yards or so from the base of the hill. He also saw what looked like a low, barbed-wire fence about fifty yards out. The barbed wire didn't bother him as much as the thought there might be dogs protecting livestock. In Afghanistan, he had dispatched a few dangerous and some unfortunately curious dogs that endangered his mission. A quick grab of the muzzle and blade through the throat. He hoped he wouldn't have to take out someone's pet, but he would if he had to. Drew reached into the pocket of his cargos and pulled out his tactical knife. He opened the blade and got up in a crouch. He took a deep breath and bolted low and hard.

He ran as fast as he could in a direct line. Drew held the strap to the rifle hard against his chest to minimize the movement of the weapon but holding down an eight-pound piece of steel in a dead sprint was difficult. Drew flew through the field. In the dark, his senses were naturally heightened. He could hear a few cars on the road behind him, the cicadas in the trees off to his right and, then, the distant bark of a dog.

Fuck. A dog coming my way, he could sense it.

He was now within sight of the fence. It looked to be about four feet high. A fence meant to keep dumb-ass livestock in a particular area rather than for security. Still four feet is four feet. When was the last time he had to throw himself over a four-foot barrier at a full sprint?

The dog stopped barking, but he caught movement in his periphery. The dog was heading his way. A quick moving, silent dog meant a trained dog. Some type of German Shepherd or Malinois headed his way to tear off a chunk of his ass. He decided he wasn't going to stop for the fence. There was no time. Straight up and over was the only way to make it. Drew pushed his pace hard and streaked toward the fence. As he ran, he folded his knife back up and shoved it in his pocket. In the back of his mind, he tried to remind himself he wasn't twenty-five and in peak combat shape, but it really didn't matter out here on some crappy field in the backcountry with a dog coming to blow up his mission.

What was it that gunny used to say?

Acceleration will save your ass.

He was in a full sprint. The fence coming up fast. This was it. He gave himself a two-foot buffer from the fence and leaped up and forward. He reached his arms out like Superman to extend over the fence. Drew could feel the tip of his right boot make contact with something, but it didn't snag. He cleared the fence and landed with a muffled thump in the loose dirt. Drew rolled over his right shoulder and got up to run. He didn't think about anything but getting to the base of the hill. He didn't think about what certainly was going to be the throbbing pain in his shoulder. He didn't think to look back for the dog. He could hear a few intermittent barks. He didn't even think to look up at the hill. The most important thing was to make it to the hill. He ran. He ran faster and with more determination than he ever had in his life. He wasn't running to complete some mission or save his life. He was running to save Katie.

Be ready, you fuckers, because I'm coming for you.

I am the Weapon. I am the Dark. I am the Silence. I am Death.

FORTY-ONE

Chino led the group off the road and down to the turnoff. In the dark, the cover from the trees lining both sides of the turnoff was better than he expected. From their position, it looked like they had about three hundred yards to cover until they got close enough to post up near the house. The leafy trees provided some cover, and the thick, dark trunks would allow them to hide in between movements.

"Okay," Chino said in a low voice, "here's the way it's going to go. I'm going to need to call an audible. No rabbit here. The road is too isolated and will draw too much attention." He looked to see if they all understood.

"I head out first to a secure location. Look for my hand signal. When I wave you up, everyone come at once. Fluid and quick. Don't run."

"Copy that," Chance said as he craned his neck to get a better look at things.

"When you get to me everyone stays set for a full twenty seconds without movement. Clear on that?"

"Got it." Ramirez did not have to ask why since he knew silhouettes moving in the dark would be the only thing visible to the naked eye.

"Okay," Chino said. "It's time to get our people back."

Chino flew out of his crouch and kept a quick, steady gait. His eyes stayed on the house. He could see no movement outside it. He passed one tree and made it to another thick oak about forty yards from the others. Going down on one knee, he pulled out his binoculars. He looked up the hill for any sign of Drew but saw nothing but a dark hillside. Sweat trickled down his brow and ran off his nose. He wiped his face with the back of his hand.

Forty-yard sprint and I'm sweating like a pig. Fuck, I'm out of shape.

Now came the tricky part. He stood up and gave a wide wave of his arm from behind the trunk. The muffled impact of footfalls from the three men was noticeable but did not create an inordinate amount of noise. Chino kept an eye up the road for any sign of movement. Ramirez arrived first, followed by Chance and then Gerardo. Chance was breathing hard. All three went down and waited for instruction from Chino.

"Nice work, boys," he said. "So far so good. Everyone stay set for a solid twenty now. Gather your breath and wait for my sign."

At that, Chino was off again. He noticed the road to the house dipped and rose slightly ahead of him. The small rise would provide a good place to post up until they figured out their next move. It was further out than the fifty yards he had planned to run, but it provided decent cover, so he went for it. As he was running, he noticed some activity ahead of him. He was still about one hundred yards from the house. His heart was pounding and his lungs were screaming for air as he drove the last ten yards. He dropped to his stomach. He tried to control his breathing and bring his heart rate down. He waited a few more moments, his head down in the crook of his right arm.

Okay, he told himself. Let's pull it together.

He lifted his torso to survey the scene. The lights were on outside of the house as well as inside. He saw no movement outside of the house. He looked to the hill for Drew. Nothing. Chino rolled over on his back and sat up. He waved back to the others. He couldn't see them, so Chino got up to expose more of his arm. Just as he rose, he heard the unmistakable sound of a car door closing and engine turning over.

Shit, he thought. Someone is leaving the house. He got up to wave the others off but could now see the headlights starting to illuminate the road. Chino dove into the high brush to the side of one of the trees. He pulled out his Glock and readied himself for what might happen next.

The group kept the same order as they started toward Chino. Ramirez was moving more quickly than before because Chino put more distance between them. He had been moving for about thirty yards before he saw the headlights moving toward him down the road. He stopped dead in his tracks.

"Car coming our way," he said as he turned to the others to stop them.

"Everyone down!"

They all hit the high grass and flattened themselves.

Gerardo was watching the car move down the road toward them. He looked over at Ramirez.

"*Oye, Migra!*" He pulled his weapon out and had it in his right hand down in the dirt. "We can't let this car leave."

"We don't even know if it is connected to the house," Ramirez said.

"There are only two visible houses on this road, so it looks like pretty good odds that these are the *putos* trying to kill us."

"But what if . . ." Ramirez started to say.

"We don't have a choice. You and Gordo catch up to Chino."

Gerardo was up and running low back toward the end of the road where they started.

* * *

Chino was positioned out of the beam of the headlights. He looked back to where he believed the others were and held his breath as the car continued slowly down the road. It slowed midway, and the driver tapped his brakes for a second and then continued. In the distance, he saw the car reach the intersection to the highway. It stopped and wasn't moving.

* * *

Gerardo ran hard to the foot of the road. He had one chance—surprise the driver as he came to a stop. He hoped he could make the determination, in a split second, that the driver was one of the men holding the hostages. Whoever was in the car would be either a *ranchero narco*, like the ones from the restaurant, or ex-military *guero*. It wouldn't be that hard to figure out. The only thing that bothered him, other than being out on a backroad facing unknown gunmen and firepower, was he didn't know how many men might be in the car.

He ran low about twenty yards behind the car. Gerardo saw the car was an American-made sedan. Light colored, four doors. Not a usual narco vehicle. The car began to slow as it reached the highway. This was the only chance he would have. He swept up on the driver's side window with the Sig Sauer in his right hand. The driver did not see him until Gerardo knocked on the window with a knuckle on his left hand. The driver turned, and Gerardo was close enough to see the man's eyes widen. Not the surprise of an innocent civilian seeing a strange person at their window but of someone identifying a threat. In that instant, Gerardo could see he was one of the ex-military *gueros* they had seen earlier. Before the man could react, Gerardo crashed the butt of the Sig Sauer across the window. The glass shattered, and he quickly struck it a second time. His hand entered the vehicle, and he was able to strike the man across the nose with the barrel of the gun. The glass left in the window ripped into his forearm, but he couldn't feel any pain. His heart was racing as he pulled on the exterior handle to open the door. The man inside grabbed the gun and Gerardo's wrist with both hands and started to pull him into the vehicle through the window. Gerardo reached in with this free arm and rammed three fingers into one of the man's eyes. He drove the fingers hard and could feel tissue tearing. The man let out a quick scream but then tightened his grip on Gerardo's gun hand and began to twist.

Gerardo kept his fingers in the eye socket and drove the man's head back as he tried to pull the other hand and weapon free from the driver's grip. He had enough room to pull the gun back and swing it hard against the bridge of the man's nose. He heard the familiar sound of crushing bones as he brought the gun down hard again and again. The man's hands dropped and went limp. Gerardo struck him four more times in the same place with all the force he could muster. He pulled away from the window for a second. He was breathing hard. Looking back down the road toward the house, he could not see the others or any movement at the house. Gerardo knew he needed to act quickly. He opened the door and pushed the limp body of the man into the passenger seat and got in. As he was pushing the legs of the driver, Gerardo could see the ankle holster and gun hidden under his pants leg.

"*Puta madre!*" he said aloud to himself.

No gangsters use ankle holsters. The only people who use them are law enforcement. One more *pinche problema,* he thought.

He fired up the engine and entered the highway heading away from the border. He needed to move the car quickly from the scene and dispose of it. As he looked back toward the house, Gerardo tried not to think about the fact he was driving a car with a shattered, bloody driver-side window and a dead man with his face caved in.

FORTY-TWO

Drew was at the base of the hill that overlooked the house. His oblique position meant he could not see the slope facing the house. He would have to climb up from behind and then move downhill on any shooter. He checked his watch. Thirteen minutes had elapsed. He had seven minutes to get up the hill and locate the threat.

He looked up and saw a small game trail zigzagging up the side of the hill. Even in the dark, he could tell the slope was dense with manzanita and prickly sage scrub. He started up the narrow path. The night was clear, and without city lights, the stars dazzled in the sky. Drew kept his pace quick, but his footfalls were deliberate to avoid making noise. He tried to control his breathing as he pushed up the hill. He was about three-quarters of the way up when he saw an alternate route. A barely noticeable single track headed straight for the top. It looked to be about sixty yards but a steady climb.

Drew cinched up the strap to the rifle even more. He moved up the trail taking long strides and using his hands to touch the ground and maintain his balance. Thorny spines of low cacti and dried brush scraped his forearms. His boots caused loose rock and dirt to fall back down the trail. He knew this might draw the attention of the shooter, but he had no choice.

When Drew was about twenty yards from the top of the hill, he slowed his pace and carefully placed each step. When he spotted the large boulder that made up the bulk of the summit, he dropped to his stomach and crawled the last few yards. The boulder was much larger than it appeared from a distance. It was over twenty feet to the top. From behind the boulder, he could see a crevice it made with smaller rock beside it. Drew carefully made his way up the crevice. He dug his fingers into any crack he could find. Scaling along the back of the boulder, he carefully placing each foot and hand securely before moving. His heart was beating hard, and he restrained his intake of air. Drew reached the top and slid on his stomach over the boulder. Looking down he could see the entire valley below. The house was clearly visible. This was an optimal position for a shooter. He could see the road leading up to the house and the highway about a quarter mile away. He could not see Chino or any of the others, which was good because it meant they were well hidden. He lifted his head a few inches to look for the shooter.

Nothing. Damn it! Where the hell was he?

At that moment he heard the faintest rustling below him. It might have been a small animal, but the sound was more of a large mass moving against the dirt. He had been trained in distinguishing acoustic clues and knew the physical movement of men was fundamentally different than that of animals. Animals at night were foragers, hunters, or prey. The noise below him was a hunter.

Drew slowly dragged his body across the top of the boulder. He crept to the edge. Then he saw it. The slight movement of a rifle barrel. It was an unmistakable silhouette for him. He caught the exposed top three inches of the barrel. The rest was covered by netting and camouflaged by dry brush. Drew now knew the man was a trained military sniper just like him. Drew also knew the sniper's mission was to kill them. No loose ends.

Drew leaned back away from the edge and checked his watch. Two minutes left. He would have to move soon. He reached down to his pocket, retrieved his tactical knife and opened it to expose the six-inch blade. Drew kept the edge razor sharp and was confident in his ability to wield it lethally. He rolled to move the rifle bag forward across his body. Drew carefully unzipped the outer pocket of the bag and searched for something to secure the knife. His fingers made contact with the soft outline of a roll of what he could only guess was electrical tape.

Ramirez, he thought, you are one magnificent bastard.

Drew slowly pulled the tape off the roll. He grabbed the knife with his right hand, blade facing down from his palm. Drew wrapped the

177

tape slowly around the handle and his palm multiple times until it was secure. There was no chance he was going to lose the knife in a scuffle. Drew rolled back and repositioned the rifle behind him. He moved slowly back across the rock and lowered his head. He took in a deep, slow breath to clear his mind. He knew the task at hand. He knew the importance, and he knew the danger.

I am the Weapon. I am the Dark. I am the Silence. I am Death.

Drew rose to a crouch and then stood on top of the rock. Across the ridge in front of him, the bright orange glow of a rising moon began to shed light on the valley.

He jumped.

FORTY-THREE

Jimmy Connors was duct taped around his torso to a chair and watched the three men in front of him make preparations for what he could guessed was a slow torture session. He looked around at what would be a living room if a normal family lived here. To his left, he could see the entry to the kitchen. Directly in front of him, past the tripod, was the front door. Three men and twenty feet separated him from freedom. He refocused on the two men adjusting the tripod. The cellphone attached to the tripod meant they were most likely going to record his agony to send to his no-good nephew.

Jesus Christ, Chester! If I make it out of this, I am going to kick your ass.

Jimmy saw that one of the men, the larger Mexican, was one of those who kidnapped him a few days ago. He was also the fucker who cut off the top of his ear. He never said a word to Jimmy. The other two were new to the show. Two Americans. One looked like he could be working at Walmart. Nothing distinctive about him. Not tall, not short. Not dark, not pale. You could pass him a hundred times and never notice him. Only the haircut gave away his military past. The other man, however, was something else. He stood at least six four, maybe 250 pounds. He had his dark hair cut short and blunt across his forehead, with a dark mustache, razor cut straight at the corners. Everything about him screamed "I am a serial killer."

Fuck it all. These assholes are working with the greasers!

"What the fuck?" Jimmy yelled. "I could take being fucked up by these narco losers, but by my own fellow citizens?"

The men said nothing.

The big ugly—a bit of John Wayne Gacy to him, Jimmy thought—walked over and stood square in front of him. He looked down at Jimmy and smiled.

"Fuck you! You piece of . . ." Jimmy started to tell.

The man swung a hard, open-hand slap to Jimmy's already mangled ear. For a few seconds, Jimmy could see nothing but bright lights. A second blow came crushing down on his nose. He heard the crack of the bones in his nose and could taste the salty tang of the blood on his lips. As his vision began to refocus, he saw the man moving away from the table against the wall.

"Fuck you all, you motherfuckers!" he yelled as he spit up blood.

Jimmy began to panic. He knew they were capable of anything. They already took his ear, what was next? No. Fuck this, he thought. The time was now to make a move. He could see through the window in the kitchen that it was dark outside. If badass ninja girl was going to do something, it had to be before he lost another part of his body.

"You assholes are going to get what's coming to you now that it's DARK!" he hollered at the top of his lungs. He rattled in his chair as hard as he could to make noise, but he stopped cold when he saw the scary large man approaching him with a short paring knife.

"This fucker is going to peel off my skin!" Jimmy screamed.

* * *

Katie heard the screaming. She looked outside and saw it was dark enough for Drew to try to rescue her. Of course, she had no way of knowing whether he was out there. She had no way of knowing how many men were inside the house or outside. She had no way of knowing whether Drew was alive or dead. But in her heart, she knew Drew would do whatever it took to get her back. She stood up and positioned herself in the center of the room. Her right leg back ready to sprint. She rechecked the leather lacing around the pen in her palm.

She watched the door for any sort of movement and readied herself for what was to come. Remember your footwork, she told herself. Quick strikes, vulnerable places. The mantra from her instructor over the last five years was etched into her consciousness, and now it would be put to the test.

Fuck it. No more waiting. It's time to do something.

Katie ran at the front door and buried her shoulder into it. She felt the cheap, tract home door bend and crack a bit. She stepped back, her shoulder now throbbing, and started to kick hard at the door and scream.

The man had started to insert the point of the knife into Jimmy's chest just to the inside of his right armpit when he heard the noise. Jimmy was screaming as the man began dragging the blade across his chest. The noise from the room became louder, and it became clear the woman inside was loose now. The man pulled the blade back and walked over to the door. The woman inside kept banging on the door. He looked back at the other two and smiled.

Katie backed away from the door as she heard the key being inserted into the lock. She crouched low into a sprinter's stance. She was all in. Whoever came in through the door, whatever his size or strength, she was going to charge. Katie could count on a few connecting strikes with her palm stick based on sheer surprise, so she needed to make them count.

The door swung inward. Katie did not have time to register the man's size as she bolted at him. He had taken a full step into the room when Katie rammed her head into his chest. She drove him back to the right of the door. She felt a stab of pain in her upper back. The man pushed her off a foot or two and reached out with his right hand, which Katie could see held a knife. Without thinking, as she practiced in her training, she ducked below and moved to his left. She slapped the extended arm with her left hand across the man's body exposing his face. Katie drove an open palm directly up and into his nose. She heard a crack and felt the immediate warm rush of blood on her hand. She pulled her hand back and threw her right elbow into the man's throat. The blow stunned the man, and she could hear him gasp for air.

She brought the same hand back and drove the pen point hard into the side of his neck. She felt the pen pierce flesh. She pulled it back out and then drove the pen into the same spot five more times as fast as she could. The man was flailing at her but could not get a firm grip. Katie threw a quick tomahawk chop with the pen point into his eye. She could feel the blood pour out of the eye socket. She delivered four more blows to the same area, driving the pen point as deep as she could manage. The man dropped to the ground. Blood was pulsing out of the ragged hole in his throat, but he was holding his eye. Oddly, Katie was thinking at that moment, he was not screaming.

Katie knew she had to run for it.

* * *

Jimmy Connors heard the commotion in the room. He knew Katie had begun her desperate attack. He was not going to check out of this world duct taped to a chair with a flap of skin dangling from his chest and minus one ear. He rose up with the chair still attached to his body and ran toward the two men inside the room. The larger Mexican gave him a look of disbelief as Jimmy buried his head into his chest. Jimmy fell to the ground on top of the man with half of the chairback pressing against the man's chest. The other man ran over and started striking Jimmy in the face with his closed fist. Jimmy couldn't block the blows, but he kept driving the chair into the chest of the man under him. Two or three more blows came raining down when he heard movement from the room. Katie was out. He caught her moving out of the corner of her eye and saw her stop.

"Keep moving!" he yelled.

The man beating Jimmy spun around and saw Katie standing in the middle of the room. Blood was splattered over the front of her shirt, and her right hand was completely red. The tip of the pen was dripping blood.

She looked one more time at Jimmy and bolted for the door. The man flew after her.

FORTY-FOUR

Drew landed on top of the shooter. The weapon the man was holding fell down the side of the hill into the brush. Drew's knee crashed into the man's back, and he quickly shoved the knife blade into the guy's back. Drew was surprised at the man's size. He held his left forearm across the would-be shooter's back, and he could feel the solid strap of muscle. Drew was a solid six feet two and 210 pounds. He could tell this man outweighed him by fifty pounds. The shooter instinctively rolled on his side and grabbed Drew's knife hand at the wrist. He drove his open palm hard under Drew's chin. Drew used his left hand to punch the shooter in the throat. He hit him again and again in the throat until the man loosened his grip on the knife hand.

Drew drove the knife into the shooter's side trying to puncture a lung. The shooter threw an elbow into the bridge of Drew's nose. For a moment he was stunned but maintained his position on top of the man. Drew came across the side of the man's face with the blade and brought it back down hard into the top of his shoulder. The man jammed his elbow into Drew's neck and tossed him off into the dirt. Drew landed hard on the rifle still attached to his back.

The position of the gun on his back had him lying vulnerable with his chest exposed. The shooter threw himself onto Drew. He fought hard to keep the guy off his torso, but the man used his weight to gain a prone position over Drew. He crashed three thunderous hammer fists to Drew's face and then got both hands around Drew's throat. The power of his grip was paralyzing, and Drew could feel that the man was trying to crush his hyoid bone with his thumbs. Drew was well trained in the move and knew it was lethal.

Drew tried to push the man off his chest by bucking his torso, but he was too heavy. The shooter continued to drive his thumbs into Drew's throat. Drew pulled his right hand out from under his back and sent two quick strikes with the blade into the upper part of the shooter's back. He released his grip of Drew's neck and rolled off his chest. Drew immediately rose to his feet while the shooter did the same. Both men squared off with Drew moving the knife, still taped to his hand, in a figure eight in front of him.

Holy fuck! Five stab wounds and this asshole is still standing!

The man was enormous. He was at least six foot six, maybe taller. Drew could see the bleeding wounds from his knife strikes, but he was still standing and ready to attack. Drew felt small, but he was the only one holding a weapon. The beast moved toward Drew with both hands out in a martial arts pose. Drew couldn't tell what type of martial art, but the guy was not afraid of the knife. Drew moved laterally with the man waiting for an opening. As Drew stepped to the right, his foot caught the edge of a large rock embedded in the dirt. He stumbled for a second. The man seized the opportunity and delivered a roundhouse kick to the side of Drew's head. Drew staggered but kept on his feet. With amazing speed, the shooter came forward and threw two quick, powerful punches to Drew's chest. The force sent Drew crashing through the brush and backed him against the large boulder he had jumped off. The shooter closed on Drew.

This is it. I have to end it now.

Drew dropped his torso, rotated his hips, and delivered an open hand under the man's chin. The forceful blow stopped the man and knocked his head back hard, exposing his neck. Drew drove the knife blade in and across the man's neck in one fluid motion. The shooter backed up and stared at Drew. His hands were hanging loose to his side, and he seemed unsure of what to do next. The blood was spraying out of the neck gash, but he was still standing. With no time to waste, Drew threw his body into the shooter. They fell downhill and through brush. Drew scrambled on top of the man's stomach and drove the knife into his heart and slashed upward before pulling the blade out. Drew got up and stepped away. The large tree of a man lay face up and silent, staring at stars but not seeing them.

Drew dropped his hands to his knees to catch his breath. His heart was pounding, but he snapped back to reality. Get into place. Katie's still down there.

Drew dropped the gun bag and pulled the rifle out. He hurried back up the scrub and climbed to the top of the boulder. The nearly full moon now lit up more of the valley, and he could make out the house below. He could see some of the movement from where he thought Chino might be. He then noticed movement from about fifty yards from the house. Multiple bodies.

Shit, he thought. They had men ready to come in from the flank. This was a trap.

Before Drew could start thinking about what to do, he saw a small figure bolt from the front door of the house. The figure ran through the fields and was moving away from the house and toward the road. Another figure was in pursuit. As the chase got into the open field, Drew saw the outline of something familiar. A ponytail.

Katie was running.

FORTY-FIVE

Chino and Ramirez edged up to a dark tractor that was parked off the side of the road. Judging from the grass growing high around the tires, the tractor had not moved in a while. Chance was back at the embankment about forty yards behind them. Chino checked his watch. Nineteen minutes. One minute until go time.

"You ready, Ramirez?"

"As ready as I'm going to be."

Ramirez checked his Glock and ran his fingers back through his hair. His head was sweating, and his heart was pounding.

"I'm going out another forty yards lateral to the house." Chino pointed to the area to the left of the front of the house. "You and Chance flank to the right when the shooting starts."

"Copy that," Ramirez said as he waved Chance up to them.

Chino started a swift crawl across the dry grass running along the side of the road. The moon illuminated the valley, but the grass was high enough to keep him hidden.

Chance came over in a near sprint. He was breathing hard by the time he reached Ramirez. Chance threw himself onto his stomach behind the tractor. He landed in a loud thump. Ramirez let out a chuckle.

"What's so fucking funny?" Chance asked.

"It's just that you need a little training on effective foot-to-ground transition."

"Foot to what?

"Falling on your face, Gordo."

Chance looked up at Ramirez. The lampblack from the cork had now smeared over his face from the sweat. The overall appearance made him look like he was trying to do a half-assed Halloween costume. He smiled at Ramirez. The white in his eyes shined like small lights against the dark smear on his face.

"Where the fuck is Gerardo?" Chance asked looking back down the road.

"I don't know," Ramirez said. "But if he's not dead, I expect him to be blazing back through here soon."

Ramirez looked down the road and saw that Chino was in position.

"Okay, we move on Chino," Ramirez said.

"Copy that, boss," Chance said as he pulled out his Glock. He was still lying on his stomach next to Ramirez and held the weapon in his right hand in front of him.

Ramirez looked over to Chance.

"Remember," he said. "Center mass. Two shots at a time. Don't waste any shots. You are not going to hit anything from more than thirty yards."

"Got it, dude. I've done this before."

"I know." Ramirez reached over and pushed the barrel of Chance's gun away from him. "But there is nothing normal in a situation like this."

"Got it."

"And for God's sake, Chance. Hold the gun like it's supposed to be held. No gangster-style nonsense."

"Yeah, yeah, yeah. Nag, nag, nag," Chance said in a sing-song voice.

* * *

Gerardo had been driving now for five minutes. He looked around and assessed the situation. He was a Mexican national, albeit under witness protection, driving a stranger's vehicle with a shattered driver's side window. The interior of the vehicle was covered with broken glass and blood. He was armed with a gun registered to a Border Patrol agent and, of course, there was that dead man whose face was a pulpy mess. There would be no explaining this to any *policía* who might happen to wonder what this death wagon was doing driving down a country highway.

Pinche madre! he thought. Gerardo figured enough time had passed that the men in the house would believe that the car had left the area. He needed to get back into the fight. Time to pay a visit to the men who wanted to kill him.

Gerardo skidded through a U-turn and accelerated down the road back to the house.

* * *

Katie was running across a grassy field. She could hear footfalls behind her. She pumped her arms hard and sprinted toward the road. She could hear someone gaining on her, so she took a second to glance back. It was one of the men who had been beating on Jimmy. He was uninjured and moving fast, quickly gaining on her. At this rate, she thought, he would catch her before she reached the road. Katie looked again and shifted hard to her right. The sudden change caused the man in pursuit to skid to a stop. He lost his balance and stumbled. Katie saw this and sprinted as hard as she could. The man got up and bolted toward Katie. She couldn't see him, but she knew he was angry. Katie made a hard left and veered to the road.

Drew, where are you?

Katie was breathing hard. She worried that if Drew weren't here, she would still be exposed on the open road. There was not much traffic moving at this time of night. She looked back over her shoulder. The man was twenty feet behind her. She started to panic. She wanted to give up. Fall to the ground. Surrender to the pain. But she thought about her children. She thought about Drew, and she put her head down and drove for the road.

FORTY-SIX

Drew scrambled over the top of the rock and took up a position. He pulled the rifle out of the bag and locked a round in the chamber. He dropped to a shooter's position—on his stomach. With his left hand, he dropped the small bipod attached to the barrel end and sighted. It was not a night vision scope, but he was close enough to the targets and had enough moonlight to make out the outline of any body. His heart rate was still elevated, and he knew that he would have to lower it before shooting.

Drew went back to his training. He closed his eyes for two seconds. Clear your mind, he told himself. He let out a deep, cleansing breath and opened his eyes. He scanned the area where he had seen Katie running. He followed the path with the scope until he saw the two figures nearing the road. The one in front was a female. The male pursuer was gaining. No time to think. No time to consider technical aspects to the shot: wind, distance, elevation, humidity. No time to think about the fact that he had never fired this weapon. Even if he had a spotter, there was no time to consult about drop and angles. The only thing to consider was that Katie was running for her life. The only thing for him to believe was that he was a weapon. He was the dark. He was the silence. He was death.

Drew concentrated on the pursuing man. He was running a direct line toward the road. He spotted a point inches above the top of his head to account for movement. Drew exhaled. He steadied himself. He blocked out the environment around him. All he could hear was his own heartbeat.

He squeezed on the trigger in a fluid and deliberate pull.

* * *

Katie heard the crack of the shot behind her. She had been with Drew to the firing range, and she knew the sound of a rifle. She stopped, unsure of whether the man behind her had fired a warning shot. She held her hands up and slowly turned around. The man lay face down about ten yards from her. The level of damage stunned her. It looked like a round entered the back of the man's head and plowed off the top of his skull. The bullet skidded through the top of his head like a plane crash landing in an open field. Flesh and blood spatter fanned out in a half moon for about five feet. Katie stood silently for a second. She regained her wits and looked in a direct line from the dead man in front of her, down the field, up the hill to the top where the boulder sat like a crown.

"Drew!" she said aloud to no one but herself.

Katie smiled and moved away from the body and toward the road.

* * *

Chino heard the shot and knew someone fired from the hill. It was a sniper shot. Just who shot it was the question. It didn't matter, Chino thought. They had to move. He looked back to Ramirez and waved. The plan was for him to go left of the home and Ramirez and Chance to go right. Wherever the fuck Gerardo was at this moment was anyone's guess.

Chino started to move low and quick as he tried to stay out of sight from the windows. He got to within ten feet of what looked like a kitchen window. The light was on, and he could make out the top part of a white refrigerator. The front door was around the corner from the window. Chino figured that any professionals in the house would have heard the gunshot and be alert. There was no good time to start the assault so now was as good as any other.

Time to fuck shit up.

He got up to charge the house. As he did, Chino was thrown to the ground by a crush of weight. He was stunned, and the blow knocked the wind out of him. He turned and struggled to breathe. A man quickly moved on top of his chest and began punching him in the face. In the dark, with the moonlight to the rear of the man, Chino could not make out any details other than a fist was making painful contact to his face. After two blows and the man pulling back for a third, Chino heard

190

a loud crack. The man's head disintegrated. Blood sprayed diagonally to the ground through the exit wound. The body went limp and fell on Chino.

Drew's alive. He also quickly processed that they had been waiting for them. This was a trap.

Chino turned and saw something move his way through the high grass. He readied himself with his weapon in front of him, both hands extended. He could not look back over to Ramirez and Chance but figured they were facing the same type of ambush. He saw three men headed his way. They were dressed in black and holding rifles. They were approaching in a V formation. Military training. Chino knew he had an advantage with Drew in "the tower."

The dry grass around Chino rose two feet and provided cover as he watched the men moving toward him. He assessed the combat situation. With his Glock, Chino could expect to hit two accurately if they were within twenty yards. That left the third man able to react with his weapon.

Able to react, he thought. Able to kill me.

The men's approach was methodical, and he would have to commit soon. He looked back over his shoulder for signs of Ramirez and Chance but saw only the dark field he left them in. The men were forty yards away and closing. The decision was being made for him with every step they took.

Fuck it, he thought. Chino had placed his life in Drew's hands on numerous occasions and came out alive. He would just have to believe Drew was up on the hill with his scope trained on the mercenaries heading his way.

Chino got up to one knee. He dug his right foot into the dry, loose soil and got ready to launch into a sprint. The instant he rose to run, he heard three loud shots.

It was on. No time to think. He sprinted low and hard and fired three rounds at the lead man.

* * *

Did you hear that?" Chance whispered to Ramirez.

191

"One round, long distance." Ramirez looked up to the hill. "It was either Drew firing my rifle, or their own shooter has spotted Chino."

"Either way," Chance said as he looked back toward the road. "We need to move. The shooting has started, we're going to have to move fast. Even though this seems like we're out in the middle of nowhere, we've got about twenty minutes until the cops start arriving."

"Ramirez said, "I'm going to move toward the front door. You work to the rear and find a way in through the back."

"Copy . . ."

A loud crack broke the silence. Ramirez was struck from behind in the left shoulder. He felt the searing pain course through his shoulder and down his arm.

"Fuck! Fuck!" he yelled. "They've been waiting on us. You go! Now! I'll hold these fuckers off."

Chance did not wait for further explanation. He ran hard to the rear of the house. He was about forty yards out but, to him, it looked like a mile.

Ramirez turned on his stomach. His weapon drawn in front of him with two hands. He spotted the movement. Two men holding rifles. He had to have faith that Drew had been successful and was his guardian angel from up on the hill. Ramirez rose and began to fire as he ran to his left away from Chance.

* * *

Drew watched it all unfold from his position atop the rock. He saw the men approaching Chino. One man acting as point. Definitely military trained. He watched them in his scope and was waiting for Chino's move. He knew Chino would shoot the point man and naturally trail to his left, so he spotted the man in the right rear of the formation.

"Come on, Chino," he said aloud to himself.

Drew's finger was on the trigger ready to fire. He was in his own zone. The exterior noises were muffled. Drew could feel the deliberate beat of his heart thump in his head.

Thump. One, two, three. Thump. One, two, three. Thump.

Chino was up and running. He saw the muzzle flash from the weapon. Drew had the dark outline of the man behind the point in his scope. He pulled the trigger and fired. Drew watched the upper torso of the man come apart and the body drop to the ground when he heard a shot come from the other side of the house. He swung the rifle over and scanned the field. He spotted a figure running toward the back of the house and one running toward the front. The figure running to the front was firing at something behind him. Ramirez. Drew could make him out now. Two men were pursuing him.

Drew sighted one of the men after he caught a muzzle flash. Drew fired. The man kept moving. Drew sighted him again. Fired again. In his scope, Drew saw the top of the man's head erupt in two directions. He went down instantly. Drew swung the rifle back to where Chino had been firing.

* * *

Chino was moving fast as he fired at the point man. He capitalized on the surprise and buried two shots into the man's chest. Before he could even register the success, he heard the loud crack from above him. He saw another man go down and was distracted for a second. Just then he felt pain rush through his right hand and saw his weapon fly away. He could feel blood spurting, but he kept running at the man standing and pointing a gun at him. A second round missed, and Chino barreled into him. They went down into the hard-packed ground. Chino rolled over the man face first into the dirt. He could taste the dry, wheatlike bits plastered to his mouth. He rose quickly and threw himself into the gunman who was scrabbling for a weapon. Chino crashed his bloody right forearm into the man's neck, holding him down as he used his left hand to deliver blow after blow to the bridge of the man's nose. Every punch seemed to increase the adrenaline pumping through Chino and mask the pain in his wounded hand. His opponent did not put up any defense. Chino could hear the bones or cartilage or whatever they were, crushing under each punch and felt them moving away from the nose. He couldn't tell how long he had been hitting but stopped when he heard gunfire from the other side of the house.

Chino rolled off the lifeless body and crawled back to where he lost his Glock. The moon was high enough above the valley that he could see well across the field. Ramirez was on the move and firing at men behind him. Chino found his weapon and ran toward Ramirez.

* * *

Chance made it to the back of the house and dropped to the ground with his back against the porch. He was breathing hard, and the danger level was making it difficult for him to slow his heart rate. He took a few deep breaths and turned toward the house in a crouch. He bolted to the rear door and stood with the door to his right. To his left was a small window. He moved slowly over to the window and could make out a galley kitchen, the sink piled high with used carry-out containers. He saw what he could only guess were Jimmy's legs at the end of the kitchen. He was upside down on the ground in a chair, his feet hanging over the edge of the seat. Chance could also make out the movement of another man. His back was to Chance as he was looking out one of the other windows. Chance pulled his head back from the window. The sound of gunfire was coming from all directions.

Well, fuck. Here we go again.

Chance reached over and checked the door handle. Unlocked. The thought crossed his mind that it would be kind of funny for a houseful of armed men to be worried about security. He pulled back from the door again and tried to calm himself. Surprise. That's what Drew would say. Surprise is the best weapon. He knew what to do. Now he just had to do it.

Chance moved away from the door to take one last look through the window before making his move. Now he saw Jimmy had flipped the chair and was now on his side looking through the kitchen. Chance could see that he was duct taped to the chair, but his legs were free. Jimmy was beaten and bloody. At that instant of eye contact with Jimmy, Chance knew his mean-tempered, son-of-a-bitch uncle was about to do something stupid.

Jimmy looked over and smiled. He rolled the chair over and was now on his knees.

194

Chance knew he had to move.

* * *

Gerardo could see the flash from the gunfire as he came down the highway. Luckily the sounds from the gunfire were muffled by the terrain. They might have a little time before the law came to investigate. Gerardo hoped that, since he was returning in a gunman's vehicle, he would be able to get close to the house without getting shot by his friends or anyone else. He neared the turnoff and skidded to a stop at the top of the road.

Gerardo could see muzzle flashes from both sides of the house. There seemed to no activity in the front of the house, so he decided to make a run for the front door. Gerardo pulled out his Sig Sauer and placed it on his lap. He looked down at the body of the man folded into the floor of the passenger side. The gun in the ankle holster of the body was wedged onto the floorboard. Gerardo reached over and opened the glove compartment, reached in, and moved his hand around. He felt soft rubber against blunt steel.

"Échale, guero!" he said aloud as he admired the gun he had just pulled from a holster.

A Desert Eagle 50 AE. He had fired one back in his days in the narco world. Very expensive and very powerful. He popped the clip and saw it had the full load of seven rounds. The weight of the gun in his hand felt deadly. Gerardo put the gun opposite the Sig Sauer with the grips facing out on his lap. He scanned the field ahead of him and stepped on the accelerator.

"Ya vengo, pendejos!" he yelled.

FORTY-SEVEN

Jimmy was still taped to the chair and on his back when he heard the gunfire start outside. His head was throbbing, and he could feel the blood flowing out of the large gash across his chest. One of the men bolted out the door chasing Katie, and the big ugly was nowhere to be found. Jimmy smiled at the thought of that badass woman ramming an ink pen into his head. There was still one man standing in the home, the guy Jimmy had been trying to pin with the chair. The guy had shaken loose and was by the window with his gun out.

Chester and his friends must be out there. The idea his nephew was coming to his rescue against professional gunmen was almost laughable, but someone was out there, and these guys were worried.

Jimmy could see the man by the window was distracted by the shooting outside. With the duct tape around his torso, there was no chance he was going to get free from the chair. But he could get up and run. He didn't know where he could run to or how far a beaten-up man bound to a kitchen chair could go, but it was better than sitting in this death trap.

Jimmy slowly rocked his body to the side and turned the chair on its side. The slight impact with the ground sent a wave of pain through his upper torso. Jimmy kept silent and watched the man standing near the window and taking sporadic glances outside to see who was attacking. He turned his head to get a view down the aisle of the kitchen toward the door to look for his exit. Then he saw him. Chester was in the window. Jimmy had never been so happy to see his nephew, and he knew he needed to do something. He looked over at Chance and smiled.

Time to get into the fight.

Jimmy got up to his knees and brought one leg up. He charged at the man by the window.

* * *

Ramirez was running. The ground was uneven and pocked by gaping gopher holes with loose mounds of dirt surrounding them. He stepped deep into one and lost his balance. He put his hand down and kept himself from falling, and continued to race toward the house. At least two men were still behind him. Bullets whizzed by his ears as he got within yards of the house. He could make out Chino coming from the other direction with his gun in his left hand. Ramirez saw that Chino's right hand was bloody.

He saw Chino waving his gun side to side, so Ramirez took it as a sign to get out of the way. He veered toward the house as Chino fired at the men chasing him. Ramirez caught the muzzle flash out of his peripheral vision as he made it to the raised concrete porch. Ramirez dropped to the opposite side of the porch and used the concrete bank for cover. He turned and fired back. The men had dropped into the field and were firing from prone positions. At least one of them had a rifle. Ramirez could tell by the rounds snapping all around him.

Ramirez looked over to Chino. He was behind a tractor using his right wrist to steady his left shooting hand. The high grass made it difficult to mark any target. If this continued, he thought, the county sheriff would arrive soon. Something needed to break the stand-off.

* * *

Drew could not get a line of sight on the activity on the right side of the house. He determined that he was combat ineffective from his position. He also did not know where Katie was or whether she was safe. He made a quick descent using a game trail and ran for the right rear of the house. He covered a distance hoping to flank the shooters and made it to a spot about seventy-five yards from the muzzle flashes visible in the grass. Drew dropped to a prone shooter position and adjusted his scope.

The targets were still too low in the grass. In the dark, he could not make out any identifiable parts of the shooters. Drew knew he would have to wait for a shot, but time was running out.

* * *

197

Chance knew he had to get close and surprise the guy inside. Shooting him through the window seemed impossible because he kept doing those damn head bobs. *If you would just stand still, I'd fuck you up good.* Out of options, Chance pulled the exterior door open and rushed into the kitchen. He saw Jimmy crash his body into the man standing to the side of the window. Chance could not fire because Jimmy and the chair he was strapped to were close against the man. He ran hard across the galley kitchen and barreled his shoulder into the man. The force knocked everyone to the floor. Chance landed on top of the man and tried to use his body weight to pin him down. The man lost his weapon but quickly grabbed Chance's right wrist and started to twist hard. The man was strong, much stronger than him. He needed to do something, or he was going to lose the weapon. Jimmy was still taped to the chair and was on his side trying to kick at the man with his feet.

"Get up, Jimmy!" Chance yelled.

Jimmy started to rock side to side to turn over and get up.

"Get out of here!"

Chance was using both his hands to push against the man's grip. He kept his finger on the outside of the trigger guard waiting for the right moment. The man released his left hand and threw three punches into Chance's side. The blows crushed into his ribs and made it hard for him to breathe, but he would not let go of the pistol. The man threw two more punches to the same spot and Chance felt himself almost bending at the impact. He was face to face with the man now and could make out his facial features. The pale blue eyes and hawk nose stared down at him. The man looked into Chance's eyes and saw a breaking point.

He smiled.

"You are going to die, fat boy," he said in a malicious whisper.

Chance kept his hands tight around the gun despite the blows to his ribs. The man's fingers dug into his wrists, and he could feel the sharp edges of his nails. The man's grip on the handle would soon overpower Chance, and he knew it. The man was now straddling Chance with his right knee on his chest, pinning him. His face was so close that the sweat of his forehead was dripping onto Chance. He could taste the salt on the corners of his mouth. The gun barrel was pointing right, and Chance's right wrist was bent back against the force of the man pushing down.

Chance was losing the battle to the man's strength.

Chance looked over for Jimmy. He was still crashed in the corner trying to right himself on the ground. He looked at the weapon. The barrel still pointing away. His finger was on the outside of the trigger guard. Then it came to him.

Chance dropped his finger into the trigger well. The weapon was still pointed away and to the right of the man. He could not turn it toward the man on top of him. In one quick movement, he released his left hand and reached up behind the man's head, pulled the head down and toward his right shoulder. He pushed the weapon, still sideways, as far left as he could. He closed his eyes and fired. The bright white muzzle flash singed across the man's face. The man released his grip and reached for his eyes. Chance pulled the weapon back, shoved the barrel of the gun into the man's chest and fired two quick rounds. The man jolted up and crumpled to the floor onto his back.

Chance rolled away from the dead man, the sulfur signature from the Glock filling the air. Chance got up to one knee trying to catch his breath. He looked over at Jimmy who was staring at him from the floor.

"You okay, Jimmy?"

Jimmy did not respond. He just stared.

"What?" Chance asked.

"Holy shit, Chester!" Jimmy said with a smile. "When did you stop being a lazy sack of shit and become a fucking badass?"

Chance laughed.

"It's a long story. I'll tell you later, but we need to get the fuck out here quick."

Chance grabbed a knife from the kitchen and cut away the duct tape holding Jimmy to the chair. He looked at Jimmy. The thick purple clot of blood over his mangled ear hid a lot of the damage, but Chance could see the jagged cut. Jimmy's face was a mess. Two black eyes and a swollen lip. The gash across the upper part of his chest left a curtain of blood cascading down his torso.

"You sure you're okay?" he asked.

"Never better," Jimmy said and laughed.

He looked around the room. Chance saw two phones and a black spiral notepad on the kitchen table. He gathered them up and moved to the back door. Chance heard gunfire to the right of the house.

"We need to get out of here."

"We need to find the girl," Jimmy said.

Chance had almost forgotten about Katie.

"Is she okay? Did they hurt her?" Chance asked.

Jimmy laughed.

"She is a certified ass kicker! I'm pretty sure there's a dead fucker in the back room who wasn't expecting to get his throat opened up by a girl with a ballpoint pen. She's out there in the dark somewhere."

"Let's go find her," Chance said as he pushed Jimmy out the door.

FORTY-EIGHT

Katie watched from behind a wide oak tree near the road. She was about one hundred yards from the house and could see the dark shapes of men converging on it. In the dark, she could see the fight unfold by the muzzle flashes. Katie was scared. She was scared because her life had been upended by forces she could not control. She was the mother of two boys. Two days ago, she was making arrangements to carpool for a baseball tournament in Irvine. Now she was in a dark field somewhere in East County, tired and scared. She had most likely killed a man with a ballpoint pen and was covered in blood.

She knew Drew was in the thick of it somewhere. Men were trying to kill him. There was nothing she could do but wait it out. She noticed figures moving out of the back of the house. One of the men was holding up the other by waist and shoulder. It had to be Jimmy, she thought. He made it out!

Katie got up and started walking slowly toward the house. She heard a noise and turned to her left. A car was speeding down the road heading for the house.

* * *

Drew knew they could not just sit out here in a field firing back and forth. Law enforcement would soon arrive. From what he could tell, two men were left firing at Ramirez and Chance. There was no activity he could see from inside the house, so he figured these two were the only ones left.

Running toward the sound of a gunfight was nothing new to him. He had done it in Afghanistan and Iraq. The adrenaline of armed combat in uniform in a foreign land was different than this. Military assaults were ordered and mostly free of concerns of conscience. It was war, and he was trained to accomplish his mission. The purpose and justification for the mission were decided by others with a security

201

clearance higher than he could imagine. This allowed him to separate himself from the danger and death. His sole purpose was to accomplish his mission and get out alive. This was different. This was a danger of his creation. He could not divorce himself from the thought it was his fault he was out here. Drew was killing people and trying to save his wife because of decisions he made five years ago.

This had to end here.

Drew bolted off the ground with the rifle at his shoulder and ran toward the men in the field.

Death is coming.

* * *

Gerardo flew down the road toward the house. He could see the men firing at the Ramirez and Chance. He jumped the low berm on the side of the road and barreled into the field directly at the shooters. Gerardo started firing rounds with his left hand keeping his head low in behind the wheel. One of the men spun and began firing at him. Two quick rounds shattered the right half of the windshield. Gerardo could see the two men standing twenty yards apart. One was turned and firing at him. The other was still facing the other way and shooting at Ramirez and Chance. Off to the side, he saw a figure running toward them.

Drew was on the move.

Gerardo punched the accelerator and went directly for the man shooting at him. Two more rounds went through the windshield. Small glass pieces bounced off his face. One thick piece of something burrowed into his upper right arm. He looked at it but could not register any pain as the car bounced on the uneven terrain.

"Chingada madre!" he yelled to himself. The danger increased the adrenaline rush every second he advanced.

Just like old times.

He lifted his head for a second and saw the man shooting at him only a few feet away. The headlights lit up his face. A *guero*, an American. He could see the pale skin and goatee. He could see the man's military-style haircut. He could even make out the Sig Sauer M11 the man was holding in both hands and firing. The impact of the

202

car on flesh and bones made a loud thump. He watched the man fold over the front of the car. The body flipped sideways and slammed against the windshield, but the head stayed clear of the impact and racked back with such a savage swing that Gerardo could hear the neck snap. The body rolled off the windshield. Gerardo cranked the wheel hard to the right, and the car slammed into the house.

* * *

Drew sprinted through the high, dry grass. The men shooting at Chance and Ramirez were about fifty yards away. They were not looking in his direction, so he ran hard to a spot in the open field about fifty yards from the shooters. Drew dropped to one knee and brought the rifle up to his shoulder. As he brought the shooters into view in the scope, he saw the headlights piercing the dark. He tracked the scope to his left and saw the vehicle careening through the open field.

It must be Gerardo.

Within seconds the car had made impact with one of the shooters. Drew watched the other man stand and turn his weapon toward the vehicle. Drew had the man in his sight. He steadied his arms and squeezed the trigger.

The round demolished the man's head. Drew could see the halo of blood spatter. The body went limp to the ground. The shooting stopped.

Drew ran toward the house where he last saw Ramirez. Katie! Katie was in the house! Ramirez and Chino rose from their positions and made their way to the front of the house. Drew ran up to them breathing hard.

"Everyone good?" he asked.

"Chino!" he said looking down at the hand, "You all right?"

Chino held his bloody right hand up.

"Looks like a clean shot through and through." He winced as he opened and closed his fingers. "Doesn't look like any major damage. Just need to get this hole cleaned up and closed."

The light-colored sedan had smacked into the side of the house. Smoke was rising from the crumpled front end. Gerardo climbed out of the driver's side open window. He spilled out on the ground with a thud.

"*Puta madre!*" he said. "That shit hurt."

Drew cracked a smile with the knowledge they were still alive. He walked over to Gerardo. Ramirez and Chino followed. Drew scanned the field and the road in the distance. He could see some lights on in a house off in the distance.

"We need to clear the house and get out of here. Anyone seen Katie or Chance and Jimmy?" he asked.

No one spoke.

"Let's go in," Drew said. "Chino and Ramirez take the back. Gerardo, you're with me. Start a ten count on my mark, and we blow in at ten. Copy?"

They all nodded in agreement.

Drew looked over at Chino and nodded his head. The nod was all Chino needed.

"Go!" Drew said in a low tone.

Ramirez started to run, audibly counting out "one-one thousand, two-one thousand."

Drew's pulse was racing. The stalking of the sniper, hand-to-hand combat and the familiar feel of sighting a target spiked everything inside him. He made it to the front door and looked over to Gerardo. He gave him a nod and backed up, ready to kick the door down. Gerardo held his hand up to stop him. He reached over and tried the door handle. Unlocked. He looked back at Drew and smiled. Gerardo opened the door and charged into the house.

Drew could hear a commotion from the back of the house but no gunfire. They met Chino and Ramirez in what might have been the dining room but now only was a room with a table and a couple of wooden chairs. Off to the right, Drew saw the aftermath of a struggle in the galley kitchen. Another broken chair with straps of duct tape still attached lay next to a large mass on the floor. He walked over with his weapon extended. A body was sprawled face up on the floor. The blood from the holes in his chest was still pooling on the yellow linoleum tile under the body. Drew could see what looked to be a flash burn across the man's face.

He looked around. No Katie or Jimmy.

"Clear the house!" Drew said looking around the room. "Take any identification or intelligence we can use. Fast! We are gone in . . ."

Drew stopped dead when he saw Katie appear in the rear doorway. He couldn't breathe. His wife stood locking eyes with him. Blood covered her hands and forearms. Dried blood caked the top of her forehead. She smiled. Katie ran to Drew and threw herself into his arms.

"Are you all right, darling?" Drew said into her ear as he held her.

Katie did not say anything. Drew could feel Katie nod her head as she cried into his shoulder. The few seconds he held her were the best moments in Drew's life since his boys were born. Drew looked up and saw the others start to move about the room.

A voice came from behind him at the front door.

"If any of these motherfucking shit bags is still alive, I am going to poke their eyes out with a fork!"

Drew looked over and saw Chance holding up a bruised and bloody middle-aged man with half an ear.

"You must be Jimmy."

"You must be the Marine."

"Sorry about all this mess."

"Well," Jimmy said. "I got the shit kicked out me, half my ear cut off and they were just starting to peel my skin off."

Jimmy gave a crooked smile.

"But still, I have to say it was the most exciting thing that ever happened to me."

Jimmy looked at Katie.

"And I have to tell you, Devil Dog. That girl of yours is one certified badass. I think if you look in the back room, you're going to find some dead contract killer who found the wrong end of ballpoint pen and fucked with the wrong soccer mom."

"Travel club baseball mom," Katie said.

Drew looked down at Katie and brushed the hair back from her eyes.

"You sure you're okay?"

"I just want to go home."

Drew smiled.

The others had swept the house and gathered back in the living room.

"I've got the wallets off the two dead guys and two cell phones," Chino said.

"We don't have time to check the other bodies," Drew said. "We have to bolt. Now!"

They went out the back door and made their way across the field to where two of the cars were parked. The moon had risen two hands above the mountains and now lit up the valley like a spotlight. Chance was supporting Jimmy by the shoulder as he made his way across the field. Ramirez trailed behind, his shoulder slumped from the pain radiating from the wound. Chino led the way with Katie following closely. Drew and Gerardo brought up the rear, scanning the field in all directions to look for any possible shooters.

As they made it safely to the road, Drew took one last look over the valley. The car crashed into the side of the house was still smoking and visible under the lights from the house. He could see light coming out of both the front and rear open doors. There were two dead men in the house. There were six dead men in the field and one dead sniper in the brush on the hillside.

Jimmy and Katie were both safe now, but Drew knew it was not over. These men were not normal cartel *sicarios*. There were at least six armed ex-military American gunmen. Whoever hired them needed something from Drew, and it was in the thumb drive.

FORTY-NINE

Chino, Ramirez, and Jimmy drove into Tijuana to get treatment for their wounds. Going into Mexico was a fairly easy proposition for any United States citizen. There were no questions asked. The car was sent snaking through a series of harsh speed bumps and then deposited onto the roads of Tijuana. The border city was a place where cash could get anything you wanted. There was the usual—drugs, alcohol, women. Most importantly, plastic surgery, medication, and emergency medical treatment were available without any questions or follow-up documentation.

They arrived at Hospital Modera within a mile of the border. As they sat in the emergency waiting room, Chino could not help but notice the scene they may have created. A beaten man with a blood-clotted, duct-taped ear, another man with a blood-soaked T-shirt wrapped around his hand, and a third with a visible wound to his upper left shoulder. He also noticed that none of the twenty or so people in the waiting room gave them a second glance.

You gotta love TJ, Chino thought.

It had been a long night. The primal drive to defend one's self supercharged his body during the evening. Now, holding his wounded hand draped over his shoulder, Chino could feel his body begin to crash. He tried not to examine the gunshot wound, hoping it had not caused any permanent damage. He could open and close his fingers, which made him feel better. But overall, he felt like he had been rolled down a mountain. His forearms were bruised and scraped. He wasn't a medic, but he was pretty sure he had cracked a few ribs during the fight. Every step he took made him wince.

He looked over at Ramirez, sitting directly across from Chino on a hard plastic chair. Ramirez appeared to be in shock and stared blankly into the yellowish din of the waiting room.

"You good, Ramirez?" Chino asked.

Ramirez snapped out of his trance.

"Yeah, I can tell the bullet just grazed the top of my shoulder. I'm just trying to figure out where this is all going to end."

"Drew has the thumb drive. He'll check it out to see what we have on our hands."

"I can tell you one thing." Ramirez leaned forward. "Those men were government all the way. From the haircuts to the fleet sedans they were driving."

"I kind of figured that, too."

"This thing goes way up the ladder. They weren't acting alone. They were soldiers tying up loose ends." Ramirez leaned back.

"And we are the loose ends," Chino said.

Jimmy Connors sat back listening to the two talk.

"Well, if it isn't too much of a problem for you all," he said while rubbing the stump at the end of his ear, "I'd rather be left alone in my shitty apartment, on my ratty couch with a Bud in my hand."

It hurt like hell for Chino to laugh, but he laughed hard.

FIFTY

Drew and Katie sat in the kitchen of their home with Gerardo. The knuckles of Drew's right hand were scraped raw. Katie had cleaned up the caked-on blood from her forehead and was calmly leaning back in her chair. Gerardo sat next to Drew in front of an open laptop.

"*Órale,*" Gerardo said. "Let's see what this *pinche mierda* is all about."

Drew inserted the thumb drive and opened the file. Katie got up and came around the table, standing behind Drew.

"Holy shit!" she said.

Drew was silent. He scrolled up and down the list of names.

"Holy shit!" Katie said again.

The screen had a list of thirty names. Some of the names were clearly aliases, but seven were spelled out in full. It was as if the list maker wanted them to be seen. Below the name was a series of numbers. They were no hyphens, but the number pattern was easily discernible as phone numbers. To the right of each name was a date. On the far right, another number.

"Could it be this easy?" Drew asked.

"Yeah, no encryption, passwords. Nothing. How stupid can you get?"

"I don't think Caritas was worried about security for this information. He was just using this as leverage. Protection. Just in case things started to fall apart," Gerardo said.

"So, this is it. We just need to find out who these people . . ." Katie stopped midsentence.

Drew looked up at Katie.

"Henry Harrison," Katie said as she scanned the other names. "He is a big political donor from Point Loma. Real big in party politics. I

209

met him when I was in high school with my dad at the Varsity Club and . . ."

Katie stopped again.

"Oh my God!" she said.

Drew spun the laptop screen toward Katie.

"James Purcell! If this is the same guy, Purcell is one of the biggest defense contractors for Homeland Security. His company just closed on a contract to build a detention facility to house undocumented immigrants before they have hearings."

Drew looked up at Katie. "How do you know all this?"

"NPR, you ingrate!" she said. "There's more to life than sports talk radio."

"Well, now we know we're up against corrupt politicians and big money."

"Don't forget about a *muy* pissed off narco *jefe*," Gerardo added.

"This is never going to end," Katie said as she dropped back onto the kitchen chair.

The group sat silent.

"There is something," Gerardo said.

"What's that?" Drew asked.

"Caritas," Gerardo said as he placed both his hands on the table as if to brace himself.

"He's dead."

"That's right, and these *pendejos* had him killed."

Drew and Katie still did not understand where Gerardo was going.

"Caritas is," Gerardo paused, "or was the nephew of Cicatriz. His only nephew. If he knew who was responsible for his death, Cicatriz would want blood. He wouldn't care who he had to kill. He would also be upset with any of the child traffickers doing business with Caritas."

"How's that?" Drew asked.

"There is a code, *Un código de conducta dentro malditos.*"

Drew and Katie gave him a blank look.

Gerardo gave them a half smile. "*Narcotrafficantes* are not child molesters. They may be thieves, liars, and murderers, but they draw the line at children."

"Honor among thieves," Katie said.

"Something like that," Gerardo said. "I'm pretty sure that if Cicatriz knew about his, he'd get involved in the revenge business."

"Wait a minute!" Katie gave him an incredulous look. "You mean to tell me he had no idea what his own nephew was up to?"

"Most likely not until it all fell apart in the desert. Cicatriz would never condone this sort of business. I'm sure that once he found out, he did everything he could do distance himself from his nephew's actions."

"That would make him some sort of honorable criminal."

"At the very least," Gerardo said. "It would give him some time to figure out what to do and who needed to punished."

"So, he's been waiting for five years?" Drew asked.

"That's the thing. I think that for as much as Caritas was a pampered blowhard, he made some pretty high-up connections in order to pull this off. We know this by what we learned over the past few days—"

"And the well-armed gunmen at the ranch," Drew said.

"*Asi es.* My guess is that Cicatriz was trying to get to the bottom of this and find out who was involved. Punishment and retribution would go a long way with the other narco bosses."

"Only he never got the info from his nephew," Katie said.

"Because they had him executed," Gerardo said. "And he knows it."

"So, let me get this right, because we now know you boys aren't the best planners. You're thinking this narco boss is going to be pissed beyond belief at these high-level pedophiles and is willing to help us out by putting an end to their miserable lives?"

Gerardo looked at Drew and Katie, who began to see the shape of his plan.

"Well, that's what I think he will do," he said.

"So, you are going to make your way deep down into Mexico—"

"With a price on your head," Drew said.

Katie nodded. "To ask the sociopath who wants you dead for help with our problem."

Gerardo also nodded. "Look, I made decisions. My sins have put me where I am today. I will have to live the rest of my life looking over my shoulder, or I can grab the *toro* by the horns. What's the worst that can happen?"

"Two bullets in the back of the head," Drew was quick to answer.

Face down in the dirt like I deserve. "I need to do this. If any of you want to live a normal life, you need to understand it is the only way." Gerardo locked his gaze with Drew.

"I'm going with you," Drew said.

Katie's eyes widened.

"Not this time, *amigo*." Gerardo looked over to Katie. "Too dangerous for you."

"What about for you?" Drew asked.

"It's what I deserve."

FIFTY-ONE

Three days passed since the shootout at the house. While there was some news coverage about a disturbance near Tecate, there was no mention of gunfire or fatalities. It seemed almost impossible the death of six men in a gun battle would go unnoticed by the media. It could only mean there was a cleanup operation that moved quickly to the scene and coordinated a complete blackout.

"I don't even know what to think about this," Ramirez said as he reached for the printout to examine the numbers.

They all sat in a booth in the back of Gordo's in Santee. Drew and Chino sat across from Ramirez and Chance. Chino's hand was bandaged, and the throbbing pain from the hole in his palm was persistent. He held the hand up with his elbow on the table.

Ramirez recognized the numbers as soon as he saw them. The area code and individual phone numbers were DOJ issued. He knew because he had the same sort of number. Someone on the list was government. The fact that at least two of the names were prominent political players, as Katie pointed out, meant the government numbers were connected to prominent officials. Ramirez spread the sheet out and took a photo of the numbers with his phone.

"We need to think long and hard about how we are going to deal with this," Drew said.

Ramirez was silent as he studied the list from the thumb drive.

"Well, boss." Chino winced in a brief jolt of pain as he brought his hand to rest across his shoulder. "At the very least we need to have multiple copies of everything and be ready to go to the press on this."

"Copy that shit," Chance said. "We need to detail this to anyone who will listen. That's the only way to protect ourselves."

"Well, we aren't talking to anyone until we hear," Drew paused, "or don't hear from Gerardo."

Drew told the others about Gerardo's suicide mission. Travel back to confront the king cobra. Gerardo left before Drew or anyone else could convince him otherwise. He left Drew a detailed itinerary. He would cross into Tijuana on his motorcycle and zoom down the Baja California peninsula to La Paz, where he would text Drew that the fishing was good. Gerardo would then take his bike across the Gulf of California on the ferry to Topolobampo.

"Topopo... what?" Chance asked.

"It's a fishing port outside of Los Mochis in Sinaloa," Drew said.

Drew explained that once in Topolobampo, Gerardo would text him that he landed a marlin. From the time of that text, Drew explained, if he hadn't heard from Gerardo within twenty-four hours, it would mean he was not coming back.

"Not coming back?"

"*Never* coming back."

"Did he land the marlin?" Ramirez asked.

Drew looked at his Luminox.

"Three hours and twenty-two minutes ago."

The men were silent as they considered the enormous risk Gerardo was undertaking on their behalf.

"Well, when that *vato* gets back, I'm taking him to Disneyland." Chino laughed.

"Copy that," Drew said with a smile as he grabbed the list and thumb drive. "In the meantime, Katie has an idea of how to protect and distribute this stuff when we need to."

"It's a good thing we have someone with some brains helping us out this time," Chino said.

"Could have used her five years ago," Chance said.

Drew laughed out loud. "You got that right. Instead, we got our intel from some gangster wanna be in triple X Laker gear."

Chino took his bandaged hand off his shoulder and rested it in his open palm.

"No shit," he said. "and look what that got us."

FIFTY-TWO

The ferry arrived in Topolobampo at four o'clock in the afternoon. Gerardo stood on the top deck of the *California Star* as it motored into the tranquil blue waters of the bay. The town consisted of a handful of houses pushed up against a low hill that rose along the edge of the bay. A short, five-block *malecón* was bordered with shops and homes. *Pangas* and commercial fishing boats were secured to a few scattered docks.

Late August in Sinaloa. Gerardo had forgotten how miserably hot it was in this part of the world. The temperature hovered at a sweltering 110 degrees. The hot air blasted through his nostrils, and he found it difficult to breathe. He moved down to the ferry's covered lower level where his motorcycle was stored along with a few cars. It was only a few degrees cooler in the shade of the lower deck. He found his motorcycle, once again thankful it had not been left behind at the shootout, and pushed it between the cars to be ready to get off the ferry. He scanned the area for pedestrians and men milling about the port. To the untrained eye, it would be difficult to discern a *sicario* from a *campesino*. Gerardo, however, was a trained eye. *Sicarios* and lookouts usually traveled in pairs. They might be two men watching pedestrian traffic and not talking to each other. Gerardo had been there before. There was nothing to talk about. There was only the job.

The port was unusually slow moving at this time of the day. It was the heat. Even by *Sinaloense* standards it was hot. No one wanted to make any unnecessary movements. The small group of people leaving the ferry moved quickly to the people waiting for them so they could seek refuge in air-conditioned cars. A few of the poorest of the poor milled about asking for handouts from the passengers. The walkway and vehicle ramp emptied onto the terminal plaza. Small curio stands selling marionettes, baskets and T-shirts lined both sides of the plaza. A taco stand with three customers clustered beneath a thatch overhang was off to the far right. On the opposite side, a *mariscos* restaurant with six or seven tables. Three tables were occupied. Gerardo removed his black Wayfarers for a better look. Then he spotted them. There was nothing unique about the way they were dressed. Two men. One wearing a black western shirt, dark jeans and a beige cowboy hat with a black band. He was lazily leaning back in his chair twirling a Pacifico. It was the bulge in the waistband that captured Gerardo's attention. The other man was extremely dark skinned and had his jet-black hair slicked back. He was heavyset and wearing black slacks over silver tipped boots. The light *guayabera* strained across his bulk and only made his skin look darker. Even from fifty yards, Gerardo could see the sweat making dark rings under his arms.

They hadn't spotted him, but they would. Gerardo knew it. They would hear the Ninja fire up and immediately take notice. Gerardo knew there was no way they would be able to get their lazy, overheated asses off the chairs and into their cars before he was miles away down the road. They would make a call to report an unidentified player entering the game. If he moved fast enough, they would not be able to give a description of anything but the bike and even that would only be a general one. A fast, black motorcycle.

Gerardo knew he was about fifteen miles from Los Mochis. Traveling at 100 miles per hour, he would be there in minutes. Once in the city, Gerardo would find an alley, ditch the bike, and make his way on foot. Whether the bike would be there when he got back was a question. Whether he got back at all was the biggest question.

Bueno, pues, Gerardo thought. He was still on the ferry, but the ramp was now clear of vehicles and people. He secured his leather riding jacket to the rear of the bike and brushed his sweaty palms against the front of his black jeans. Bending down, he secured the laces on his tactical boots. Just in case, he thought. He was always ready to run. He rolled the sleeves up on his dark gray shirt to the forearms, pulled out his cellphone from his front pants pocket and typed out a text.

Landed a marlin, see you in 24. He hit SEND.

Gerardo fired up the engine and mounted the bike. He put his helmet on and disappeared behind the smoke-black visor. Leaning over the bars, he gunned the throttle. The bike flew down the ramp and jumped onto the pavement. In his peripheral vision, he saw movement from where the men in the restaurant were sitting. He tore out of the terminal and onto the road within seconds.

Knowing this might be a one-way trip was almost liberating to Gerardo. When he looked down at his speedometer it read 125.

If it ended here in his homeland, Gerardo would be okay with it. Face down in the dirt might be what he deserved. Dirt had always been part of his life and now, if it was the end, at least it was his dirt.

FIFTY-THREE

It started out piecemeal for Ramirez. That sneaking suspicion about Winters. He had to get past the basic knowledge from everyone in the office. Winters was a prick. It was the way he carried himself. Like he was better than everyone. He had no close friends in the office, and no one could remember any of his field work or how he got promoted. He didn't look like the type of guy who could crawl in the desert brush if he had to. He did look like the type of asshole who would figure out a way for you to have to do the crawling for him.

At a regional meeting a few months ago, an HSI field supervisor asked Ramirez how the Corriente-Torres case was proceeding. Ramirez knew it was stalled in pretrial proceedings. Henry Bowles, the HSI supervisor, saw the hesitation in Ramirez.

"Your bossman, Winters, came by and asked for all of our internal memorandums on the case."

"Internal memos?"

"Yeah," Bowles said. "I thought it was kind of strange for a dead investigation. I was under the impression that the defendant was already wearing the rat jacket."

Ramirez knew there wasn't any official notification of informant status for Caritas, but everyone knew a case lingering in pretrial for so long meant a snitch agreement was in the works. Any request for internal memos would also include handwritten notes of investigators as well as audio recordings of interviews.

"He wanted audio as well?"

"All audio and written logs."

The standard protocol was for investigators to release the reports of all interviews to the US Attorney. In turn, the assistant US attorney on the case would make the summary of the interviews available to defense attorneys. Since most cases settled out early, there was usually no need

218

for producing the actual audio for the interviews. In trial cases, the audio discovery would be produced in advance of the trial. The report of the audio did not include details the investigators believed irrelevant to the prosecution of the case. The live recordings, however, were frequently replete with spontaneous statements from witnesses as well as background information that might be useful to defense attorneys.

Winters was looking for something.

There would be no reason he would need to review the files and ROIs in the case since his role as deputy director did not entail active case supervision. This fact, coupled with the Department of Justice phone numbers, gave Ramirez all he needed to know that Winters was involved. The trick was finding out a way to confirm it.

Katie listened as Ramirez detailed his suspicions about Winters. Drew sat next to her in the booth at Gordo's. Chino was on his way back to the booth holding three cold Pacificos. Chance was sitting back at the bar on the phone checking in on Jimmy.

"It seems that sometimes the most effective way is the easiest," she said to Ramirez.

"What do you mean?"

"Well, think it out," she said looking at all three. "You know the general exchanges for the DOJ numbers."

Ramirez nodded in agreement. "And HSI, ICE, FBI, and US Marshal."

"Right," Katie said with a smile. "We have three of the cellphones left by these guys the other night. I think we can just power them on and start calling numbers."

Ramirez smiled at the simplicity. "And just see who answers."

Drew took a deep swallow of the Pacifico and nervously gave the bottle a little spin as he put it back down on the table.

"We also know these guys are probably law enforcement or military so they will have the phone location systems on waiting for these things to activate."

"Which is why we need to do this fast. No more than five minutes and in a public, crowded place."

"Do you know how long it will take to get a track on the cell phone?" Katie asked.

"Depends on the agency and the money," Ramirez said.

The group was silent for a second.

"Look," Ramirez said. "As you probably can guess, the higher levels of government law enforcement and anti-terrorism groups have access to cutting-edge technology. I can't even begin to tell you what we have here. It depends on who we are dealing with, where they are located and how fast they can move."

Ramirez paused to consider his next thought.

"What I can tell you," he said in a measured tone, "is they are at high levels of the government and heavily involved in child sex trafficking and Mexican cartels. Just let that sink in. They have a lot to lose."

"It also doesn't take a rocket scientist to figure out this is very bad press for government law enforcement," Katie said. "They will do whatever they need to do to keep it quiet."

"Just like they whacked Caritas," Chino added.

"That's why we need to see this through." Ramirez paused and looked around. "Otherwise we spend the rest of our lives looking over our shoulder waiting for some asshole to put an icepick in our back."

Katie winced at the thought.

Ramirez looked over at Katie and Drew.

"Sorry, Katie," he said.

"No need. I'm a big girl, and I agree with you one hundred percent. But I also think we need a fallback."

"Fallback?" Drew asked.

"Insurance. We need to have this whole story ready to go. Everything. Names, locations, dates," she looked around, "you name it. We package it all up and get it ready for the press. And not just the local rag. No. This goes straight to national. *The New York Times.*"

No one disagreed with Katie's assessment.

"I wish we had a little more time to plan this out," Chino said.

"No choice in the matter." Drew was adamant. "Gerardo is down in Narco Land throwing a Hail Mary, and we are running out of time. We take these phones out to a public place and start making the calls."

"I was thinking maybe Balboa Park." Ramirez knew that the city's signature park was heavily trafficked by locals and tourists, and there were many places in it where no vehicles were allowed. That would afford them even more time because anyone reading the phone GPS would have to get to the coordinates by foot.

"That's perfect! We set up a perimeter." Drew nodded to Chino and Chance. "You make the calls."

"Don't forget," Chino said, "you need to pull the SIM cards and trash the phones before you leave."

Ramirez gave him a nod and explained he could sit in the park and scroll the three phones quickly to scan for numbers he felt might be connected to government agencies. He would also try some of the numbers on the list from the thumb drive, but he could only spend a few minutes doing it. Once those phones were activated, they would send out a search beacon.

"Let's hope that at least one of the phones is a burner with no password lock," Ramirez said.

"No sense in waiting," Drew said. "Let's get on this."

FIFTY-FOUR

Gerardo stood beneath the canopy of a large pepper tree across the street from El Gallito. A streetlight diffused a weak glow over the roadway and sidewalk. The air was still blow dryer hot at 9:00 p.m., and his throat was parched as he watched men going in and out of the cantina. Pacifico and Modelo neon signs hung below the bright red and yellow sign depicting a fighting rooster. He had been here before. If not this specific cantina, many just like it. It was the type of place that men in *la vida* frequented. *Sicarios* sat next to federal police. Drug runners sat across the table from judges and lawyers. It was neutral ground until it was not. Gunfire could break out at any moment. The danger is what made the bar exciting and drew the crowd.

Gerardo knew Cicatriz based his operations in Culiacan but had his wife and children in Los Mochis. He was here every weekend, along with a band of men for security. To get an audience with Cicatriz, he would have to go through his men first. He hoped El Mono was not one of them.

He looked at his watch. Six hours left.

Órale, pues, he told himself. Time to get things in motion.

He crossed the narrow street and slowed before reaching the door. A large sliding window was open to the street. Ranchera music wafted out of the bar. He took in the familiar aroma of cantinas in deep Mexico. The taste of humidity and warm beer raced through his mouth and dry throat. The back of his long-sleeve shirt was drenched with sweat. He had the front of the shirt out over his pants to cover the gun butt across his waist. Gerardo ran his hand through his damp hair and started toward the door.

He stepped in to see the cantina half full. Three tables with two or three men each. No women. As he entered, every man in the bar stopped whatever he was doing to look at him. Gerardo scanned the faces for anyone who looked familiar. He couldn't identify any of the men, but he was certain that they were associated with Cicatriz. He made his way over to the bartender, an older man with a mop of bright white hair who stood with both hands atop the cobalt blue tiled bar watching Gerardo come to him.

"*Buenas noches, jefe. Tecate, por favor.*" Gerardo turned back to the room and noticed the men still watching him. The bartender reached down into a cooler of ice and came up with a dripping, cold can of Tecate. He slid over a small wooden bowl with lime wedges and small shaker of salt. Gerardo brushed the crushed ice off the top of the can and popped the tab. He squeezed a lime wedge over the opening and shook salt over the top of the can. Gerardo paused for a second, wondering whether this might be the last beer he ever tasted. He put the can to his lips and took a deep swallow. The salt and lime tang followed the cold beer down his throat. *The best beer I've ever drunk in my life.*

He turned again to look at the tables. At one, men were engaged in a competitive dominos game. He could tell that money was at stake by the way the men were loudly insulting each other. At another table, three men diverted their attention back to the *narco novela* on the television mounted in the upper corner of the cantina. He looked over to the table closest to the door. The two men seated there were staring at him. Both men, overweight and sweating, were leaning back in their chairs with arms folded across chests. Gerardo did not recognize them, but he gave them a nod. One of the men was dressed in typical *ranchero Sinaloense* style. Stiff fitting dark jeans over cowboy boots. They looked like rattlesnake from a distance. He had his beige western hat on the table. The sleeves on his dark colored dress shirt were rolled tightly up his forearms. The other was wearing a classic white *guayabera* that worked hard to cover his prodigious stomach.

Gerardo walked over to their table. The cowboy sat up.

"*Buenas noches, caballeros.*" Gerardo gave them a low wave across his chest.

The men said nothing to him.

Gerardo reached across to the near table and pulled a chair over. He flipped it and sat down facing the men.

"I need to speak with your boss," Gerardo said calmly in Spanish.

"Who the fuck are you?" the cowboy asked.

"Someone who needs to talk to your *patrón,*" Gerardo said in a commanding tone.

The cowboy laughed and adjusted himself in his seat.

"I have no problem with you." Gerardo kept his eyes on the hands of the two men. "Just call your *jefe* and tell him that Gerardo Rios is here and would like to speak to him."

The men were silent. Gerardo could not tell if they knew who he was. After a few long, awkward seconds, the fat one in the *guayabera* stood up from the table and walked toward the door. As he exited, Gerardo saw that he pulled a phone out of his front pocket. The cowboy stayed silent at the table staring Gerardo down. These men were hired help, but they weren't *sicarios.* Gerardo could tell the difference. These men were expendable worker ants. He could tell they were armed, but he knew they would not be quick on the draw. From what he could tell, the cowboy had his gun in his rear waistband. He would have to make a strong effort to lift his giant torso from the chair and reach the gun. Gerardo stayed seated and took another sip from his beer.

Seconds later, the other man walked back into the cantina. He nodded to the cowboy. The man stood up and grabbed his hat. He looked over to his friend who was now standing by the door. Gerardo stood up.

"*Vámonos!*" the man said as he grabbed Gerardo by the shoulder and pushed him toward the exit.

The moment he got outside of the bar, the cowboy reached into Gerardo's front waistband and pulled out his weapon. In one quick movement, he swung the barrel end of the gun into the side of Gerardo's face. Gerardo was not ready for such rapid movements from the man. He was staggered but stayed on his feet. Just as he began to get his bearings, a dark hood came draping down over his face. The hot smell of his breath inside the hood caused him to gag. He knew this would probably happen. After all, he had done the same thing to countless men over the years. He just wasn't ready for it to happen to him.

Calm down. He knew Drew would tell him to take a deep cleansing breath. Control your heart rate.

Easier said than done, *guero.* Drew may have been to war, but Gerardo doubted he had ever been tossed in the bed of a pickup with a hood on his head on his way to see a narco boss who wanted him dead.

FIFTY-FIVE

Ramirez sat on a wooden bench in the main promenade of Balboa Park. Built in the early 1900s, the park was the host of the 1915 Panama-California Exposition. City planners hoped it would garner some international respect for the growing city, so they poured money into building a showcase. The result was a beautiful 1,200-acre park nestled in the center of the city. El Prado, a long pedestrian boulevard that runs the length of the park's core, is lined with ornate Spanish Colonial Revival buildings that house museums and restaurants. The California Tower, a familiar site for passengers landing at the city's airport, stands tall over the Museum of Man near El Prado's western end.

It was a lazy Friday afternoon in August. The heat was a manageable eighty degrees. Tourists and locals strolled down the promenade, and Ramirez spread the three phones to his side on the bench. He looked to his right and could see Drew posted up about one hundred yards away. To his left, he could see Chino sitting near the large fountain in front of the Natural History Museum. He could not see Chance, but he guessed that he was somewhere behind him.

He picked up the first phone. An older model iPhone. He powered the phone up, but it went straight to lock mode. He turned it off and tossed it back on the bench. Ramirez grabbed the second phone, a Samsung, and powered it up. The screen came up. No security code. He was in. Ramirez looked at his watch. It was 4:05 p.m. He needed to get off the phone as quickly as possible. He pulled from his shirt pocket a folded list of numbers from the information on the thumb drive. Scrolling down the phone's call log, Ramirez checked to see if any numbers matched what was on the sheet. He was having difficulty tracking the numbers as they seemed to dissolve into each other. He paused to focus. None of the numbers were matching and time was

226

ticking away. He looked at his watch. Eleven minutes had passed. The longer he stayed connected, the greater his risk of detection. He needed to finish and shut the phone down. He put the sheet on his thigh and went back down the phone log. Then he saw it. The first time around he was too busy trying to match up numbers so he didn't notice. The number exchange was for Homeland Security. He knew the prefix.

Ramirez looked up to see Drew and Chino still standing guard. No activity yet. He looked back down at the phone. The last call came in about an hour before the shootout at the house. Fifteen minutes now since he turned on the phone. Fuck it, he thought. Let's find out who is on the other end.

He pushed redial. The phone connected and rang. One ring, two rings, three rings, four rings. Ramirez was nervous about the time. Six rings, seven. Then someone picked up. There was silence on the other end. Ramirez did not speak. Dead air on the phone. After a few long seconds, the voice on the other end said "Speak."

Ramirez immediately hung up the phone and powered it down. He gathered up the phones and started walking quickly through the Prado. He passed Drew and nodded. Drew threw a hand signal to Chino and peeled away in the opposite direction. Ramirez continued down the Prado past the California Tower and onto the Cabrillo Bridge that spanned the 163 freeway. He hurried back to his car.

"That motherfucker!" he said loudly to himself.

He knew the voice.

FIFTY-SIX

Gerardo was lying face up in the bed of a pickup. This wasn't the best choice for transportation in a Sinaloan narco town, but it wasn't like he had another option. They had been driving for about fifteen minutes, so he figured he was on the outskirts of town. The vehicle rolled to a stop. He heard the doors open and the unmistakable sound of boots crunching gravel. He heard the tailgate of the truck swing open. One of the men grabbed both of his ankles and pulled him across the bed and down to the dirt. The impact knocked the wind out of him. Gerardo tried to catch his breath as one of the men grabbed him by the collar and pulled him up. The cowboy ripped the hood off Gerardo, and he found himself standing in front of Cicatriz's home. Gerardo had been to the Los Mochis house before. One of several *narco palacios* spread over large lots. The Jurassic Park-sized front gate to the compound was guarded by two armed men. The fat guy in the *guayabera* from the cantina pushed him forward. The house was Cicatriz's attempt to achieve South Beach Miami cool. He had seen a photo of a home in a magazine and had his architects construct a replica. All white, sharp angles, and glass, the home was crippled in its quest for cool because it wasn't sitting on the sand next to the ocean. Instead, Gerardo always thought, the home looked like a building where you might visit your dentist.

Gerardo was headed to *la oficina*, a square, single-level concrete building with transom windows near the top but no other openings except a reinforced steel front door. The building stood alone and away from the main house. Cicatriz referred to it as his office so his children would believe he was engaged in some legitimate business instead of the torturing and murder that occurred inside. The men pushed Gerardo through the door. There was no turning back now. Either he would be successful in his attempt to reason with Cicatriz, or he would be dead.

228

He had been rehearsing in his mind what he might say and how to explain his flight from the organization. There was no good way. The only hope was to set aside the moral ambiguities tumbling around in his head and show Cictariz that intervention in the clusterfuck happening in the US would benefit the cartel.

The men shoved him down onto a metal chair in the middle of the room. Cowboy grabbed Gerardo's arms and yanked them back, but before Gerardo could register the pain in his shoulders and arms, he felt the tight binds of the plastic zip ties cinch at his wrists.

Both men moved out in front of Gerardo. The one in the *guayabera* walked over to a table along a wall. Neither of them had spoken since the cantina. The man picked up a pair of speed bag gloves from the table, and Gerardo knew what was coming. A *calentada*. They were going to touch him up. Beat him. A bit of pummeling before the next act. The man worked his pudgy hands into the gloves and walked over to Gerardo. He stood in front of him with his legs straddling Gerardo's thighs.

Now it begins.

The first blow did not register the pain Gerardo was expecting. The soft cover of the glove did not break the skin. The next shot came crashing down on his right cheekbone, and its force got Gerardo's attention. The man was left-handed. He pulled Gerardo's head back with his right hand and used his left to deliver another powerful blow to the side of his face. Gerardo's ears were ringing, and his eyesight was distorted. He was thinking he had underestimated *guayabera* and that he must have once been a boxer. The next five blows came in rapid succession. The pain radiated at the base of his skull as his head whipped back with each blow. He tried to breathe but felt unable to control his lungs. He started to cough up blood. The world around him was bright white. Is this what the end looks like? The last image in his mind before it went black was a barren expanse of bright red dirt.

FIFTY-SEVEN

They were seated in a corner booth at Gordo's. Katie had her laptop open with the thumb drive inserted in a port. Drew was next to her waiting for the information to appear on the screen. Chino and Ramirez sat across from them, and Chance was at the end of the table on a wooden chair.

"We're ready to go," Katie said.

"We need to hear from Gerardo first," Drew said.

He looked at his watch. Six hours remained until the full twenty-four hours had run. Drew knew the mission was a suicide run. They had all learned the level of senseless violence of which the cartel was capable. More so now that Gerardo had returned to the man who put a price on his head. He also returned with the details of Caritas's execution. Of course, the only reason Caritas was in a position to be murdered was Gerardo and his collaborators in the US. Cicatriz would not hesitate to torture Gerardo for the names of anyone else who was involved. But Gerardo had committed himself to the plan and, as he put it, dying with their names if he had to.

He was banking everything on what he knew about the inner workings of Cicatriz's operations. Cicatriz operated his *plaza* under the blanket of the larger Sinaloa cartel. The cartel was a business run by psychopaths with a twisted set of ethics. They were criminals, and they were proud. They were cold-blooded murderers and peddlers of narcotics that wrought havoc on families and children, but they were not child abusers. Sexual abuse of children was dealt with quickly and severely within the cartel. Gerardo knew that news of the involvement of Cicatriz's organization in child sex trafficking would cause enormous problems for him. It might even result in execution of the crime boss. Cicatriz would have a motive to keep silent about what happened in the desert. Gerardo's problem was getting in front of Cicatriz and being able to lay out the details before they executed him.

It was Gerardo's plan to rope Cicatriz into the mix, but Katie orchestrated the backup. She put together a detailed narrative of the events in the desert five years ago. She identified the men by aliases, at least for now. Katie cross-referenced the phone numbers of those individuals she could readily identify. At present, there were at least four prominent political figures and two high ranking Homeland Security officials. She also detailed the shootout at the house in Tecate a few days earlier. Word still had not reached the media, which meant the coordinated effort to keep it quiet was succeeding.

Katie had three packages ready to go. All the information was scanned and attached to the summary. She had identified the border-issue reporters at the New York Times, Washington Post, and the Los Angeles Times. The package for the newspapers was well-written and provided guidelines for verification, which would separate their offering from the wild-eyed screeds that landed on reporters' and editors' desks every day. She had also prepared a package to go out to the FBI one week after alerting the press.

"If this all falls to shit, I'm going to take the heat," Drew said.

"What good would it do?" Katie asked.

"I can put a face to the carnage, crime, and coverup," he answered.

"But—" Katie started to interrupt him with concerns about jail and her family.

"No. No. No!" Chance cut Katie off. "If anyone goes public it is me. I'm the one that brought everyone into this. I'm the asshole that put everyone in contact with that sociopath Caritas."

"Well," Drew pushed his beer aside. "We can talk about this when the time comes."

"There is no discussion. I'm doing it. I have no kids, no real family except for an angry uncle with half an ear." He gave a quick chuckle at the thought. "And all because of me."

Everyone at the table looked around at each other. A nod in agreement from Chino.

"If that's the case," Katie said, "you and I are going to spend a lot of time prepping you with the right things to say."

"Yeah, I know," he said with a smile. "Saying the right thing has never been my strong suit."

FIFTY-EIGHT

Gerardo was awakened by the crash of an open hand against the side of his face.

"Despiértate, puto!" The voice was loud and rang in his ears.

He awoke to find himself in *la oficina.* Bright can lights in the ceiling illuminated the space. His arms were tied behind him to the metal chair. Three or four men milled about the room in front of him. He spat blood onto the floor and tried to catch his breath. His vision was still blurry, but he could make out the men gathered around a table pushed against the wall on the far side of the room. One of the men had his back to Gerardo. He recognized the figure. Cicatriz was short, maybe five feet, six inches. He was chunky, with most of his extra weight hanging over his belt buckle. Gerardo saw him as he turned from the table. Cicatriz had aged considerably since Gerardo last saw him. Maybe the years of frustration trying to get his nephew out of prison had taken its toll. Gone was the almost jet-black hair swept back with Tres Flores Brilliantine. Short gray hair dominated his head, and the eyebrows were near white. The scar for which he was named remained the same. It took the form of a deep, downward Z that started at the outside of his right eye and continued to his mouth. The origin of the scar was the subject of folklore, but no one had the courage to ask him about it.

He made eye contact with Gerardo and pursed his lips. The short mustache was still dark brown and looked like a movie prop against his weathered face. In a pair of dark blue slacks and gingham-patterned, short-sleeve shirt, Cicatriz would fit right in at any retirement community in Southern California.

"Gerardo Rios," he said in a low-pitched voice. "My prodigal detective has returned."

Gerardo was still trying to gather his senses before attempting to form the words that might save his life.

"*Tienes unos huevotes!*" Cicatriz said as he cupped his own crotch with his veiny hand. "I will give you that."

He walked over and stopped three feet in front of Gerardo. Two men stood next to him. Both taller, younger, and waiting for orders to inflict pain or death.

"You have one minute to convince me why I should not have these *soldados*," he looked over at the two men standing next to him, "snap your neck, gut you like a wild pig and hang you from an overpass with a sign around your neck."

Gerardo sat paralyzed. His mouth could not form any words.

"Do you know what that sign would say?" Cicatriz took a step forward.

Gerardo was starting to regain his composure. He kept his gaze locked on Cicatriz.

"It will say 'This is what happens to *pinche traidores!*" Cicatriz emphasized every syllable of the word for traitor.

This was it, Gerardo thought. Now or never. This is why he came.

"I know I let you down, *jefe.*" Gerardo spat out what was left of the warm blood in his mouth. "But I have come back to tell you the truth of what happened in the desert five years ago and what happened to your nephew."

Cicatriz was silent. He stood still and stared at Gerardo.

"Caritas was partnered up some pretty powerful gringos." He looked for any sign that Cicatriz already knew this. "He got involved in his own deal to move *niños* to *pervertidos.*"

Cicatriz's eyes widened. Gerardo saw his face begin to contort; the corners of his mouth drooped.

"He used your organization, your *sicarios*, your money to broker a deal for himself." Gerardo was stern in the accusation. Cicatriz still did not respond.

"I know," Gerardo paused. "I have proof that he was in league in with some *gringo politicos* and members of the government law enforcement to deliver these children to abusers."

Gerardo saw Cicatriz close his eyes and take in a deep breath. He knew. Gerardo could tell that he knew. *Pues*, except for that last part. The original media accounts alluded to the presence of children in the trafficking operation, but the public indictment only alleged conspiracies to distribute narcotics and trafficking in undocumented aliens. Gerardo's news was problematic for Cicatriz since he did not appear to be aware of the involvement of government agents and higher ups. This could be very embarrassing for him and his organization. Gerardo took the opportunity and started to tell the story. He explained how he witnessed the children being led through the desert. He told him about the dirty Border Patrol agents assisting Caritas and about the shootout at the ranch. He left out the part about the beating inflicted upon his nephew.

"What good does it do to tell me this now?"

"Because someone is cleaning up all the loose ends. They enlisted *La Eme* to murder Caritas because," he paused because he knew the next words might cause Cicatriz to fly into a rage, "he was cooperating with the government."

"Caritas was not a *pinche rata!*" he cried.

"I know it is hard to believe, *pero tú sabes,* five years and no plea in the case. No deal. No trial. He was giving information, more than the *mierda* you had him feeding the feds, and these powerful men needed to put an end to it, so they had him killed."

Cicatriz stepped forward and delivered a crushing blow to the bridge of Gerardo's nose. The blow snapped his head back. When Gerardo's head came back up to face Cicatriz, all he could see was a white blur.

"You are just tossing *pinche mentiras* to spare your worthless life," Cicatriz bellowed.

Gerardo's vision slowly reset. He could feel the warm blood flowing over his mouth from his nose.

"Why would I travel from *el norte* to this," Gerardo looked around the room, ". . . this death pit? I could have dropped back into witness protection and disappeared for another five years."

Cicatriz stepped back away from Gerardo.

"Explain to me how Caritas could have been placed in the same holding cell as mafia and gang members," he said.

Gerardo knew he had Cicatriz's attention.

"This comes from high up in the system," he told the *jefe*. "People with the power to move federal inmates. The power to access federal files. The power to order the murder of your nephew. And now, I am here to tell you. And to ask for your help."

"My help?" Cicatriz laughed and walked away from Gerardo. "Why don't I just end your miserable traitor life right now and move on with business?"

"Because," Gerardo said with a smile, "we know who they are."

Cicatriz stopped and turned back.

"You also need to know this information will be made public soon. The names, the organization and," Gerardo paused to let his words sink in, "the involvement of your cartel. *Tú sabes,* the Sinaloa cartel will not take the news well. *Pinche violadores de niños.* That does not sit well with business. You can strike ahead of the news."

Cicatriz smiled at Gerardo.

"You have my attention," he said.

"We need your protection and your help. Some of these men need to be dealt with. We can establish they have ties to criminal activities here in Mexico and," he steadied his gaze at Cicatriz, "with Caritas's renegade operation. If something were to happen to them, it would be kept under wraps. At least as much as possible. The American government does not need the bad publicity. Dirty agents, dirty politicians, child sex ring. Not good for morale, *que no?*"

Gerardo could sense that he was getting through to Cicatriz.

"On the other side," Gerardo knew he was getting to the tricky part, "we are ready to release two sets of information."

"Who is we?" Cicatriz was angry.

"*Mis amigos del norte.*"

"Tell me why I shouldn't just peel the skin off your chest until I get the answers I want?' Cicatriz reached over and pulled up a metal chair and dropped his large body into the seat.

"Two reasons." Gerardo straightened up in his seat. "First, I am prepared to die to protect them. I know that I deserve to die for the things I have done for you. You had me deliver my lifelong friend to a dirt field outside of Culiacan and watch him take a bullet to his skull."

Gerardo looked around the room at the other men behind Cicatriz.

"I deserve to be face down in the dirt. That is the just punishment for my sins as it may be yours." Gerardo was feeling more confident.

"All of that can be arranged."

Gerardo smiled. "But second, we have all of the information. Names, phone numbers, emails of everyone involved. It is very big news. We have the details of the operation and the facts of what occurred that evening in a written statement. Absent from the declaration is the name of Caritas or mention of your organization."

Gerardo paused to see if he was making an impact on Cicatriz.

"Now they may eventually figure out who else was involved, but the last thing the American government will want is an open investigation of law enforcement and political ties to a child smuggling ring." Gerardo could tell Cicatriz was weighing his options.

"If you don't want to help us," he continued. "Or you decide to end my miserable life right here, we will make the entire story public. This will include identifying Caritas and this organization. It is all ready to be sent to the media."

"Are you threatening me, *cabrón?*"

Gerardo swallowed the spit and blood that had accumulated in the back of his throat and considered his response.

"*Sí, jefe.* That is exactly what I am doing."

Cicatriz sat silent for a long minute staring at Gerardo. The men behind him stood at attention awaiting his orders. In *la oficina,* those orders usually involved snuffing out a life. Gerardo locked eyes with Cicatriz. He could see the years of violence and death had taken its toll.

The gaze that would have broken most men five years ago had given way to the tired annoyance of an old man.

"*Bueno, Gerardo Rios.*" Cicatriz leaned forward on the seat of the chair and put his meaty hands on his knees. "I will allow you an opportunity to rectify the situation in *el norte.* Make no mistake. *Me debes,* you owe me your miserable life, and I have not decided what I will do with it. But for now, you will go back and bring me the names and information. You will also deal with the problem and these men."

"I will need your help with . . ." Gerardo started to say.

"You will go with El Mono." Cicatriz smiled. "And he will make sure you return."

Let's be serious, *jefe,* Gerardo thought. He knew what a trip with El Mono meant. It guaranteed Gerardo would not return. To anything.

FIFTY-NINE

The text came in at two in the morning. Drew's phone vibrated on the nightstand. Drew reached over for the phone. Katie was up and watching him. The glow from the phone lit up Drew's face.

Very successful fishing trip. Be back tonight at six. Won't need you to pick me up.

The text outlined one of the contingencies they had planned for. Gerardo was bringing someone back with him. He explained that, if Cicatriz did not murder him, he might be sent back with one of his *sicarios* to make sure the job was done. It would also mean Gerardo would have to accompany the *sicario* on the job. Gerardo explained if that were the case, it would be far too dangerous for the rest of them to become involved. If he sent the text, it meant he would have to proceed alone.

Drew handed the phone over to Katie. She read the text and gasped. "This is bad, Drew."

"I know, but not unexpected. We have to stick to the plan."

"I'm so scared, Drew," Katie whispered.

Drew reached over and pulled Katie closed to him. She rested her head on his chest and then buried her face into the crook of his arm. She fought back the urge to cry. Drew stroked her hair and tried to remain calm.

"Nothing is going to happen to you, darling. I promise."

Katie turned her face up to Drew.

"We need to end all this." she said.

"I know. I'm working on it."

Drew typed out a prearranged text to Chino, Chance, and Ramirez. He hit send and put the phone back on the nightstand. He dropped his head back onto the pillow and Katie wrapped herself tightly around Drew. He stared at the ceiling until the sun came up.

SIXTY

Cicatriz had his *licenciado* make the arrangements. A small plane flew
Gerardo and El Mono to the airport in Tijuana. They were picked up
at the airport and driven to a law office off Avenida Revolución. The
lawyer there provided Mono and Gerardo with tourist visas and
Mexican National Identification Cards. They walked across the
pedestrian port of entry at San Ysidro. Gerardo was surprised at how
easy it was to cross. The customs officer checked the visas and IDs and
asked them how long they would be visiting in the United States.
Gerardo told him they had family in Los Angeles and wanted to visit
Disneyland on the way back. Mono stayed silent.

It was 4:00 in the afternoon when they crossed into the United
States. Gerardo had been living in Southern California for the past five
years and forgotten how different it seemed just a few steps away from
Mexico. The air smelled different. The people milling about had a
lesser sense of desperation. Mono had not said a word since the
lawyer's office. The pedestrian walkway from the port of entry dropped
them into a strip mall in San Ysidro. They walked past the *casas de
cambio* and the kiosks offering Mexican auto insurance and stopped at
the McDonalds. In the parking lot, Mono made a call to one of
Cicatriz's men.

They were picked up fifteen minutes later and driven to Barrio
Logan. The driver stopped in front of a faded blue, two-story Victorian-
style home. When it was built seventy years ago, the home no doubt
stood tall and proud against the downtown San Diego skyline. Since
then, the neighborhood had become a place to house the lowest
income workers in San Diego. Years of crime and gang violence made
some parts of the neighborhood dangerous. Only recently had the
gentrification process begun to change the area. The high cost of
housing in San Diego brought in double-income young people. The

result was a nascent but spotty hipster community with the requisite coffee shops and craft-beer saloons. Nevertheless, there were pockets where even the bravest skinny-jean-wearing, mustache-twirling twenty-something dared not venture. This street was one of them.

Gerardo looked up at the house. Black iron security bars covered all the windows. He wondered if they were to keep people out or keep people in. The curtains were drawn on all of them. The driver turned and nodded back for them to get out of the vehicle. Gerardo and Mono followed the driver past the chain-link gate and up the pathway to the front door. An angry looking man with a shaved head opened the door before they got to it and stood in the doorway. His loose, oversized white T-shirt hung over ink dark jeans. Both his arms were prison tattooed, no color, and a giant LOGAN across his neck. He motioned them inside. Gerardo stepped into near darkness. A light at the end of a long hallway leading to the stairs was the only illumination. He could hear a television above him in one of the rooms. The sound of foot traffic from above gave him the impression there were at least four or five people upstairs.

The man turned his back and walked down the hallway. He stopped short of the stairs and opened the door to a bedroom. After flipping the light on, he moved to the edge of the room. When Gerardo's eyes adjusted to the light, he saw weapons laid out on a bed. One Mossberg shotgun, three Glock nine millimeters, one ridiculously oversized .357 Magnum, one Sig Sauer .380, three military-style knives, a pile of plastic zip ties and, strangely, a can of pepper spray.

Mono stepped forward and picked up a Glock. He stuck the gun in the waistband at his back and reached for the shotgun to examine the barrel. He tossed it back down on the bed.

"Wrap this up with a least ten rounds and give me two magazines for the Glock."

Gerardo picked up the Sig Sauer and put it in his waistband in front.

Mono motioned for Gerardo to pick up the zip ties. He reached for a handful and was tempted to grab the pepper spray, but he could sense Mono watching him. The bald gangster returned with a blanket and wrapped the shotgun and ammunition. He handed it to Mono and left the room. Mono motioned with his head to Gerardo it was time to leave. They walked out the door and down the steps back to the car. The driver stood outside the vehicle. When they arrived at the car, the driver handed the keys to Gerardo and walked away down the street.

Gerardo walked around to the trunk and opened it. Mono dumped the bundled blanket into the trunk and walked back to the passenger door. He looked back at Gerardo and got in the passenger seat. Gerardo got into the driver's seat and shut the door. The silence during the transaction and now in the car was unnerving to Gerardo. He placed his hands on the steering wheel and looked straight ahead.

"*Ahora qué?*" He already knew the answer.

"*Ahora viene el muerte.*"

Death was certainly coming. He hoped it came for the right people. He fired up the ignition and drove in silence to Point Loma.

SIXTY-ONE

They sat in the car on a tree-lined street in Point Loma. The road sloped gently to reveal a postcard view across the bay to downtown San Diego. The sun had dipped behind them, but a red-orange reflection off the glass-faced buildings in the downtown cityscape lit up San Diego Bay. The house sat at the end of the narrow road. A lighted brick fence and security gate surrounded the two-story mansion. From his vantage point, Gerardo could not tell how many people were inside the residence. He couldn't tell if there was armed security. He couldn't tell if the man they were looking for was inside. He looked over to Mono and saw the same cold, vacant stare he had seen before on jobs for Cicatriz. He knew that Mono didn't care how many people were inside or whether there was security. He would complete his mission.

They sat silently in the car for another twenty minutes. The orange and purple gloaming bled into a full moon night sky. Without saying a word, Mono opened the passenger door and walked toward the gate. Gerardo got out of the driver's seat and followed about ten feet behind. Mono stopped at the gate and examined the entrance. Metal bars interlocked at the connection between the two gates. He turned and walked along the concrete fence that stood about six feet high. Gerardo could see the house in his periphery. When they reached a point from where they could see the rear of the house, Mono grabbed the top of the fence with his hands and pulled himself up.

He didn't look for security cameras, listen for dogs or do any other investigation before leaping over the fence.

Gerardo shook his head.

"How about giving me a hand?" he asked in a loud whisper.

He stood waiting at the bottom of the fence. No response.

Puta madre. Looks like I'm on my own.

He jumped for the ledge on top but slipped his grip and came crashing back to the ground. He got up and backed up to make a run for it. He took in a few breaths and strode for the wall. He caught the ledge with the tips of his fingers and pulled himself up. He rolled over the top and landed on his feet on the other side. He saw Mono was already at one of the back French doors. Gerardo sprinted to catch up to him.

By the time Gerardo reached him, Mono was crashing the metal barrel of his Glock through one of the small windows in the French door. Gerardo knew the man was in murder mode. He was focused on the task without regard to Gerardo or any other person who might get in his way. Mono reached his hand in through the broken window and opened the door.

Gerardo was relieved when he did not hear any alarm trip. They entered what looked like a large ballroom. A wide-open room with minimal furniture, it seemed like it could hold a hundred people. A large iron chandelier dominated the ceiling. A grand stairway of dark wood and red carpet across the room led to the upper floor. Mono walked across the room, his Glock in his right hand. Gerardo was two steps behind when they reached the landing. Mono looked both ways in the upper floor's hallway and started to his right. A door opened about ten feet away. Gerardo froze.

When the door opened completely, Gerardo saw a woman in a dark pantsuit. She looked to be in her mid-fifties, blonde hair brushed back tight in a bun. A thick pearl necklace and the look of impertinence at the strangers in her house was all Gerardo needed to determine she was the lady of the house.

She stood in the doorway. The realization there were two armed intruders in her home flashed across her face. Her mouth formed a silent O and was about to let out a scream when Mono raced across the hall and delivered a savage blow with the barrel end of his gun to her face. The sound of steel on flesh caused Gerardo to recoil. The woman's body bent back like a rag doll, arms out in front of her. Blood from her nose spouted out and up as she fell back to the floor.

Mono looked back to Gerardo.

"Tie her up." He wiped the blood from the barrel of the gun on the leg of his jeans.

Gerardo pulled out one of the zip ties in his back pocket and moved over to the woman. He leaned down to turn her over and made sure she was still breathing. He wondered if she knew her husband was involved with trafficking children. It didn't matter. He dragged her into one of the bedrooms and shut the door. When he came out of the room, Mono was standing in the hallway staring at him.

"Give me your phone," he said with his palm out.

"Why do you want my phone?" Gerardo knew why.

He did not respond but kept the same cold gaze on him that he had seen countless times.

Gerardo expected this. Mono had always been thorough when it came to closing off escape routes. Gerardo hoped the last text he sent after they crossed into the United States made it through. He handed over the phone to Mono, who put it in the front pocket of his jeans, turned, and walked down the hallway. Along the way, Mono paused at each of five doors to listen for movement. As they approached the end of the hall, light was visible underneath the last door.

Mono did not look back at Gerardo. Without hesitation, he opened the door.

The room was a large study. A wall of bookshelves took up the far wall. A gleaming wood floor gave way to a large Persian rug. A man sitting at a desk looked at them and froze. He did not speak. He was wearing a polo shirt and khaki pants. The banker's light on his desk illuminated his pale features. His white hair was brushed back, from a deeply creased forehead. The loose skin of his face was offset by steel blue eyes.

Mono looked back at Gerardo.

"*Este es el pendejo?*" he asked.

Gerardo had only seen a picture on the internet that Katie showed him. Sitting behind his oversized desk in this movie set of an office, he looked like every rich white man Gerardo had ever imagined. He looked over at a wall to his left. The entire wall was covered with framed photos and certificates. The photos showed the man, blazer and tie, shaking hands with other white men. The smile of money and power in every photo. There were photos of white men in golf clothing grinning for the camera, cigars and drinks in their hands. Gerardo scanned the certificates and saw all he needed. He read the last name, Harrison.

Gerardo looked over to Mono and nodded.

The man stood up from his desk, his arrogance and self-confidence recovered.

"Who do you think you are, coming in—".

He stopped mid-sentence because in the instant he saw Mono walk toward him, he realized the lifetime of deceit and greed had a balance due. He knew why these men were here. He knew that no amount of money, power, or persuasion would stop what was about to happen.

He dropped back into his seat. The corners of his mouth drooped to a cartoonish pout. Gerardo thought he saw a tear fall from the corner of an eye.

Mono stopped at the edge of the desk in front of the man. He raised his weapon. The man looked down at his desk. Mono fired twice into the top of his head. The rounds blew skull and flesh into the leather chair. Blood began to pool onto the desk. Mono turned to leave and started to walk. On his way out, Gerardo looked back. The image of the powerful white man, bent face down over his desk, seared into his mind. He should have felt some sort of sympathy. He did not.

This was how it was done. No speeches, no reasons given to the man before he was killed. They knew why. They always knew it was coming.

Fuck that *guero.* He got what he deserved.

He followed Mono out the back door and over the fence.

SIXTY-TWO

Katie read the narrative to herself again. She laid out everything and included Gerardo and Ramirez since their names were already associated with the events. She included a list of the names and numbers she was able to discover through basic internet searches. Even without the evidence of the shootout five years ago, the mere presence of the names together looked suspicious. Politicians, law enforcement, and power brokers connected to child sex trafficking was a story that would lead newscasts and front pages across the nation.

She sat alone at the desk in her bedroom. The boys were at a sleepaway camp in Julian, a town in the San Diego County mountains. Drew was with Chino, Ramirez, and Chance. They had set the next phase of their plan to action. She laughed to herself when she considered the word "plan." It was more of a Hail Mary than any plan. The plan required every moving part be successful and then, still, a pile of luck.

The individual emails were addressed to the *New York Times, Washington Post,* and *Los Angeles Times,* and the group had decided to add *The San Diego Union-Tribune,* CNN, NBC and ABC to the distribution. She sat silently, staring at the bright screen in her dimly lit bedroom. Katie had nothing to do but wait. Wait for a message from Drew, who had often told her that warriors never leave a brother behind on the battlefield. Wait to see if everyone made it out alive. Wait for the final instructions to hit send and the next phase of their lives to begin.

SIXTY-THREE

Agent Matthew Winters was finishing his PowerPoint presentation highlighting the recent success of Operation Clean Sweep. There were other places he would rather be on a Friday night than the Scottish Rite Event Center on Hotel Circle. He had been committed by his agency to give the speech to county business owners outlining the program to eradicate undocumented workers in the hospitality industry. Right-wing, anti-immigrant nut jobs and protesters were, of course, screaming from the back of the auditorium. Luckily, he was the first of three speakers, which meant he could deliver his presentation and be out of the auditorium early with little chance of getting cornered with a barrage of questions from people who had nothing better to do on a Friday night.

Winters mechanically proceeded through the presentation. Detention and arrest statistics. Individual case anecdotes of apprehending illegal workers in hotels with criminal histories. Winters had other things on his mind. There was the fiasco at the house in Tecate. The cleanup of the shootout required him to commit serious resources and to falsify government reports to account for the unmistakable gunfire that echoed through the canyon. While his arrogance shielded him a bit, Winters knew the walls were closing in on him.

Winters completed the last slide and thanked the audience for their attention. There was a smattering of applause, and several people scooted their metal folding chairs to get up to leave. Winters deferred questions to the end of the last speaker's presentation because he knew he would not be there. He gathered up his notes and laptop. The drone of the follow-up speaker sounded like a cartoon as he made his way past the audience and out of the auditorium.

It was a little past 9:00 p.m. and the parking lot was fairly well lit. He could see his DOJ sedan on the far end of the lot. As he walked between cars, he was lost in thought. He was trying to figure out what to do with the problem. Men were dead, the names of several prominent individuals might become public, and there were some very live witnesses to his illegal operation out there waiting to bring his world to a crashing end.

Winters pulled his phone out of the inside pocket of his blazer. He started to scroll down his email messages and dreaded the phone call he was going to have to make to Hank Harrison. He didn't notice the slow-moving car to his right. Winters reached his car and popped the trunk. He laid down his laptop bag and a white note binder. As he was about to shut the trunk lid, he felt his cell phone vibrate in his jacket pocket. He stopped and reached for the phone. As he read the incoming call number, a blow to the side of his head knocked him off his feet. His head slammed into the concrete in a dull thud. Before he could focus, another blow came crashing into his nose and forehead.

SIXTY-FOUR

As they exited the parking lot, Gerardo asked Mono where he should drive. Mono looked straight ahead.

"East, *al desierto.*"

Back to the desert. Back to where it all began. Gerardo resigned himself to this appointment with his life's common thread. The dirt. He knew there was no place in the city where Mono could complete his mission. Just like old times, just like Sinaloa. Find a dirt road and end this *vato's* life, and his. Gerardo knew the chances of him making it out of the desert were very slim. The alternative was a return trip to Los Mochis and a slow, painful death. On second thought, he would prefer the desert.

"Hand me your *pistola.*" Mono held his open hand out.

With his gun tucked into his waistband, Gerardo considered handing Mono a round to the face. But then what, he would be in a car with a dead *sicario* splattered all over the front seat and windows and a high-ranking Homeland Security official in the trunk. He couldn't take the chance of running into the CHP or Border Patrol. If that happened, Winters would walk, and nothing would be solved. He needed to see this through. If this was the hand dealt to him, then so be it.

He carefully pulled the Sig Sauer out from his waistband and handed it to Mono. Gerardo kept his eyes on the road and started to weigh his unappealing options. The miles passed away in silence. After El Cajon, the terrain became rural and sparsely populated. They passed Viejas Casino where idiots were losing money and making tribal members rich. Maybe they weren't so dumb. He was the one in a rolling car of death.

Mono remained silent. The same cold stare. He looked at the passing terrain looking for a turnoff that might just be the right place to execute two people. The silence continued as they passed over the Pine Valley Bridge. Gerardo eyed the valley below, at least a three-hundred-foot drop. He considered driving off the bridge and doing everyone a favor, but he couldn't trust that he could break through the side railings. *Pinche gringo* engineering was nothing to take a chance on.

The terrain had now given way to classic Southern California scrub. Almost desert but with enough cover to let Mono finish the job. He sensed it coming as he saw the exit for Kitchen Creek Road. The moon provided enough light to be able to see the start of a run of mountains to the northeast. Mono lowered his head in the passenger seat for a better view across the driver's side.

"*Aqui.*" He motioned with the Sig Sauer in his hand for Gerardo to pull off.

The ramp came to a stop sign where they made a left turn and traveled under the freeway. The two-lane road was curvy and dark. To his left, Gerardo could see several single-track dirt trails leading up to the start of steep mountains. The trails meandered through low manzanita and mesquite. Large boulders dotted the mountainside.

About a quarter mile from the freeway, Mono signaled for Gerardo to stop. He pulled off to the right onto a dirt turnout. He cut the lights and pulled the car over as far as possible. He looked across the road and saw a trail entrance. The sign on the iron gate prohibited motorized vehicles. The foot trail veered around the padlocked gate. To the right of the gate and closer to the road was an official-looking sign marker. Gerardo strained his eyes to make out the letters in the moonlight.

It read: Pacific Crest Trail.

Mono tossed the Sig Sauer into the glove box. If it wasn't clear to Gerardo before it certainly was now. This was the last stop. Mono gave him a head motion to get out of the vehicle. Gerardo looked up into the night sky. This might be the last time he would see the stars.

SIXTY-FIVE

Winters came to in the dark. The hard steel against his back and the chemical smell informed him that he was in the trunk of a moving car. Whoever had him didn't care he was a federal agent. He knew law enforcement was usually off-limits in the criminal world *unless* that agent made the leap to criminal conduct. Then all bets were off. He knew what he had done. He started to gasp for air. He was scared.

He could feel the car slowing, rolling over gravel and dirt, then coming to a stop.

I fucked up, I fucked up, he kept telling himself. He could feel a warm fluid spreading across his groin. He had pissed in his pants and hadn't noticed until now. He heard both doors open. The driver's side closed and then the passenger's. Footsteps. A delay of a second or so and then he could hear the beep from the key fob and the trunk lid unlatched.

Two figures stood looking down at him. They were backlit by moonglow. He tried to focus, but he could not make out any details. The two figures were just dark shadows. The crash of cold steel across the side of his face sent him rolling back into the trunk. He felt like his head was about to shatter.

"*Ya es tiempo, pendejo!*"

Winters could speak only a few words of Spanish, but he knew his time was up.

SIXTY-SIX

Chino did his best to maintain his distance but cars on the eastbound 8 at this hour were few and noticeable. When he saw the car pull off the highway, Chino pulled his foot off the accelerator and allowed some distance before he started to make his way over.

Drew looked out at the terrain.

"Dark as fuck out here." Drew said, straining his head forward to keep his eyes on the taillights.

The two-lane blacktop curved into the side of a steep, rocky grade. Chino turned off the headlights and was navigating by the running lights.

"I know this area," he told Drew. "The road ends up in a campground about three miles up."

"Then they are going to need to stop somewhere in between."

Chino leaned forward over the steering wheel trying to get a better view of the road.

"This is pretty fucking sketchy out here," he said as he scanned the terrain. "Looks like the type of place you take people to . . ."

"You got that right." Drew didn't need to finish the thought.

Just then the bright red flash of the brake lights about one hundred yards away lit up the road. Chino quickly braked and pulled off to the narrow shoulder. They waited for a few seconds and the red lights went out.

"They're stopped," Drew said.

"Looks like it's go time."

Drew didn't answer but got out to the car and headed to the trunk. Chino met him at the rear of the vehicle while Drew kept his eyes trained on the area where the lights had been. Chino popped the trunk and handed Drew his rifle bag.

"We good, boss?" Chino asked as he tucked his handgun into his front waistband.

"Let's end this."

Drew didn't wait for a response. He turned down the road and started a moderate, measured run. As his legs began to loosen up and circulation pulse through his body, he picked up his pace. Chino was close behind on his right shoulder.

Drew was now in a near sprint down the curvy road in the dark. They were each locked into combat mode. Clear minded, single purpose. Each footfall was carefully placed to avoid turning an ankle or making undue noise. Drew held the strap of the gun bag tight against his chest to keep it from moving. They rounded the bend and Drew threw up his hand for Chino to halt. Chino stopped dead. Drew motioned for him to go left. They scampered up a low hillside and dropped behind a charred oak stump.

Drew leaned back against the stump and took a second to catch his breath. He took the rifle bag off his shoulder, peeled it open, and pulled out a spotter scope secured inside by a Velcro strap and handed it to Chino. Drew readied the weapon. In his mind, he reviewed the training from sniper school he recited to himself every day on deployment. He noted his conditions. Nighttime. No breeze of note. Elevated angle firing. He knew when firing from an elevated position, the effect of gravity on the bullet is less than firing across a level plane. He needed to take this into account.

He looked over to Chino who had been adjusting the spotter scope.

"Let's sight the target," Drew said in a low voice.

"Copy that."

They both turned and popped up over the stump.

"Looks like 200 yards," Chino said using the scope to mark the area.

"I confirm," Drew said, scanning the area with the scope on his rifle.

Chino examined the trail up and down again.

"Target moving uphill," Chino said. "If he moves another hundred yards, we won't have a shot."

"Copy that." Drew turned the focus ring on his scope. "Let's give it another minute."

"That's cutting it close, boss." Chino reset the chronometer on his Luminox. "One minute starting now."

"Looks like a clearing ahead." Drew spotted it through his scope. "If the target stops there, I should have a shot."

"Sure wish I could give you more help, boss. Maybe a quick angle formula but . . ."

"Yeah, I know, we both don't have the time or the equipment. What I wouldn't give for a Slope Doper or laser imaging right now."

The thought of breaking out military-issue targeting and range devices caused Chino to laugh.

"But you've got the natural born skill our Lord and Savior gave you to blow motherfuckers' heads off from a mile away." Chino did his best impression of a preacher in a hushed tone.

Drew couldn't help but smile.

"We are going to need to move over to flat ground for a shot. Standing over this stump is too awkward," Drew whispered.

"Copy that, boss."

"And remember, send the text if and when I tell you."

Drew knew from his training that the fundamentals of marksmanship depended on a steady position. A prone position would enable him to focus on the other elements of the shot-aiming, breathing, and trigger control. He knew it was important to establish the natural point of aim for the rifle. To do so, his body would have to be relaxed and under no undue strain.

They dropped down and crawled across the dirt to a flat clearing on the side of the hill. Drew turned the rifle toward the target. He dropped the bipod on the front of the rifle and rested the butt on his arm and shoulder. Even though it had been years since his last mission, aside from the Tecate business, all the training came rushing back to him. First, preparation. He closed his eyes and placed his hands in the firing position and brought the aim to the target area. With his eyes still closed, he told himself, *Relax.* He brought his heart rate down and slowed his breathing. He was trained that holding in a breath creates instability. The lack of oxygen can induce a tremble. Breath normally and under no circumstances push air out of your lungs. Create the natural rhythm to which the body is most at ease. He was trained to break the trigger at the bottom of the natural respiratory pause. He would fire in that one-second break between inhaling and exhaling. Finally, he needed his mindset. His consistency.

And so he started.

I am a Weapon. I am the Dark. I am the Silence. I am Death.

SIXTY-SEVEN

Gerardo made his way slowly up the trail. With no flashlight, he had to rely on the moon's help to navigate the path. Low cacti and dry brush made barriers on each side of the trail. The thought crossed his mind that an ankle twist might buy him a few moments before the end, but he figured he would be postponing the inevitable. Behind him, he could hear Winters whimpering. The usual bargaining and pleading with God men do before death.

"I'm telling you, I can give you guys what you need. Protection, money, LEGAL STATUS." He emphasized legal status.

Mono pushed him hard from the back, and sent Winters face down in the dirt.

"Goddamn it!" Winters turned back to look at Mono. "I am a federal agent! If you do anything to me, you can bet the government will do everything in their power to hunt you and your bosses down."

Mono said nothing. Instead, he took a step toward Winters and gave him a soccer style kick to the face. Winters flailed on the ground and covered his bloody face. Mono motioned for Gerardo to pull Winters up.

Gerardo walked over to Winters. He surveyed the area. High brush on both sides, the mountain range to the right and a smaller ridge to the left. If he could overpower Mono, he could easily drag both bodies into the gnarly branches and cover of the manzanita and cactus. It would take a few days for them to turn up. Then he thought about trying to cash in a favor with Mono, for old time's sake. For all the jobs he had accompanied him on. But in the end, he knew that was exactly why he was here . . . in the dirt.

Gerardo pulled Winters up to his feet and backed away. Winters was sobbing. All the years of scheming meant nothing now. His shoulders were slumped, and he did not look up. Mono stepped in front of Winters and lifted his forehead with the barrel of his gun.

"*Mírame, pendejo!*" Mono always wanted his victims to look at him.

Winters slowly lifted his head, and his eyes rose to meet Mono's gaze. Mono glanced over at Gerardo. No emotion. Cold as ice. He took a step back and fired into Winter's forehead. The shot echoed in the small valley and against the mountain ridge. The top of Winter's forehead blew back away from his skull, and his limp body went backward into the dirt. Mono stepped forward and stood over the body. He kicked the body in the ribs and then fired another round into Winter's face, at least what was left of it.

* * *

Drew heard the shot, and it sent a wave of adrenaline rolling through his body. After the second shot echoed across the mountains, he rechecked the target in the scope. His heart was racing. Relax, he told himself. Breathe. Breathe. In the dark, without laser sighting, he would need a clear shot. Chino was lying prone to his right with the spotter scope.

"Gerardo has his back to us," Chino was urgent. "He's in the shot."

They had prepared for this contingency, among two hundred other things that could go wrong.

"Get ready," Drew said. He closed his eyes and let out the last of his calming breaths. He closed off the noise around him. He concentrated on his heartbeat. He worked to bring his breathing down to a normal pace. Inhale, exhale. Inhale, exhale. Inhale, exhale.

"Now," he said calmly to Chino.

Chino reached for his phone.

* * *

Gerardo did not move. He stood staring as Mono fired off his second shot. Mono turned to him and motioned for him to come closer.

"You know what's next," he said.

"I was considering calling in a favor but . . ."

"But you know this is the life that you and I chose."

La vida se cuesta su vida. This life, the life of outlaws, narcos, and guns would one day cost you your life. He knew the saying well. Gerardo was silent because he knew Mono was right.

At that moment, Gerardo heard the buzz and alert from his phone. The chirp from the alert was loud and clear on the silent trail. He could see the light from the phone in the front pocket of Mono's jeans. The vibration startled Mono for a second. He reached into his pocket to retrieve the phone. He peered at it. Mono looked puzzled.

"*Qué es 'duck'?*" he asked. "*Un pato, no?*"

His phone. One word. Duck. One second that seemed like an eternity passed between Mono and Gerardo. The instant Mono realized the text was not about waterfowl, Gerardo threw himself into the dirt.

* * *

I am the Weapon. I am the Dark. I am the Silence. I am Death. Exhale. Squeeze the trigger.

* * *

A 175-gram bullet from a .308 caliber rifle has a muzzle velocity of 2,600 feet per second. The bullet travels at supersonic speed at the beginning of its flight and then transitions to subsonic as it moves away from the firing point to the target. Over two hundred yards, it takes less than two seconds to strike the target with enormous velocity. Drew sighted Mono's face at the top of his forehead to take into account the elevated angle. The round entered Mono's head above the bridge of his nose. The round dismantled his face and carved its way through the back of his neck. The mangled bit of bullet landed in the dirt ten yards away.

Gerardo opened his eyes. The side of his face was plastered against the loose, dry dirt. Here I am again. In the dirt. But alive. He kept his head against the ground and could see the bodies of the two men around him. Only one man could have taken the shot. He didn't know how Drew did it or when they started following him, but he was sure glad they did.

He lifted himself off the dirt and stood up. He could see the outline of two men coming at him on the run. He did not doubt who they were. When Drew and Chino made it to him, Gerardo nearly tackled both at once.

"*Ay, cabrón!*" he yelled. "*El pocho y el guero mas chingónes!*"

Drew stopped and examined his shot. Not bad, he thought, in the dark and with an unfamiliar weapon.

"You knew we weren't going to leave you alone with him," Drew said.

"I was ready for it to end," Gerardo said solemnly, but then his face split into a wide grin. "But I am good with letting *el muerte* wait for my Mexican ass a little while longer!"

"Well, boys," Chino said, "we need to get the hell off these trails. The sign below said this was an egress to the Pacific Coast Trail. People are going to be on this trail bright and early."

Drew surveyed the area using the flashlight on his phone. The trail was well traveled. Multiple hiking footprints were visible.

"We leave the bodies where they lay," he said. "We run the risk of leaving our DNA on them if we try to move them into the brush. Besides, they would be found in a matter of days."

"Copy that," Chino said. "Let's drag out our tracks back to the road and get that vehicle out of here."

Drew and Gerardo walked quickly down the trail while Chino moved slowly dragging the fan of a shrub distorting most of the prints on the trail. When they arrived at the car, Drew saw the keys were still on the console.

"We saw you driving," he said to Gerardo. "You need some time to wipe this down before you dump it."

"Time is something I have," he smiled at both of them. "Thanks to you two."

Chino gave him a nod and turned to run back down the road to his vehicle.

"How did you find me?" Gerardo asked.

"Ramirez tracked your iPhone when you sent the first text after you reentered the US."

"How did he . . ." Gerardo started to ask.

"Don't ask," Drew said. "Some government program we know nothing about."

"So, you have been following us this whole time?"

"We figured he wouldn't try anything with you until after he finished with Winters. Believe me, it was touch and go. Chino wanted to drop this asshole when you were in Barrio Logan."

Gerardo laughed, thinking about what a dilemma it would have been if they shot Mono at the gang safe house where they got the weapons.

"Well," he said, "it looks like we saw it through. I hope it works."

"We're going to have to wait and see," Drew said.

Chino rolled up in the white Nissan rental car. He got out with a backpack in his hand. He walked over to Gerardo and handed it to him, but did not look inside.

"One hundred thousand dollars cash," Chino said. "We figured you could use it to get lost."

"You need it more than we do," Drew said. "You need to take this car as far as you can before you dump it."

"Then," Chino said, "just disappear."

Gerardo could not form the words. He was seconds short of being executed before he was saved by the same men who had his back in the desert five years ago. He knew they were forever tied together and would defend one another when the time called for it.

"*Bueno, amigos.*" He stepped forward to shake hands. "This is it, again."

"You know how to reach us," Drew said.

"If you see anything," Chino emphasized anything, "You call, and I will be there. Wherever you are."

"Copy that," Drew said shaking Gerardo's hand.

"Tell Gordo and Ramirez I said *adiós.*"

"Most definitely." Drew patted him on the shoulder.

Gerardo opened the car door and threw the backpack into the passenger seat. He paused for a second and then turned back to Drew.

"Take care of that badass wife of yours, and Chino," Gerardo looked over to him, "get off your ass and marry that Azteca princess!"

Drew and Chino laughed. Gerardo gave them one last smile and got into the car. He fired up the engine and U-turned onto the road. He was gone.

They watched the taillights fade in the distance and for a good sixty seconds without a word.

"Well, boss," Chino broke the silence. "Let's get the fuck out of the badlands."

"Copy that, son. Let's see the shitstorm we're about to unleash.

SIXTY-SEVEN

Chance, Ramirez, Sonya, and Katie waited at Gordo's for the men to return. Katie was relieved to tears at the thought it might be over. She was grateful Drew was coming back alive and everyone was safe. At least for now.

They sat together in a large booth at the restaurant. Chance was silent, nervously turning a shot glass of Don Julio. He was partly upset he hadn't been out there with Drew and Chino. Gerardo was his friend and someone for whom he would put his life on the line. But he knew Chino and Drew represented the best chance of success.

Ramirez kept running different scenarios through his mind. The execution of a law enforcement official would result in a dragnet of monumental proportions. They would be checking border crossings, airports, highways. They'd look at anything that had wheels or wings. They would gather recordings from security cameras, analyze shell casings. The federal law enforcement machine was a juggernaut. The group's best chance was that the second part of their plan would muck up the waters so badly that the feds would find a convenient way to come up short on the investigation. In any event, they could only wait.

Drew and Chino walked in the front door. Locals at the restaurant gave them friendly hellos, and they both tried to act as normal as possible. They made their way to the booth. Katie started crying as she stood up to hug Drew. She grabbed him as tightly as she could. Drew knew the display of emotion might be a bit noticeable, so he patted Katie on the back.

"It's all over, darling," he whispered in her ear. "Everything is going to be all right."

The words entered her ear and filled her body with warmth. She kissed him on lips and sat back down into the booth.

Sonya held on to Chino.

"Okay, baby," Chino whispered, trying to calm her down. "Remember, to everyone else here, I'm still your stupid-ass boyfriend."

She laughed and punched him in the chest. "You sure are a dumb-ass, but you're my dumb-ass."

Chance and Ramirez stood waiting for a confirmation from Drew. They needed the look. The look of recognition from Drew that this might be all over.

"What do you think, Drew?" Chance asked.

Drew looked at everyone at the table.

"I think we did everything we could."

"The threat here has been neutralized," Chino added.

"We have to wait and see what happens on the fed level after we let Plan B go," Ramirez said.

"Well then," Chance let out a big breath of air. "Let's get the show on the road."

Drew looked to Chino and Ramirez. They both nodded in agreement.

Katie was already seated with her laptop open.

"You sure this is safe?" Drew asked.

"I worked with her on this," Ramirez said. "Four different email accounts, five servers, and six IP addresses. I checked this out with forensics a while back as part of an investigation. There is no chance it's coming back to us."

"We also bought this refurbished laptop just for this one-time use," Katie added.

Tristan, the bartender, walked over to the table to hand cold Pacificos to Chino and Drew. After he walked away, Drew took a long sip from the beer and put it back down on the table.

Damn, that beer tasted good.

"Let's fire that rocket and blow up the Death Star," he said to his wife.

Katie smiled. She moved the cursor and hit SEND.

* * *

Drew and Katie were silent on the drive home. Drew drove while Katie stared straight ahead in the passenger seat. Katie shed an occasional tear as she ran down all the things that happened over the last few days. She was angry at Drew for having put them all in danger, but now, at this moment, she had never loved anyone as much as she did him. Drew could sense her concern but knew that words were not enough to make things right. He reached over with this right hand and placed it on her hand.

She looked over between the tears and smiled.

"Hey, Drew," she said.

"What darlin'?"

"You're not gonna make me start taking defensive driving or some weird ass martial arts knife-throwing classes. Are you?"

Drew laughed out loud.

"No, baby," he was still laughing. "You are as badass as they come."

They pulled up the driveway to their home and sat silently in the car for a while.

"You know what sounds good right about now?" Katie said.

"What, darlin'?"

"Disneyland."

Drew smiled and leaned over to kiss her. Katie held her cheek against Drew for a minute before she let go of him.

"Let's go inside," she said.

"I'm right behind you. Always."

CPSIA information can be obtained
at www.ICGtesting.com
Printed in the USA
JSHW031022030121
10599JS00007B/23